THE SUN IS ALSO A STAR

nicola yoon

DOUBLEDAY CANADA

Doubleday Canada and colophon are registered trademarks of Penguin Random House of
Canada Limited

Library and Archives Canada Cataloguing in Publication data available upon request.

HC ISBN 978-0-385-68368-5
EL ISBN 978-0-385-68369-2

Printed and bound in the USA

Published in Canada by Doubleday Canada,
a division of Penguin Random House Canada Limited

www.penguinrandomhouse.ca

10 9 8 7 6 5 4 3 2 1

Penguin
Random House
DOUBLEDAY CANADA

*For my mom and dad, who taught me about
dreams and how to catch them*

*It does no harm to the romance of the
sunset to know a little about it.*

—*Pale Blue Dot,* Carl Sagan

*Do I dare
Disturb the universe?
In a minute there is time
For decisions and revisions which a minute will reverse.*

—*The Love Song of J. Alfred Prufrock,* T. S. Eliot

prologue

CARL SAGAN SAID that if you want to make an apple pie from scratch, you must first invent the universe. When he says "from scratch," he means from *nothing*. He means from a time before the world even existed. If you want to make an apple pie from nothing at all, you have to start with the Big Bang and expanding universes, neutrons, ions, atoms, black holes, suns, moons, ocean tides, the Milky Way, Earth, evolution, dinosaurs, extinction-level events, platypuses, *Homo erectus,* Cro-Magnon man, etc. You have to start at the beginning. You must invent fire. You need water and fertile soil and seeds. You need cows and people to milk them and more people to churn that milk into butter. You need wheat and sugar cane and apple trees. You need chemistry and biology. For a really good apple pie, you need the arts. For an apple pie that can last for generations, you need the printing press and the Industrial Revolution and maybe even a poem.

To make a thing as simple as an apple pie, you have to create the whole wide world.

daniel

Local Teen Accepts Destiny, Agrees to Become Doctor, Stereotype

It's Charlie's fault that my summer (and now fall) has been one absurd headline after another. Charles Jae Won Bae, aka Charlie, my older brother, firstborn son of a firstborn son, surprised my parents (and all their friends, and the entire gossiping Korean community of Flushing, New York) by getting kicked out of Harvard University (*Best School,* my mother said, when his acceptance letter arrived). Now he's been kicked out of *Best School,* and all summer my mom frowns and doesn't quite believe and doesn't quite understand.

Why you grades so bad? They kick you out? Why they kick you out? Why not make you stay and study more?

My dad says, *Not kick out. Require to withdraw. Not the same as kick out.*

Charlie grumbles: *It's just temporary, only for two semesters.*

Under this unholy barrage of my parents' confusion and shame and disappointment, even I almost feel bad for Charlie. Almost.

natasha

MY MOM SAYS IT'S TIME for me to give up now, and that what I'm doing is futile. She's upset, so her accent is thicker than usual, and every statement is a question.

"You no think is time for you to give up now, Tasha? You no think that what you doing is futile?"

She draws out the first syllable of *futile* for a second too long. My dad doesn't say anything. He's mute with anger or impotence. I'm never sure which. His frown is so deep and so complete that it's hard to imagine his face with another expression. If this were even just a few months ago, I'd be sad to see him like this, but now I don't really care. He's the reason we're all in this mess.

Peter, my nine-year-old brother, is the only one of us happy with this turn of events. Right now, he's packing his suitcase and playing "No Woman, No Cry" by Bob Marley. "Old-school packing music," he called it.

Despite the fact that he was born here in America, Peter says he wants to live in Jamaica. He's always been pretty shy and has a hard time making friends. I think he imagines that Jamaica will be a paradise and that, somehow, things will be better for him there.

The four of us are in the living room of our one-bedroom apartment. The living room doubles as a bedroom, and Peter and I share it. It has two small sofa beds that we pull out at night, and a bright blue curtain down the middle for privacy. Right now the curtain is pulled aside so you can see both our halves at once.

It's pretty easy to guess which one of us wants to leave and which wants to stay. My side still looks lived-in. My books are on my small IKEA shelf. My favorite picture of me and my best friend, Bev, is still sitting on my desk. We're wearing safety goggles and sexy-pouting at the camera in physics lab. The safety goggles were my idea. The sexy-pouting was hers. I haven't removed a single item of clothing from my dresser. I haven't even taken down my NASA star map poster. It's huge—actually eight posters that I taped together—and shows all the major stars, constellations, and sections of the Milky Way visible from the Northern Hemisphere. It even has instructions on how to find Polaris and navigate your way by stars in case you get lost. The poster tubes I bought for packing it are leaning unopened against the wall.

On Peter's side, virtually all the surfaces are bare, most of his possessions already packed away into boxes and suitcases.

My mom is right, of course—what I'm doing is futile. Still, I grab my headphones, my physics textbook, and some comics. If I have time to kill, maybe I can finish up my homework and read.

Peter shakes his head at me. "Why are you bringing that?" he asks, meaning the textbook. "We're leaving, Tasha. You don't have to turn in *homework*."

Peter has just discovered the power of sarcasm. He uses it every chance he gets.

I don't bother responding to him, just put my headphones on and head for the door. "Back soon," I say to my mom.

She kisses her teeth and turns away. I remind myself that she's not upset with me. *Tasha, is not you me upset with, you know?* is something she says a lot these days. I'm going to the United States Citizenship and Immigration Services (USCIS) building in downtown Manhattan to see if someone there can help me. We are undocumented immigrants, and we're being deported tonight.

Today is my last chance to try to convince someone—or fate—to help me find a way to stay in America.

To be clear: I don't believe in fate. But I'm desperate.

daniel

REASONS I THINK Charles Jae Won Bae, aka Charlie, Is an Asshole (In No Particular Order):

1. Before this epic and spectacular (and wholly delightful) failure at Harvard, he has been unrelentingly good at everything. No one is supposed to be good at everything. Math and English and biology and chemistry and history and sports. It's not decent to be good at everything. Three or four things at the most. Even that is pushing the bounds of good taste.

2. He's a man's man, meaning he's an asshole a lot of the time. Most of the time. All of the time.

3. He is tall, with chiseled, sculpted, and every-romance-novel-ever adjective for cheekbones. The girls (*all* the girls, not just the Korean Bible study ones) say his lips are kissable.

4. All this would be fine—an embarrassment of riches, to be sure; a tad too many treasures to be bestowed on a single human, certainly—if he were nice. But he is not. Charles Jae Won Bae is not kind. He is smug and, worst of all, he is a bully. He's an asshole. An inveterate one.

5. He doesn't like me, and hasn't liked me for years.

natasha

I PUT MY PHONE, headphones, and backpack into the gray bin before walking through the metal detector. The guard—her name tag says Irene—stops my bin from traveling onto the conveyor belt, as she's done every day.

I look up at her and don't smile.

She looks down into the bin, flips my phone over, and stares at the case, as she's done every day. The case is the cover art for an album called *Nevermind* by the band Nirvana. Every day her fingers linger on the baby on the cover, and every day I don't like her touching it. Nirvana's lead singer was Kurt Cobain. His voice, the damage in it, the way it's not at all perfect, the way you can feel everything he's ever felt in it, the way his voice stretches out so thin that you think it's going to break and then it doesn't, is the only thing that's kept me sane since this nightmare began. His misery is so much more abject than mine.

She's taking a long time, and I can't miss this appointment. I consider saying something, but I don't want to make her angry. Probably she hates her job. I don't want to give her a reason to delay me even further. She glances up at me again but shows no sign that she recognizes me, even though I've been here every day for the last week. To her I'm just another anonymous face, another *applicant,* another someone who wants something from America.

irene

A History

NATASHA IS NOT AT ALL correct about Irene. Irene loves her job. More than loves it—needs it. It's almost the sole human contact she has. It's the only thing keeping her total and desperate loneliness at bay.

Every interaction with these applicants saves her life just a little. At first they barely notice her. They dump their items into the bin and watch closely as they go through the machine. Most are suspicious that Irene will pocket loose change or a pen or keys or whatever. In the normal course of things, the applicant would never notice her, but she makes sure they do. It's her only connection to the world.

So she waylays each bin with a single gloved hand. The delay is long enough that the applicant is forced to look up and meet her eyes. To actually see the person standing in front of them. Most mumble a reluctant *good morning,* and the words fill her up a little. Others ask how she's doing and she expands a little more.

Irene never answers. She doesn't know how. Instead, she looks back down at the bin and scrutinizes each object for clues, for some bit of information to store away and examine later.

More than anything, she wishes she could take her gloves off and touch the keys and the wallets and the loose change. She wishes she could slide her fingertips along the surfaces, memorizing textures and letting the artifacts of other people's lives seep into her. But she can't delay the line too long. Eventually she sends the bin and its owner away from her.

Last night was a particularly bad night for Irene. The impossible hungry mouth of her loneliness wanted to swallow her in a single piece. This morning she needs contact to save her life. She drags her eyes away from a retreating bin and up to the next applicant.

It's the same girl who's been coming every day this week. She can't be more than seventeen. Like everyone else, the girl doesn't look up from the bin. She keeps her eyes focused on it, like she can't bear to be parted from the hot-pink headphones and her cell phone. Irene lays her gloved hand on the side of the bin to prevent its slide out of her life and onto the conveyor belt.

The girl looks up and Irene inflates. She looks as desperate as Irene feels. Irene almost smiles at her. In her head she does smile at her.

Welcome back. Nice to see you, Irene says, but only in her head.

In reality, she's already looking down, studying the girl's phone case. The picture on it is of a fat white baby boy completely submerged in clear blue water. The baby is spread-eagled and looks more like he's flying than swimming. His mouth and eyes are open. In front of him a dollar bill dangles on a fish-hook. The picture is not decent, and every time Irene looks at it she feels herself take an extra breath, as if she were the one underwater.

She wants to find a reason to confiscate the phone, but there is none.

daniel

I KNOW THE PRECISE MOMENT when Charlie stopped liking me. It was the summer I turned six and he turned eight. He was riding his shiny new bike (red, ten-speed, awesome) with his shiny new friends (white, ten years old, awesome). Even though there were lots of hints all summer long, I hadn't really figured out that I'd been demoted to Annoying Younger Brother.

That day he and his friends rode away without me. I chased him for blocks and blocks, calling out, "Charlie," convinced that he just forgot to invite me. I pedaled so fast that I got tired (six-year-olds on bikes don't get tired, so that's saying something).

Why didn't I just give up? *Of course* he could hear me calling.

Finally he stopped and hopped off his bike. He shoved it into the dirt, kickstand be damned, and stood there waiting for me to catch up. I could see that he was angry. He kicked dirt onto his bike to make sure everyone was clear on that fact.

"Hyung," I began, using the title younger brothers use for older brothers. I knew it was a big mistake as soon as I said it. His whole face turned red—cheeks, nose, the tips of his ears—

the whole thing. He was practically aglow. His eyes darted sideways to where his new friends were watching us like we were on TV.

"What'd he just call you?" the shorter one asked.

"Is that some kind of secret Korean code?" the taller one chimed in.

Charlie ignored them both and got right in my face. "What are you doing here?" He was so pissed that his voice cracked a little.

I didn't have an answer, but he really didn't want one. What he wanted was to hit me. I saw it in the way he clenched and unclenched his fists. I saw him trying to figure out how much trouble he would get in if he did hit me right there in the park in front of boys he barely knew.

"Why don't you get some friends of your own and stop following me around like a baby?" he said instead.

He should've just hit me.

He grabbed his bike out of the dirt and puffed himself up with so much angry air I thought he'd burst, and I'd have to tell Mom that her older and more perfect son exploded.

"My name is Charles," he said to those boys, daring them to say another word. "Are you coming or what?" He didn't wait for them, didn't look back to see if they were coming. They followed him into the park and into summer and into high school, just like many other people would eventually follow him. Somehow I had made my brother into a king.

I've never called him *hyung* again.

charles jae won bae

A Future History

DANIEL IS RIGHT ABOUT CHARLES. He's an asshole through and through. Some people grow out of their lesser natures, but Charles will not. He will settle into it, the skin that was always going to be his.

But before that, before he becomes a politician and marries well, before he changes his name to Charles Bay, before he betrays his good wife and constituents at every turn, before too much money and success and much too much of getting everything that he wants, he will do a good and selfless thing for his brother. It will be the last good and selfless thing that he ever does.

family

A History of Naming

WHEN MIN SOO FELL IN LOVE with Dae Hyun, she did not expect that love to take them from South Korea to America. But Dae Hyun had been poor all his life. He had a cousin in America who'd been doing well for himself in New York City. He promised to help.

For most immigrants, moving to the new country is an act of faith. Even if you've heard stories of safety, opportunity, and prosperity, it's still a leap to remove yourself from your own language, people, and country. Your own history. What if the stories weren't true? What if you couldn't adapt? What if you weren't wanted in the new country?

In the end, only some of the stories were true. Like all immigrants, Min Soo and Dae Hyun adapted as much as they were able. They avoided the people and places that didn't want them. Dae Hyun's cousin did help, and they prospered, faith rewarded.

A few years later, when Min Soo learned that she was pregnant, her first thought was of what to name her child. She had this feeling that in America names didn't mean anything, not like they did in Korea. In Korea, the family name came first and told the entire history of your ancestry. In America, the family name is called the last name. Dae Hyun said it showed that Americans think the individual is more important than the family.

Min Soo agonized over the choice of the personal name, what Americans called the first name. Should her son have an American name, something easy for his teachers and classmates to pronounce? Should they stick to tradition and select two Chinese characters to form a two-syllable personal name?

Names are powerful things. They act as an identity marker and a kind of map, locating you in time and geography. More than that, they can be a compass. In the end, Min Soo compromised. She gave her son an American name followed by a Korean personal name followed by the family name. She named him Charles Jae Won Bae. She named her second son Daniel Jae Ho Bae.

In the end, she chose both. Korean and American. American and Korean.

So they would know where they were from.

So they would know where they were going.

natasha

I'M LATE. I enter the waiting room and head over to the receptionist. She shakes her head at me like she's seen this before. Everyone here has seen everything before, and they don't really care that it's all new to you.

"You'll have to call the main USCIS line and make a new appointment."

"I don't have time for that," I say. I explain about the guard, Irene, and her strangeness. I say it quietly and reasonably. She shrugs and looks down. I am dismissed. On any other day, I would be compliant.

"Please call her. Call Karen Whitney. She told me to come back."

"Your appointment was for 8 a.m. It is now 8:05 a.m. She's seeing another applicant."

"Please. It's not my fault I'm late. She told me—"

Her face hardens. No matter what I say, she will not be moved. "Ms. Whitney is already with another applicant." She says it like English is not my first language.

"Call her," I demand. My voice is loud and I sound hysterical. All the other applicants, even the ones who don't speak

English, are staring at me. Desperation translates into every language.

The receptionist nods at a security guard standing by the door. Before he can reach me, the door that leads to the meeting rooms opens up. A very tall and thin man with dark brown skin beckons me. He nods to the receptionist. "It's all right, Mary. I'll take her."

I walk through the door quickly before he changes his mind. He doesn't look at me, just turns and starts down a series of hallways. I follow silently until he stops in front of Karen Whitney's office.

"Wait here," he says to me. He's only gone for a few seconds, but when he returns he's holding a red folder—my file.

We walk down another hallway until we finally come to his office. "My name is Lester Barnes," he says. "Have a seat."

"I've been—"

He holds up a hand to silence me.

"Everything I need to know is in this file." He pinches the corner of the folder and shakes it at me. "Do yourself a favor and stay quiet while I read it."

His desk is so neat you can tell he prides himself on it. He's got a matching set of silver-colored desk accessories—a pen holder, trays for incoming and outgoing mail, and even a business card holder with LRB engraved on it. Who even uses business cards anymore? I reach forward, take one, and slip it into my pocket.

The tall cabinet behind him is a landscape of color-coded stacks of files. Each file holds someone's life. Are the colors of the files as obvious as I think they are? My file is Rejection Red.

After a few minutes he looks up at me. "Why are you here?"

"Karen—Ms. Whitney—told me to come back. She's been kind to me. She said maybe there was something."

"Karen's new." He says it like he's explaining something to me, but I don't know what it is.

"Your family's last appeal was rejected. The deportation stands, Ms. Kingsley. You and your family will have to leave tonight at ten p.m."

He closes the file and pushes a box of tissues toward me in anticipation of my tears. But I'm not a cryer.

I didn't cry when my father first told us about the deportation orders, or when any of the appeals were rejected.

I didn't cry last winter when I found out my ex-boyfriend Rob was cheating on me.

I didn't even cry yesterday when Bev and I said our official goodbye. We'd both known for months that this was coming. I didn't cry, but still—it wasn't easy. She would've come with me today, but she's in California with her family, touring Berkeley and a couple of other state schools.

"Maybe you'll still be here when I get back," she insisted after our seventeenth hug. "Maybe everything will work out."

Bev's always been relentlessly optimistic, even in the face of dire odds. She's the kind of girl who buys lottery tickets. I'm the kind of girl who makes fun of people who buy lottery tickets.

So. I'm definitely not going to start crying now. I stand up and gather my things and head toward the door. It takes all my energy to continue not being a cryer. In my head I hear my mother's voice.

Don't let you pride get the better of you, Tasha.

I turn around. "So there's really nothing you can do to help me? I'm really going to have to leave?" I say it in such a small voice that I barely hear myself. Mr. Barnes doesn't have any trouble hearing. Listening to quiet, miserable voices is in his job description.

He taps the closed file with his fingers. "Your dad's DUI—"

"Is his problem. Why do I have to pay for his mistake?"

My father. His one night of fame led to a DUI led to us being discovered led to me losing the only place I call home.

"You're still here illegally," he says, but his voice is not as hard as it was before.

I nod but don't say anything, because now I really will cry. I put my headphones on and head for the door again.

"I've been to your country. I've been to Jamaica," he says. He's smiling at the memory of his trip. "I had a nice time. Everything is *irie* there, man. You'll be all right."

Psychiatrists tell you not to bottle up your feelings because they'll eventually explode. They're not wrong. I've been angry for months. It feels like I've been angry since the beginning of time. Angry at my father. Angry at Rob, who told me just last week that we should be able to be friends despite "everything," i.e. the fact that he cheated on me.

Not even Bev has escaped my anger. All fall she's been worrying about where to apply to college based on where her boyfriend—Derrick—is applying. She regularly checks the time difference between different college locations. *Do long-distance relationships work?* she asks every few days. The last time she asked I told her maybe she shouldn't base her entire *future* on her *current* high school boyfriend. She did not take it well. Bev thinks they'll last forever. I think they'll last through graduation. Maybe into the summer. It took me doing her physics homework for weeks to make it up to her.

And now a man who has probably spent no more than a week in Jamaica is telling me that everything will be *irie*.

I take my headphones off. "Where did you go?" I ask.

"Negril," he says. "Very nice place."

"Did you leave the hotel grounds?"

"I wanted to, but my—"

"But your wife didn't want to because she was scared, right? The guidebook said it was best to stay on the resort grounds." I sit down again.

He rests his chin on the back of his clasped hands. For the first time since this conversation began, he's not in charge of it.

"Was she concerned about her safety?" I put air quotes around *safety,* as if it weren't really a thing to be concerned about. "Or maybe she just didn't want to ruin her vacation mood by seeing how poor everyone really is." The anger I've suppressed rises from my belly and into my throat.

"You listened to Bob Marley, and a bartender got you some

pot, and someone told you what *irie* means, and you think you know something. You saw a tiki bar and a beach and your hotel room. That is not a country. That is a resort."

He holds up his hands like he's defending himself, like he's trying to push the words in the air back into me.

Yes, I'm being awful.

No, I don't care.

"Don't tell me I'll be all right. I don't know that place. I've been here since I was eight years old. I don't know anyone in Jamaica. I don't have an accent. I don't know my family there, not the way you're supposed to know family. It's my senior year. What about prom and graduation and my friends?" I want to be worrying about the same dumb things they're worrying about. I even just started getting my application together for Brooklyn College. My mom saved for two years so she could travel to Florida and buy me a "good" social security card. A "good" card is one with actual stolen numbers printed on it instead of fake ones. The man who sold it to her said that the less expensive ones with bogus numbers wouldn't get past background checks and college applications. With the card, I can apply for financial aid. If I can get a scholarship along with the aid, I might even be able to afford SUNY Binghamton and other in-state schools.

"What about college?" I ask, crying now. My tears are unstoppable. They've been waiting for a long time to come out.

Mr. Barnes slides the tissue box even closer to me. I take six or seven and use them and then take six or seven more. I gather my things again. "Do you have any idea what it's like not to fit

in anywhere?" Again I say it too quietly to be heard, and again he hears me.

I'm all the way to the door, my hand on the knob, when he says, "Ms. Kingsley. Wait."

irie

An Etymological History

MAYBE YOU'VE HEARD the word *irie* before. Maybe you've traveled to Jamaica and know that it has some roots in the Jamaican dialect, patois. Or maybe you know that it has other roots in the Rastafari religion. The famous reggae singer Bob Marley was himself a Rastafarian and helped spread the word beyond the Jamaican shores. So maybe when you hear the word you get a sense of the history of the religion.

Maybe you know that Rastafari is a small offshoot of the three main Abrahamic religions—Christianity, Islam, and Judaism. You know that Abrahamic religions are monotheistic and center on differing incarnations of Abraham. Maybe in the word you hear echoes of Jamaica in the 1930s, when Rastafari was invented. Or maybe you hear echoes of its spiritual leader, Haile Selassie I, Emperor of Ethiopia from 1930 to 1974.

And so when you hear the word, you hear the original spiritual meaning. Everything is *all right* between you and your god, and therefore between you and the world. To be *irie* is to be in a high and content spiritual place. In the word, you hear the invention of religion itself.

Or maybe you don't know the history.

You know nothing of God or spirit or language. You know the present-day colloquial dictionary definition. To be *irie* is simply to be *all right*.

Sometimes if you look a word up in the dictionary, you'll see some definitions marked as obsolete. Natasha often wonders about this, how language can be slippery. A word can start off meaning one thing and end up meaning another. Is it from overuse and oversimplification, like the way *irie* is taught to tourists at Jamaican resorts? Is it from misuse, like the way Natasha's father's been using it lately?

Before the deportation notice, he refused to speak with a Jamaican accent or use Jamaican slang. Now that they are being forced to go back, he's been using new vocabulary, like a tourist studying foreign phrases for a trip abroad. *Everything irie, man,* he says to cashiers in grocery stores who ask the standard retail *How are you?* He says *irie* to the postman dropping off mail who asks the same thing. His smile is too big. He pushes his hands into his pockets and throws his shoulders back and acts like the world has showered him with more gifts than he can reasonably accept. His whole act is so obviously fake that Natasha's sure everyone will see through him, but then they don't. He makes them feel good momentarily, like some of his obvious good fortune will rub off on them.

Words, Natasha thinks, should behave more like units of measure. A meter is a meter is a meter. Words shouldn't be allowed to change meanings. Who decides that the meaning has changed, and when? Is there an in-between time when the word means both things? Or a time when the word doesn't mean anything at all?

Natasha knows that if she has to leave America, all her friendships, even with Bev, will fade. Sure, they'll try to stay in touch at the beginning, but it won't be the same as seeing each other every day. They won't double-date to prom. No celebrating acceptance letters or crying over rejection ones. No silly graduation pictures. Instead, time will pass and the distance will seem farther every day. Bev will be in America doing American things. Natasha will be in Jamaica feeling like a stranger in the country of her birth.

How long before her friends forget about her? How long before she picks up a Jamaican accent? How long before she forgets that she was ever in America?

One day in the future, the meaning of *irie* will move on, and it will become just another word with a long list of archaic or obsolete definitions. *Is everything irie?* someone will ask you in a perfect American accent. *Everything's irie,* you will respond, meaning everything's just okay, but you really don't feel like talking about it. Neither of you will know about Abraham or the Rastafari religion or the Jamaican dialect. The word will be devoid of any history at all.

daniel

Local Teen Trapped in Parental Vortex of Expectation and Disappointment, Doesn't Expect to Be Rescued

The nice thing about having an overachieving asshole for an older brother is that it takes the pressure off. Charlie has always been good enough for two sons. Now that he's not so perfect after all, the pressure's on me.

Here's a conversation I've had 1.3 billion (give or take) times since he's been home:

Mom: Your grades still okay?

Me: Yup.

Mom: Biology?

Me: Yup.

Mom: What about math? You don't like math.

Me: I know I don't like math.

Mom: But grades still okay?

Me: Still a B.

Mom: Why no A yet? *Aigo.* It's time you get serious now. You not little boy anymore.

Today I have a college admission interview with a Yale alum.

Yale is *Second-Best School,* but for once, I put my foot down and refused to apply to *Best School* (Harvard). The idea of being Charlie's younger brother at another school is a bridge entirely too far. Besides, who knows if Harvard would even take me now that Charlie's been suspended.

My mom and I are in the kitchen. Because of my interview, she's steaming frozen *mandu* (dumplings) for me as a treat. I'm having a pre-*mandu* appetizer of Cap'n Crunch (the best cereal known to mankind) and writing in my Moleskine notebook. I'm working on a poem about heartbreak that I've been working on forever (give or take). The problem is that I've never had my heart broken, so I'm having a hard time.

Writing at the kitchen table feels like a luxury. I wouldn't be able to do it if my dad were here. He doesn't disapprove of my poem-writing tendencies out loud, but disapprove he definitely does.

My mom interrupts my eating and writing for a variation on our usual conversation. I'm cruising through it, adding my "yup's" through mouthfuls of cereal, when she changes up the script. Instead of the usual "You not little boy anymore," she says:

"Don't be like your brother."

She says it in Korean. For emphasis. And because of God or Fate or Sheer Rotten Luck, Charlie walks into the kitchen just in time to hear her say it. I stop chewing.

Anyone looking in at us from the outside would think things are copacetic. A mother making breakfast for her two sons. One son at the table eating cereal (no milk). Another son entering the scene from stage left. He's about to have breakfast as well.

But that's not what's really happening. Mom is so ashamed about Charlie hearing her that she blushes. It's faint, but it's there. She offers him some *mandu,* even though he hates Korean food and has refused to eat it since junior high.

And Charlie? He just pretends. He pretends he doesn't understand Korean. He pretends he didn't hear her offer of dumplings. He pretends I don't exist.

He almost fools me until I look at his hands. They curl into fists and give away the truth. He heard and he understood. She could've called him an epic douche bag, an animatronic dick complete with ball sac, and it would've been better than telling me not to be like him. My whole life it's been the opposite. *Why can't you be more like your brother?* This Reversal of Fortune is not good for either of us.

Charlie takes a glass from the cupboard and fills it with tap water. Drinking water from the tap is just to piss Mom off. She opens her mouth to say the usual "No. Drink filter," but she closes it again. Charlie gulps the water down in three quick swallows and puts the glass back into the cupboard unwashed. He leaves the cupboard open.

"*Umma,* give him a break," I tell her after he's gone. I'm pissed *at* him and I'm pissed *for* him. My parents have been relentless with the criticism. I can only imagine how ass it is for him working at the store all day with my dad. I bet my dad berates him in between smiling at customers and answering questions about extensions and tea tree oils and treating chemically damaged hair. (My parents own a beauty supply shop that sells black hair care products. It's called Black Hair Care.)

She opens the steamer basket to check on the *mandu*. The steam fogs up her glasses. When I was a little kid that used to make me laugh, and she would ham it up by letting them get as steamy as possible and then pretending she couldn't see me. Now she just pulls them from her face and wipes them with a dishcloth.

"What happen to your brother? Why he fail? He never fail."

Without her glasses she looks younger, prettier. Is it weird to think your mom is pretty? Probably. I'm sure that thought never occurs to Charlie. All his girlfriends (all six of them) have been very cute, slightly chubby white girls with blond hair and blue eyes.

No, I'm lying. There was one girl, Agatha. She was his last high school girlfriend before college.

She had green eyes.

Mom puts her glasses back on and waits, like I'm going to have an answer for her. She hates not knowing what happens next. Uncertainty is her enemy. I think it's because she grew up poor in South Korea.

"He never fail. Something happen."

And now I'm even more pissed. Maybe nothing *happened* to Charles. Maybe he failed out because he simply didn't like his classes. Maybe he doesn't want to be a doctor. Maybe he doesn't know what he wants. Maybe he just changed.

But we're not allowed to change in my household. We're on a track to be doctors, and there's no getting off.

"You boys have it too easy here. America make you soft." If I had a brain cell for every time I heard this, I'd be a goddamn genius.

"We were born here, Mom. We were always soft."

She scoffs. "What about interview? You ready?" She looks me over and finds me lacking. "You cut hair before interview." For months she's been after me to get rid of my short ponytail. I make a noise that could be either agreement or disagreement. She puts a plate of *mandu* in front of me and I eat it in silence.

Because of the big interview, my parents let me have the day off from school. It's still only eight a.m., but no way am I staying in the house and having any more of these conversations. Before I can escape, she hands me a money pouch with deposit slips to take to my dad at the store.

"*Appa* forgot. You bring to him." I'm sure she meant to give it to Charlie before he left for the store but forgot because of their little incident in the kitchen.

I take the pouch, grab my notebook, and drag myself upstairs to get dressed. My bedroom is at the end of a long hallway. I pass by Charlie's room (door closed as always) and my parents' room. My mom's got a couple of unopened blank canvases leaning against their doorframe. Today's her day off from the store, and I bet she's looking forward to spending the day alone painting. Lately she's been working on roaches, flies, and beetles. I've been teasing her, saying that she's in her Gross Insect Period, but I like it even more than her Abstract Orchid Period from a few months ago.

I take a quick detour into the empty bedroom that she uses

as her studio to see if she's painted anything new. Sure enough, there's one of an enormous beetle. The canvas is not especially large, but the beetle takes up the entire space. My mom's paintings have always been brightly colored and beautiful, but something about applying all that color to her intricate, almost anatomical drawings of insects makes them something more than beautiful. This one's painted in darkly pearlescent greens, blues, and blacks. Its carapace shimmers like spilled oil on water.

Three years ago for her birthday, my dad surprised her by hiring part-time help for the store so she wouldn't have to go in every day. He also bought a starter set of oil paints and some canvases. I'd never seen her cry over a present before. She's been painting ever since.

Back in my room I wonder for the ten thousandth time (give or take) what her life would be like if she never left Korea. What if she never met my dad? What if she never had Charlie and me? Would she be an artist now?

I get dressed in my new custom-tailored gray suit and red tie. "Too bright," my mom said about the tie when we were shopping. Evidently, only paintings are allowed to be colorful. I convinced her by saying that red would make me look confident. Checking myself in the mirror now, I have to say that the suit does make me look confident and debonair (yes, debonair). Too bad I'm only wearing it for this interview and not for something that actually matters to me. I check the weather on my phone and decide I don't need a coat. The high will be sixty-seven degrees—a perfect fall day.

Despite my irritation with the way she treated Charlie, I kiss my mom and promise to get my hair cut, and then I get out of the house. Later this afternoon my life will hop on a train headed for *Doctor* Daniel Jae Ho Bae station, but until then the day is mine. I'm going to do whatever the world tells me to. I'm going to act like I'm in a goddamn Bob Dylan song and blow in the direction of the wind. I'm going to pretend my future's wide open, and that anything can happen.

natasha

EVERYTHING HAPPENS FOR A REASON. This is a thing people say. My mom says it a lot. "Things happen for a reason, Tasha." Usually people say it when something goes wrong, but not *too* wrong. A nonfatal car accident. A sprained ankle instead of a broken one.

Tellingly, my mom has not said it in reference to our deportation. What reason could there be for this awful thing happening? My dad, whose fault this whole thing is, says, "You can't always see God's plan." I want to tell him that maybe he shouldn't leave everything up to God and that hoping against hope is not a life strategy, but that would mean I would have to talk to him, and I don't want to talk to him.

People say these things to make sense of the world. Secretly, in their heart of hearts, almost everyone believes that there's some meaning, some *willfulness* to life. Fairness. Basic decency. Good things happen to good people. Bad things only happen to bad people.

No one wants to believe that life is random. My dad says he doesn't know where my cynicism comes from, but I'm not a cynic. I am a realist. It's better to see life as it is, not as you wish it to be. Things don't happen for a reason. They just happen.

But here are some Observable Facts: If I hadn't been late to my appointment, I wouldn't have met Lester Barnes. And if he hadn't said the word *irie*, I wouldn't have had my meltdown. And if I hadn't had my meltdown, I wouldn't now have the name of a lawyer known as "the fixer" clutched in my hand.

I head out of the building past security. I have an irrational and totally unlike-me urge to thank that security guard—Irene—but she's a few feet away and busy fondling someone else's stuff.

I check my phone for messages. Even though it's only 5:30 a.m. in California where she is, Bev's texted a string of question marks. I contemplate telling her about this latest development but then decide it's not really a development.

Nothing yet, I text back. Selfishly I wish again that she were here with me. Actually, what I wish is that I were there with her, touring colleges and having a normal senior-year experience.

I look down at the note again. Jeremy Fitzgerald. Mr. Barnes wouldn't let me call for an appointment from his phone.

"It's a very long shot," he said, before basically shoving me out the door.

Observable Fact: You should never take long shots. Better to study the odds and take the probable shot. However, if the long shot is your only shot, then you have to take it.

irene

A Tentative History

ON HER LUNCH BREAK, Irene downloads the Nirvana album for herself. She listens to it three times in a row. In Kurt Cobain's voice she hears the same thing Natasha hears—a perfect and beautiful misery, a voice stretched so thin with loneliness and wanting that it should break. Irene thinks it would be better if it did break, better than living with wanting and not having, better than *living* itself.

She follows Kurt Cobain's voice down down down to a place where it is black all the time. After looking him up online, she finds that Cobain's story does not have a happy ending.

Irene makes a plan. Today will be the last day of her life.

The truth is, she's been thinking about killing herself on and off for years. In Cobain's lyrics she finally finds the words. She writes a suicide note addressed to no one: "Oh well. Whatever. Nevermind."

natasha

I'M ONLY TWO STEPS OUT of the building before I dial the number. "I'd like to make an appointment for today as soon as possible, please."

The woman who answers sounds like she's in a construction zone. In the background I hear the sound of a drill and loud banging. I have to repeat my name twice.

"And what's the issue?" she asks.

I hesitate. The thing about being an undocumented immigrant is you get really good at keeping secrets. Before this whole deportation adventure began, the only person I told was Bev, even though she's not usually that great with secrets.

"They just slip out," she says, as if she has absolutely no control of the things coming out of her mouth.

Still, even Bev knew how important it was to keep this one.

"Hello, ma'am? Can you tell me your issue?" the woman on the phone prompts again.

I press the phone closer to my ear and stand still in the middle of the steps. Around me, the world speeds up like a movie on fast-forward. People walk up and down the stairs at three times speed with jerky movements. Clouds zoom by overhead. The sun changes position in the sky.

"I'm undocumented," I say. My heart races like I've been running a very long way for a very long time.

"I need to know more than that," she says.

So I tell her. I'm Jamaican. My parents entered the country illegally when I was eight. We've been here ever since. My dad got a DUI. We're being deported. Lester Barnes thought Attorney Fitzgerald could help.

She sets an appointment for eleven a.m.

"Anything else I can help you with?" she asks.

"No," I say. "That will be enough."

The lawyer's office is uptown from where I am, close to Times Square. I check my phone: 8:35 a.m. A small breeze kicks up, lifting the hem of my skirt and playing through my hair. The weather is surprisingly mild for mid-November. Maybe I didn't need my leather jacket after all. I make a quick wish for a not-too-freezing winter before remembering that I probably won't be around to see it. If snow falls in a city and no one is around to feel it, is it still cold?

Yes. The answer to that question is yes.

I pull my jacket closer. It's still hard for me to believe that my future is going to be different from the one I'd planned.

Two and a half hours to go. My school's only a fifteen-minute walk from here. I briefly consider heading over so I can have one last look at the building. It's a very competitive science magnet high school, and I worked very hard to get into it. I can't believe that after today I may never see it again. In the

end I decide against going; too many people to run into, and too many questions like "Why aren't you in school today?" that I don't want to answer.

Instead, I decide to kill time by walking the three miles to the lawyer's office. My favorite vinyl record store is on the way. I put my headphones on and queue up the *Temple of the Dog* album. It's a 1990s grunge rock kind of a day, all angst and loud guitar. Chris Cornell's voice rises and I let it carry some of my cares away.

samuel kingsley

A History of Regret, Part 1

NATASHA'S FATHER, SAMUEL, MOVED TO America a full two years before the rest of his family did. The plan was that Samuel would go first and establish himself as a Broadway actor. It would be easier to do that without having to worry about a wife and small child. Without them, he would be free to go on auditions on a moment's notice. He'd be free to make connections with the acting community in New York City. Originally it was only supposed to be for one year, but one became two. It would've become three, but Natasha's mom could not and would not wait any longer.

She was only six at the time, but Natasha remembers the phone calls to America. She could always tell because her mom had to dial all those extra numbers. The calls were fine at first. Her father sounded like her dad. He sounded happy.

After about a year, his voice changed. He had a funny new accent that was more lilt and twang than patois. He sounded less happy. She remembers listening to their conversations. She couldn't hear his side, but she didn't need to.

"How much longer you expect us to wait for you?"

"But, Samuel? We not no family no more with you over there and we over here."

"Talk to you daughter, man."

And then one day, they were leaving Jamaica for good. Natasha said goodbye to her friends and to the rest of her family, fully expecting that she would see them again, maybe at Christmastime. She didn't know then what it meant to be an undocumented immigrant. How it meant that you could never go home again. How your home wouldn't even feel like home anymore, just another foreign place to read about. On the day they left, she remembers being on the plane and worrying about just how they would fly through the clouds, before realizing that clouds were not like cotton balls at all. She wondered if her dad would recognize her, and if he would still love her. It had been such a long time.

But he did recognize her and he still loved her. At the airport, he held them so close.

"Lawd, but me did miss you two, you know," he said, and he held them even closer. He looked the same. In that moment, he even sounded the same, his patois the same as it always was. He smelled different, though, like American soap and American clothes and American food. Natasha didn't mind. She was so happy to see him. She could get used to anything.

For the two years that Samuel was alone in America, he lived with an old family friend of his mother's. He didn't need a job, and he used his savings to cover what little expenses he had.

After everyone moved to America, that had to change. He got a job as a security guard working at one of the buildings on

Wall Street. He found them a one-bedroom apartment for rent in the Flatbush section of Brooklyn.

"Me can make this work," he said to Patricia. He chose the graveyard shift so he would have time to audition during the day.

But he was tired during the day.

And there were no parts for him, and the accent would just not go away no matter how he tried. It didn't help that Patricia and Natasha spoke to him with full Jamaican accents, even though he tried to teach them the "proper" American pronunciation.

And rejection was not an easy thing. To be an actor you're supposed to have thick skin, but Samuel's skin was never thick enough. Rejection was like sandpaper. His skin sloughed away under its constant onslaught. After a while, Samuel wasn't sure which would last longer: himself or his dreams.

daniel

Resigned Local Takes Westbound 7 Train to Childhood's End

Sure, I can be a little dramatic, but that's what it feels like. This train is a Magic Fucking Train speeding me from childhood (joy, spontaneity, fun) to adulthood (misery, predictability, absolutely no fun will be had by anyone). When I get off I will have a plan and tastefully groomed (meaning short) hair. I'll no longer read (or write) poetry—only biographies of Very Important People. I'll have a Point of View on serious subjects such as Immigration, the role of the Catholic Church in an increasingly secular society, the relative suckage of professional football teams.

The train stops, and half the people clear out. I head to my favorite spot—the two-seater in the corner next to the conductor's box. I spread myself out and take up both seats.

Yes, it's obnoxious. But I have a good reason for this behavior that involves a completely empty train one night at two a.m. (way post-curfew) and a man with a big-ass snake wrapped around his neck who chose to sit next to me despite there being one thousand (give or take) empty seats.

I take my notebook out of the inner pocket of my suit jacket.

It's about an hour to Thirty-Fourth Street in Manhattan, where my favorite barber is, and this poem won't write itself. Fifty minutes (and three very poorly written lines) later, we're only a couple of stops away from mine. Magic Fucking Train's doors close. We make it about twenty feet into the tunnel and grind to a halt. The lights flicker off, because of course they do. We sit for five minutes before the conductor decides communication would be good. I expect to hear him say that the train will be moving shortly, etc., but what he says is this:

"LAdies and GENtlemen. Up until yesterday I was just like you. I was on a train going NOwhere, just like you."

Holy shit. Usually the freaky people are *on* the train, not *driving* the train. My fellow passengers sit up straighter. *What the hell?* thought balloons float over all our heads.

"But something HAPpened to me. I had a religious EXperience."

I'm not sure where he's from (Crazytown, population 1). He overpronounces the beginnings of words and sounds like he's smiling the whole time he's evangelizing.

"God HIMself came down from HEAven and he saved me."

Foreheads are smacked and eyes are rolled in complete disbelief.

"HE will save you too, but you have to ACcept him into your hearts. ACcept him now before you reach your final DEStination."

Now I'm groaning too, because puns are the absolute worst. A guy in a suit yells out that the conductor should just shut the fuck up and drive the train. A mother covers her little girl's ears and tells the guy that there's no need for that kind of language. We might get all *Lord of the Flies* on the number 7 train.

Our conductor/evangelist goes quiet, and it's another minute of sitting in the dark before we move again. We pull into the Times Square station, but the doors don't open right away. The speakers crackle on.

"LAdies and GENtlemen. This train is now out of SERvice. Do yourself a FAvor. Get out of here. You will find God if you look for him."

We all get out of the train, somewhere between relieved and angry.

Everyone's got someplace to be. Finding God is not on the schedule.

natasha

HUMAN BEINGS ARE NOT REASONABLE creatures. Instead of being ruled by logic, we are ruled by emotions. The world would be a happier place if the opposite were true. For example, based on a single phone call, I have begun to hope for a miracle.

I don't even believe in God.

the conductor

An Evangelical History

THE CONDUCTOR'S DIVORCE had not been easy on him. One day his wife announced that she'd simply stopped loving him. She could not explain it. She wasn't having an affair. There was no one else she wanted to be with. But the love she once felt had vanished.

In the four years since his divorce became final, it's fair to say that the conductor has become something of an unbeliever. He remembers their vows spoken in front of God and everyone. If the person who's meant to love you forever can suddenly stop, then what is there to believe in?

Unmoored and uncertain, he's drifted from city to city, apartment to apartment, job to job, anchored to the world by almost nothing. He has trouble falling asleep. The only thing that helps is watching late-night TV with the sound muted. The endless cascade of images stills his mind and sends him off to sleep.

One night, as he's performing this same ritual, a show he's never seen catches his eye. A man is standing at a lectern in front of a huge audience. Behind him is an enormous screen with the same man's face projected on it. He is weeping. The camera pans to show a rapt audience. Some of them are crying, but the conductor can tell it's not from sadness.

That night he does not sleep. He unmutes the sound and stays up all night watching the show.

The next day, he does some research and finds Evangelical Christianity, and it takes him on a journey he did not know he needed. He finds that there are four main parts to becoming an Evangelical Christian. First, you must be born again. The conductor loves the notion that you can be made anew, free of sin and therefore worthy of love and salvation. Second and third, you must believe wholly in the Bible and that Christ died so we may all be forgiven of our sins. Finally you must become a kind of activist, sharing and spreading the gospel.

Which is why the conductor makes his announcement over the loudspeakers. How can he not share his newfound joy with his fellow man? And it is joy. There's a pure kind of joy in the certainty of belief. The certainty that your life has purpose and meaning. That, though your earthly life may be hard, there's a better place in your future, and God has a plan to get you there.

That all the things that have happened to him, even the bad, have happened for a reason.

daniel

SINCE I'M LETTING THE UNIVERSE dictate my life on this Final Day of Childhood, I don't bother waiting for another train to take me to Thirty-Fourth Street. The conductor said to go find God. Maybe he (or she—but who are we kidding? God's definitely a guy. How else to explain war, pestilence, and morning wood?) is right here in Times Square just waiting to be found. As soon as I'm on the street, though, I remember that Times Square is a kind of hell (a fiery pit of flickering neon signs advertising all seven deadly sins). God would never hang out here.

I walk down Seventh Avenue toward my barber, keeping my eye out for some kind of Sign. On Thirty-Seventh I spot a church. I climb the stairs and try the door, but it's locked. God must be sleeping in. I look left and right. Still no Sign. I'm looking for something subtle, along the lines of a long-haired man turning water into wine and holding a placard proclaiming himself to be Jesus Christ, Our Lord and Savior.

Suit be damned, I sit down on the steps. Back across the street, people are making their way around a girl who is swaying slightly. She's black with an enormous, curly Afro and almost-as-enormous pink headphones. The headphones are the kind that have giant ear pads for blocking out sound (also, the rest of the world). Her eyes are closed and she has one hand over her heart. She's completely blissed out.

The whole thing lasts about five seconds before she opens her eyes. She looks around, hunches her shoulders like she's embarrassed, and hurries away. Whatever she's listening to must be amazing to cause her to lose herself right there in the middle of the sidewalk in New York City. The only thing I've ever felt that way about is writing poetry, and that can never go anywhere.

I'd give anything to really want the life my parents want for me. Life would be easier if I were passionate about wanting to be a doctor. Being a doctor seems like one of those things you're *supposed* to be passionate about. Saving lives and all that. But all I feel is meh.

I watch as she walks away. She moves her backpack to one shoulder, and I see it: DEUS EX MACHINA is printed in big white letters on the back of her leather jacket. *God from the machine.* I hear the conductor's voice in my head and wonder if it's a Sign.

I'm not usually a stalker, and I'm not following her, exactly. I'm maintaining a noncreepy, half-block distance between us.

She goes into a store called Second Coming Records. I shit you not. I know now: it's definitely a Sign, and I'm serious about blowing with the wind today. I want to know where it leads.

natasha

I DUCK INTO THE RECORD store, hoping to avoid the stares of anyone who saw me acting unbalanced on the sidewalk. I was having a moment with my music. Chris Cornell singing "Hunger Strike" gets me every time. He sings the chorus like he's always been hungry.

Inside Second Coming, the lights are dim and the air smells like dust and lemon-scented air freshener, like it always does. They've changed the layout a little since the last time I was here. The records used to be arranged by decade, but now it's by musical genre. Each section has its own era-defining poster: *Nevermind* by Nirvana for grunge. *Blue Lines* by Massive Attack for trip-hop. *Straight Outta Compton* by N.W.A. for rap.

I could spend all day here. If today were not Today, I *would* spend all day here. But I don't have the time or the money.

I'm headed to trip-hop when I notice a couple making out in the pop diva section in the far back corner. They're lip-locked next to a poster of *Like a Virgin* by Madonna, so I can't make out the faces exactly, but I know the boy's profile intimately. It's my ex-boyfriend Rob. His make-out partner is Kelly, the girl he cheated on me with.

Of all the people to run into, today of all days. Why isn't he in school? He knows this is my place. He doesn't even like music. My mom's voice rings in my head. *Things happen for a reason, Tasha.* I don't believe that sentiment, but still, there has to be a logical explanation for the horribleness of this day. I wish Bev were with me. If she were, I wouldn't have even come into the record store. *Too old and boring,* she'd say. Instead, we'd probably be in Times Square watching tourists and trying to guess where they were from based on their clothes. Germans tend to wear shorts no matter the weather.

As if watching Rob and Kelly try to eat each other's faces weren't gross enough, I see her hand snake out, snatch a record, and then slip it between their bodies and into her very bulky, perfect-for-stealing jacket.

No. Way.

I'd rather burn my eyes out than keep watching, but I do. I can't actually believe what I'm seeing. They devour each other for another few seconds, and then her hand sneaks out again.

"Oh my God, they're gross. Why are they so gross?" The words slip out of my mouth before I can stop them. Like my mom, I have a tendency to say my thoughts out loud.

"She's just gonna steal that?" asks an equally incredulous voice beside me. I quickly glance over to see who I'm talking to. It's an Asian boy wearing a gray suit and a ridiculously bright red tie.

I turn back to watch some more. "Doesn't anybody work here? Can't they see what's happening?" I ask, more to myself than to him.

"Shouldn't we say something?"

"To them?" I ask, gesturing at the little thieves.

"The staff, maybe?"

I shake my head without looking at him. "I know them," I say.

"Sticky Fingers is your friend?" His voice is slightly accusatory.

"She's my boyfriend's girlfriend."

Red Tie turns his attention away from the crime in progress and onto me. "How does that work, exactly?" he asks.

"I mean *ex*-boyfriend," I say. "He cheated on me with her, actually." I'm more flustered about seeing Rob than I realize. It's the only explanation for me volunteering that piece of information to a stranger.

Red Tie shifts his attention back to the petty larceny. "Great pair, a cheater and a thief."

I half laugh.

"We should tell someone," he says.

I shake my head. "No way. You do it."

"Strength in numbers," he says back.

"If I say something, it's going to look like I'm jealous and messing with them."

"Are you?"

I look at him again. His face is sympathetic.

"That's kind of a personal question, isn't it, Red Tie?" I ask.

He shrugs. "We were having a moment," he says.

"Nope," I say, and turn away again to watch them. Rob feels me watching and catches my eye before I can look away.

"Jesus Christ bleeding on a Popsicle stick," I whisper under my breath.

Rob gives me his patented stupid half smile and a wave. I almost give him the finger. How did I date him for eight months and four days? How did I let this accomplice hold my hands and kiss me?

I face Red Tie. "Is he coming over here?"

"Yup."

"Maybe we should make out or something, like spies do in the movies," I suggest.

Red Tie blushes hard.

"I'm not serious," I say, smiling.

He doesn't say anything, just blushes some more. I watch the color warm his face.

Rob's there before Red Tie can pull himself together to respond.

"Hey," he says. His voice is a deep, reassuring baritone. It's one of the things I liked about him. Also, he looks like a young Bob Marley, only white and without the dreadlocks.

"Why are you and your girlfriend stealing things?" Red Tie cuts in before I can say anything to Rob.

Rob holds his hands up and takes a step back. "Whoa, dude," he says. "Keep your voice down." He pastes the stupid half smile back on his stupid face.

Red Tie gets even louder. "This is an independent record store. That means it's family-owned. You're stealing from real people. Do you know how hard it is for small businesses to survive when people like you just take stuff?"

Red Tie is righteous, and Rob even manages to look a little chastened.

"Don't look now, but I think your girlfriend just got busted," I say. Two store employees are whispering furiously at Kelly and tapping the front of her jacket.

Rob's stupid face finally loses its stupid smile. Instead of going over to rescue Kelly, he shoves his hands into his pockets and walk-runs out the front door. Kelly calls out to him as he bolts, but he doesn't stop. One of the employees threatens to call the cops. She begs him not to, and pulls two records from her jacket. She has good taste. I spot Massive Attack and Portishead.

The employee snatches them from her hand. "Come back in here again and I will call the cops."

She bolts from the store, calling after Rob.

"Well, that was fun," Red Tie says after she's gone. He's smiling a big wide smile and looking at me with happy eyes. I get a sudden sense of déjà vu. I've been here before. I've noticed those bright eyes and that smile. I've even had this conversation.

But then the moment passes.

He sticks out his hand for a shake. "Daniel," he says.

His hand is big and warm and soft and holds on to mine for a little too long.

"Nice to meet you," I say, and take my hand back. His smile is nice, really nice, but I don't have time for boys in suits with nice smiles. I put my headphones back on. He's still waiting for me to tell him my name.

"Have a nice life, Daniel," I say, and walk out the door.

daniel

*Would-Be Casanova Shakes Cute Girl's Hand, Offers Her Home
Loan with Reasonable Interest Rate*

I shook her hand. I'm wearing a suit and a tie and I shook
her hand.

What am I? A banker?

Who meets a cute girl and shakes her hand?

Charlie would've said something charming to her. They'd be
having a cozy coffee someplace dark and romantic. She'd already be dreaming of little half-Korean, half–African American
babies.

natasha

OUTSIDE, THE STREETS ARE MORE crowded than before. The crowd is a mix of tourists who've wandered too far from Times Square and actual working New Yorkers wishing the tourists would just go back to Times Square. A little ways down the street, I spy Rob and Kelly. I stand there staring at them for a little while. She's crying, and no doubt he's trying to explain that he is not an unfaithful, disloyal jerk. I have a feeling he will be successful. He's very persuasive, and she wants to be persuaded.

He and I sat next to each other in AP Physics last year. The only reason I noticed him at all was because he asked for help on the isotopes and half-lives unit. I'm something of an overachiever in that class. He asked me out to the movies after he passed the following week's quiz.

Coupledom was new to me, but I liked it. I liked meeting at his locker between classes and always having plans for the weekend. I liked being thought of as a couple, and double-dating with Bev and Derrick. As much as I hate to admit it now, I liked *him*. And then he cheated. I can still remember feeling hurt and betrayed and, weirdly, ashamed. Like it was my fault he cheated. The thing I could never figure out, though, was why he pretended. Why not just break up with me and go out with Kelly instead?

Still, getting over him didn't take that long at all. And that's the thing that makes me wary. Where did all those feelings go? People spend their whole lives looking for love. Poems and songs and entire novels are written about it. But how can you trust something that can end as suddenly as it begins?

half-life

A History of Decay

THE HALF-LIFE OF A SUBSTANCE is the time it takes for it to lose one half of its initial value.

In nuclear physics, it's the time it takes for unstable atoms to lose energy by emitting radiation. In biology, it usually refers to the time it takes to eliminate half of a substance (water, alcohol, pharmaceuticals) from the body. In chemistry, it is the time required to convert one half of a reactant (hydrogen or oxygen, for example) to product (water).

In love, it's the amount of time it takes for lovers to feel half of what they once did.

When Natasha thinks about love, this is what she thinks: nothing lasts forever. Like hydrogen-7 or lithium-5 or boron-7, love has an infinitesimally small half-life that decays to nothing. And when it's gone, it's like it was never there at all.

daniel

GIRL WHO HAS NO NAME is stopped at a crosswalk ahead of me. I swear I'm not following her. She's just going my way. Her super-pink headphones are back on, and she's swaying to her music again. I can't see her face, but I'm guessing her eyes are closed. She misses a walk cycle, and now I'm right behind her. If she turned around, she would definitely think I'm stalking her. The light turns red again and she steps off the curb.

She's not paying enough attention to realize that a guy in a white BMW is about to run that red light. But I'm close enough.

I yank her backward by her arm. Our feet tangle. We trip over each other and fall onto the sidewalk. She lands half on top of me. Her phone's not as lucky, and crashes against the pavement.

A couple of people ask if we're okay, but most just make a beeline around us as if we're just another object in the obstacle course that is New York City.

No-Name Girl shifts herself off me and looks down at her phone. A few cracks spiderweb across the screen.

"What. The. Hell?" she says, not a question so much as a protest.

"You okay?"

"That guy almost killed me." I look up and see that the car has pulled over to the side on the next block. I want to go yell at the driver, but I don't want to leave her alone.

"You okay?" I ask again.

"Do you know how long I've had this?" At first I think she means her phone, but it's her headphones she's cradling in her hands. Somehow they got damaged during our fall. One of the ear pads is dangling from wires, and the casing is cracked.

She looks like she's going to cry.

"I'll buy you another pair." I'm desperate to prevent her tears, but not because I'm noble or anything. I'm kind of a contagion cryer. You know how when one person starts yawning, everyone else starts yawning too? Or when someone vomits, the smell makes you want to hurl? I'm like that, except with crying, and I have no intention of crying in front of the cute girl whose headphones I just broke.

A part of her wants to say yes to my offer, but I already know she won't. She presses her lips together and shakes her head.

"It's the least I can do," I say.

Finally she looks at me. "You already saved my life."

"You wouldn't have died. A little maimed, maybe."

I'm trying to get her to laugh, but nothing doing. Her eyes fill with tears. "I'm having just the worst day," she says.

I look away so she doesn't see my own tears forming.

donald christiansen

A History of Money

DONALD CHRISTIANSEN KNOWS the price of price-less things. He has actuarial tables in his mind. He knows the cost of a human life lost in an airplane crash, a car accident, a mining disaster. He knows these things because he once worked in insurance. It was his job to price the unwanted and unexpected.

The price of accidentally running over a seventeen-year-old girl who was clearly not paying attention is considerably less than the price for his own daughter, killed by a texting driver. In fact, the first thing he'd thought when he heard the news about his daughter was what price the driver's insurance company would pay.

He pulls over to the side of the road, turns on his hazards, and lays his head on the steering wheel. He touches the flask in his inside coat pocket. Do people recover from these things? He doesn't think they do.

It's been two years, but the grieving has not left him, shows no signs of leaving until it's taken everything from him. It has cost him his marriage, his smile, his ability to eat enough, sleep enough, and feel enough.

It has cost him his ability to be sober.

Which is why he almost ran over Natasha just now.

Donald is not sure what the universe was trying to tell him by taking away his only daughter, but here is what he learned: no one can put a price on losing everything. And another thing: all your future histories can be destroyed in a single moment.

natasha

RED TIE LOOKS AWAY FROM ME. I think he's about to cry, which makes no sense at all. He offers to buy me new headphones. Even if I let him, new ones couldn't replace these.

I've had them since right after we moved to America. When my father bought them for me, he was still hopeful for all he would accomplish here. He was still trying to convince my mom that the move away from the country of our birth, away from all our friends and family, would be worth it in the end. He was going to hit it big. He was going to get the American Dream that even Americans dream about.

He used me and my brother to help convince my mom. He bought us gifts on layaway, things we could barely afford even on layaway. If we were happy here, then maybe the move was right after all.

I didn't care what the reason for the gifts was. These way-too-expensive headphones were my favorite of them all. I only cared that they were my favorite color and promised audiophile-quality sound. They were my first love. They know all my secrets. They know how much I used to worship my dad.

They know that I kind of hate myself for not worshiping him at all now.

It seems like such a long time ago when I thought the world of him. He was some exotic planet and I was his favorite satellite. But he's no planet, just the final fading light of an already dead star.

And I'm not a satellite. I'm space junk, hurtling as far as I can away from him.

daniel

I DON'T THINK I'VE EVER noticed anyone the way I'm noticing her. Sunlight filters through her hair, making it look like a kind of halo around her head. A thousand emotions pass over her face. Her eyes are black and wide, with long lashes. I can imagine staring into them for a long time. Right now they're dull, but I know exactly what they would look like bright and laughing. I wonder if I can make her laugh. Her skin is a warm and glowing brown. Her lips are pink and full, and I'm probably staring at them for far too long. Fortunately, she's too sad to notice what a shallow (and horny) jerk I am.

She looks up from her broken headphones. As our eyes meet, I get a kind of déjà vu, but instead of feeling like I'm repeating something in the past, it feels like I'm experiencing something that will happen in my future. I see us in old age. I can't see our faces; I don't know where or even when we are. But I have a strange and happy feeling that I can't quite describe. It's like knowing all the words to a song but still finding them beautiful and surprising.

natasha

I STAND UP AND DUST myself off. This day can't get any worse. It must eventually end. "Were you following me?" I ask him. I'm crankier and testier than I should be with someone who just saved my life.

"Man, I knew you would think that."

"You just happened to be right behind me?" I fiddle with my headphones, trying to reattach the ear pad, but it's hopeless.

"Maybe I was meant to save your life today," he says.

I ignore that. "Okay, thanks for your help," I say, preparing to leave.

"At least tell me your name," he blurts out.

"Red Tie—"

"Daniel."

"Okay, Daniel. Thank you for saving me."

"That's a long name." His eyes don't leave mine. He's not going to give up until I tell him.

"Natasha."

I think he's going to shake my hand again, but instead he shoves his hands into his pockets. "Nice name."

"So glad you approve," I say, giving him my most sarcastic tone.

He doesn't say anything else, just looks at me with a slight frown, as if he's trying to figure something out.

Finally I can't take it anymore. "Why are you staring at me?"

He blushes again, and now I'm staring. I can see how it might be fun to tease him just to get him to blush. I let my eyes wander the sharp planes of his face. He is classically handsome; debonair, even. Watching him stand there in his suit, I can picture him in a black-and-white Hollywood romantic comedy trading witty banter with his heroine. His eyes are clear brown and deep-set. Somehow I can tell he smiles a lot. His thick black hair is pulled back into a ponytail.

Observable Fact: The ponytail pushes him from handsome to kind of sexy.

"Now *you're* staring," he says to me. It's my turn to blush.

I clear my throat. "Why are you wearing a suit?"

"I have an interview later. Wanna go get something to eat?"

"What for?" I ask.

"Yale. Alumni admission interview. I applied early decision."

I shake my head. "No, I meant why do you want to get something to eat?"

"I'm hungry?" he says, as if he's not sure exactly.

"Hmmm," I say. "I'm not."

"Coffee, then? Or tea or soda or filtered water?"

"Why?" I ask, realizing that he's not going to give up.

His shoulders shrug, but his eyes don't. "Why not? Besides, I'm pretty sure you owe me your life since I just saved it."

"Believe me," I tell him, "you don't want my life."

daniel

WE WALK TWO LONG BLOCKS west toward Ninth Ave and pass no fewer than three coffee shops. Two of them are from the same national coffee chain (have you ever seen anyone actually dunk a donut?). I choose the non-chain, independent one because we mom-and-pop places gotta stick together.

The place is all mahogany and dark wood furniture and smells just like you'd think it would. It's also just slightly over-the-top. And by slightly, I mean there are several oil paintings of single coffee beans hanging on the wall. Who knew coffee-bean portraiture was a thing? Who knew they could look so forlorn?

There's barely anyone else here, and the three baristas behind the counter look pretty bored. I try to spice up their lives by ordering an overly elaborate drink involving half shots, milks of varying fat content, and caramel, as well as vanilla syrup.

They still look bored.

Natasha orders black coffee with no sugar. It's hard not to read her personality into her coffee order. I almost say something, but then I realize she might think I'm making a race-related joke, which would be a very poor (on a scale from Poor to Extremely Poor—the full scale is Poor, Somewhat Poor, Moderately Poor, Very Poor, and Extremely Poor) way to start off this relationship.

She insists on paying, saying it's the least she can do. My drink is $6.38 and I let her know that the cost of saving a life is at least two elaborate coffee drinks. She doesn't even smile.

I choose a table in back as far away from the non-action as possible. As soon as we sit, she pulls out her phone to check the time. It's still working, despite the cracks on the screen. She runs her thumb along them and sighs.

"Have to be somewhere?" I ask.

"Yes," she says, and turns the phone off.

I wait for her to continue, but she's definitely not going to. Her face dares me to ask her more, but I've reached my quota of daring things (1 = following cute girl, 2 = yelling at ex-boyfriend of cute girl, 3 = saving life of cute girl, 4 = asking out cute girl) for the day.

We sit in a not-at-all-comfortable silence for thirty-three seconds. I fall into that super-self-conscious state you get into when you're with someone new and you really want them to like you.

I see all my movements through her eyes. Does this hand gesture make me seem like a jerk? Are my eyebrows crawling off my face? Is this a sexy half smile or do I look like I'm having a stroke?

I'm nervous, so I exaggerate all my movements. I BLOW on my coffee, SIP it, STIR it, playing the part of an actual human teenage boy having an actual beverage called coffee.

I blow too hard on my drink and a little foam flies up. I could not be any cooler. I would totally date me (not really). It's hard to say, but she may have smiled ever so slightly at the foam flight.

"Still happy you saved my life?" she asks.

I take too big a sip and burn not only my tongue but a path all the way down my throat. Jesus Christ. Maybe this is a sign I should just give up. I am clearly not meant to impress this girl.

"Should I regret it?" I ask.

"Well, I'm not exactly being nice to you."

She's pretty direct, so I decide to be direct too. "That's true, but I don't have a time machine to go back and undo it." I say it with a straight face.

"Would you?" she asks, frowning slightly.

"Of course not," I say. What kind of jerk does she think I am?

She excuses herself to go to the bathroom. So that I don't just sit there looking uninteresting when she gets back, I pull out my notebook to fiddle with my poem. I'm still writing when she gets back.

"Oh no," she groans as she sits back down.

"What?" I ask.

She gestures to my notebook. "You're not a poet, are you?"

Her eyes are smiling, but still, I close it quickly and slip it back into my jacket.

Maybe this wasn't such a good idea. What am I thinking with my déjà-vu-in-reverse nonsense? I'm just putting off the future. Like my parents want, I'll marry a lovely Korean American girl.

Unlike Charles, I don't have anything against Korean girls. He says they're not his type, but I don't really get the concept of having a type. My type is girls. All of them. Why would I limit my dating pool?

I'll be a great doctor with excellent bedside skills.

I'll be perfectly happy.

But something about Natasha makes me think my life could be extraordinary.

It's better for her to be mean and for us go on separate paths. I can think of exactly no ways that my parents (mostly my dad) would be okay with me dating a black girl.

Still, I give it one last try. "What would you do with a time machine if you had one?"

For the first time since we sat down, she doesn't seem irritated or bored. She furrows her brow and leans forward.

"Can it travel into the past?"

"Of course. It's a time machine," I say.

She gives me a look that says there's so much I don't know. "Time travel to the past is a complicated business."

"Say we've gotten past the complications. What would you do?"

She puts down her coffee, folds her arms across her chest. Her eyes are brighter.

"And we're ignoring the grandfather paradox?" she asks.

"Completely," I say, pretending I have a clue what she's talking about, but she calls me out.

"You don't know the grandfather paradox?" Her voice is incredulous, like I've missed some basic information about the world (like how babies are made). Is she a sci-fi nerd?

"Nope. Don't know it," I say.

"Okay. Let's say you have an evil grandfather."

"He's dead. I only met him once in Korea. He seemed nice."

"Are you Korean?" she asks.

"Korean American. I was born here."

"I'm Jamaican," she says. "I was born there."

"But you don't have an accent."

"Well, I've been here for a while." She tightens her hold on her cup and I can feel her mood starting to shift.

"Tell me about this paradox," I prod, trying to distract her. It works and she brightens up again.

"Okay. Yes. Let's say your grandfather was alive, and he was evil."

"Alive and evil," I say, nodding.

"He's really evil, so you invent a time machine and go back in time to kill him. Say you kill him before he meets your grandmother. That would mean that one of your parents is never born and that you are never born, so you can't go back in time to kill him. But! If you kill him *after* he meets your grandmother, then you *will* be born, and then you'll invent a time machine to go back in time to kill him. This loop will go on forever."

"Huh. Yes, we're definitely ignoring that."

"And the Novikov self-consistency principle too, I guess?"

I thought she was cute before, but she's even cuter now. Her face is animated, her hair is bouncing, and her eyes are sparking. She's gesturing with her hands, talking about researchers at MIT and probability bending to prevent paradoxes.

"So theoretically, you wouldn't be able to kill your grand-father at all, because the gun would misfire at just the right moment, or you would have a heart attack—"

"Or a cute Jamaican girl would walk into the room and bowl me over."

"Yes. Something strange and improbable would happen so that the impossible couldn't."

"Huh," I say again.

"That's more than a 'huh,'" she says, smiling.

It *is* more than a huh, but I can't think of anything clever or witty to say. I'm having trouble thinking and looking at her at the same time.

There's a Japanese phrase that I like: *koi no yokan*. It doesn't mean love at first sight. It's closer to love at second sight. It's the feeling when you meet someone that you're going to fall in love with them. Maybe you don't love them right away, but it's inevitable that you will.

I'm pretty sure that's what I'm experiencing right now. The only slight (possibly insurmountable) problem is that I'm pretty sure that Natasha is not.

natasha

I DON'T TELL RED TIE the complete truth about what I would do with a time machine if I had one. I would travel back in time and make it so the greatest day of my father's life never happened at all. It is completely selfish, but it's what I would do so *my* future wouldn't have to be erased.

Instead, I explain all the science to him. By the time I'm done, he's giving me a look like he's in love with me. It turns out he's never heard of the grandfather paradox or the Novikov self-consistency principle, which kind of surprises me. I guess I assumed he'd be nerdy because he's Asian, which is crappy of me because I hate when other people assume things about me like I like rap music or I'm good at sports. For the record, only one of those things is true.

Besides the fact that I'm being deported today, I am really not a girl to fall in love with. For one thing, I don't like temporary, nonprovable things, and romantic love is both temporary and nonprovable.

The other, secret thing that I don't say to anyone is this: I'm not sure I'm capable of love. Even temporarily. When I was with Rob, I never felt the way the songs say you're supposed to feel. I didn't feel swept away or consumed. I didn't need him like I needed air. I really liked him. I liked looking at him. I liked kissing him. But I always knew I could live without him.

"Red Tie," I say.

"Daniel," he insists.

"Don't fall in love with me, Daniel."

He actually sputters out his coffee. "Who says I'm going to?"

"That little black notebook I saw you scribbling in, and your face. Your big, wide-open, couldn't-fool-anybody-about-anything face says you're going to."

He blushes again, because blushing is his entire state of being. "And why shouldn't I?" he asks.

"Because I'm not going to fall in love with you."

"How do you know?"

"I don't believe in love."

"It's not a religion," he says. "It exists whether you believe in it or not."

"Oh, really? Can you prove it?"

"Love songs. Poetry. The institution of marriage."

"Please. Words on paper. Can you use the scientific method on it? Can you observe it, measure it, experiment with it, and repeat your experiments? You cannot. Can you slice it and stain it and study it under a microscope? You cannot. Can you grow it in a petri dish or map its gene sequence?"

"You cannot," he says, mimicking my voice and laughing.

I can't help laughing too. Sometimes I take myself a little seriously.

He spoons a layer of foam off his coffee and into his mouth. "You say it's just words on paper, but you have to admit all those people are feeling *something*."

I nod. "Something temporary and not at all measurable. People just want to believe. Otherwise they would have to admit that life is just a random series of good and bad things that happen until one day you die."

"And you're okay with believing that life has no meaning?"

"What choice do I have? This is what life is."

Another spoon of foam and more laughter from him. "So no fate, no destiny, no meant-to-be for you?"

"I am not a nincompoop," I say, definitely enjoying myself more than I should be.

He loosens his tie and relaxes back into his chair. A strand of his hair escapes his ponytail, and I watch as he tucks it behind his ear. Instead of pushing him away, my nihilism is only making him more comfortable. He seems almost merry.

"I don't think I've ever met anyone so charmingly deluded," he says, as if I'm a curiosity.

"And you find that appealing?" I ask.

"I find it interesting," he says.

I take a look around the café. Somehow, it's filled up without me noticing. People line the bar, waiting for their orders. The speakers are playing "Yellow Ledbetter" by Pearl Jam—another one of my favorite nineties grunge-rock bands. I can't help it. I have to close my eyes to listen to Eddie Vedder mumble-sing the chorus.

When I open them again, Daniel is staring at me. He shifts forward so his chair is grounded again on all four legs. "What if I told you I could get you to fall in love with me scientifically?"

"I would scoff," I say. "A lot."

multiverses

A Quantum History

ONE POSSIBLE SOLUTION to the grandfather paradox is the theory of multiverses originally set forth by Hugh Everett. According to multiverse theory, every version of our past and future histories exists, just in an alternate universe.

For every event at the quantum level, the current universe splits into multiple universes. This means that for every choice you make, an infinite number of universes exist in which you made a different choice.

The theory neatly solves the grandfather paradox by positing separate universes in which each possible outcome exists, thereby avoiding a paradox.

In this way we get to live multiple lives.

There is, for example, a universe where Samuel Kingsley does not derail his daughter's life. A universe where he does derail it but Natasha is able to fix it. A universe where he does derail it and she is not able to fix it. Natasha is not quite sure which universe she's living in now.

daniel

Area Boy Attempts to Use Science to Get the Girl

I wasn't kidding about the falling-in-love-scientifically thing. There was even an article in the *New York Times* about it.

A researcher put two people in a lab and had them ask each other a bunch of intimate questions. Also, they had to stare into each other's eyes for four minutes without talking. I'm pretty sure I'm not getting her to do the staring thing with me right now. To be honest, I didn't really believe the article when I read it. You can't just *make* people fall in love, right? Love is way more complicated than that. It's not just a matter of choosing a couple of people and making them ask each other some questions, and then love blossoms. The moon and the stars are involved. I'm certain of it.

Nevertheless.

According to the article, the result of the experiment was that the two test subjects did indeed fall in love and get married. I don't know if they stayed married. (I kinda don't want to know, because if they did stay married, then love is less mysterious than I think and *can* be grown in a petri dish. If they didn't stay married, then love is as fleeting as Natasha says it is.)

I pull out my phone and look up the study. Thirty-six questions. Most of them are pretty stupid, but some of them are okay. I like the staring-into-the-eyes thing.

I'm not above science.

natasha

HE TELLS ME ABOUT SOME study involving a lab and questions and love. I am skeptical and say so. I'm also slightly intrigued but don't say so.

"What are the five key ingredients to falling in love?" he asks me.

"I don't believe in love, remember?" I pick up my spoon and stir my coffee, even though there's nothing to stir together.

"So what are the love songs really about?"

"Easy," I say. "Lust."

"And marriage?"

"Well, lust fades, and then there are children to raise and bills to pay. At some point it just becomes friendship with mutual self-interest for the benefit of society and the next generation." The song ends just as I finish talking. For a moment all we can hear are glasses clinking and milk frothing.

"Huh," he says, considering.

"You say that a lot," I say.

"I could not disagree with you more." He adjusts his ponytail without letting his hair fall into his face.

Observable Fact: I want to see his hair fall into his face.

The more I talk to him, the cuter he gets. I even like his earnestness, despite the fact that I usually hate earnestness. The sexy ponytail may be addling my brain. It's just hair, I tell myself. Its function is to keep the head warm and protect it against ultraviolet radiation. There's nothing inherently sexy about it.

"What are we talking about again?" he asks.

I say *science* at the same time that he says *love,* and we both laugh.

"What are the ingredients?" he prompts me again.

"Mutual self-interest and socioeconomic compatibility."

"Do you even have a soul?"

"No such thing as a soul," I say.

He laughs at me as if I'm kidding. "Well," he says after he realizes that I'm not kidding, "My ingredients are friendship, intimacy, moral compatibility, physical attraction, and the X factor."

"What's the X factor?"

"Don't worry," he says. "We already have it."

"Good to know," I say, laughing. "I'm still not going to fall in love with you."

"Give me today." He's suddenly serious.

"It's not a challenge, Daniel."

He just stares at me with those bright brown eyes, waiting for an answer.

"You can have one hour," I say.

He frowns. "Only an hour? What happens then? Do you turn into a pumpkin?"

"I have an appointment and then I have to go home."

"What's the appointment?" he asks.

Instead of answering, I look around the café. A barista calls out a string of orders. Someone laughs. Someone else stumbles.

I stir my coffee unnecessarily again. "I'm not going to tell you," I say.

"Okay," he says, unfazed.

He's made up his mind about what he wants, and what he wants is me. I get the feeling he can be determined and patient. I almost admire him for it. But he doesn't know what I know. I'll be a resident of another country tomorrow. Tomorrow, I'll be gone from here.

daniel

I SHOW HER MY PHONE, and we argue over which questions to choose. We definitely don't have time for all thirty-six. She wants to ixnay the four minutes of soulfully staring into each other's eyes, but that's not happening. The eye thing is my ace in the hole. All my ex-girlfriends (okay, one of my ex-girlfriends—okay, I've only ever had one girlfriend, now ex-girlfriend) have liked my eyes a lot. Grace (the aforementioned singular in the extreme ex-girlfriend) said they looked like gemstones, specifically smoky quartz (jewelry making was her hobby). We were making out in her room when she first said it, and she stopped midsession to get an example for me.

Anyway, my eyes are like quartz (the smoky kind) and girls (at least one) dig it.

The questions fall into three categories, each more personal than the previous. Natasha wants to stick with the least personal ones from the first category, but I ixnay that as well.

From category #1 (least intimate) we choose:

#1. Given the choice of anyone in the world, whom would you want as a dinner guest?

#2. Would you like to be famous? In what way?

#7. Do you have a secret hunch about how you will die?

From category #2 (medium intimacy):

#17. What is your most treasured memory?

#24. How do you feel about your relationship with your mother?

From category #3 (most intimate):

#25. Make three true "we" statements each. For instance, "We are both in this room feeling . . ."

#29. Share with your partner an embarrassing moment in your life.

#34. Your house, containing everything you own, catches fire. After saving your loved ones and pets, you have time to safely make a final dash to save any one item. What would it be? Why?

#35. Of all the people in your family, whose death would you find most disturbing? Why?

We end up with ten questions, because Natasha thinks that for number twenty-four we should talk about our relationship with both our mother *and* father.

"How come mothers are always the ones most blamed for screwing up children? Fathers screw kids up perfectly well." She says it like someone with firsthand experience.

She checks the time on her phone again. "I should go," she says, pushing her chair back and standing too quickly. The table wobbles. Some of her coffee splashes out.

"Shit. Shit," she says. It's kind of an overreaction. I really want to ask about the appointment and her father, but I know better than to ask right now.

I get up, grab some napkins, and clean up the spill.

The look she gives me is somewhere between gratitude and exasperation.

"Let's get out of here," I say.

"Yeah, okay. Thanks," she says.

I watch as she navigates around the line of coffee-starved people to go outside. Probably I shouldn't stare at her legs, but they're great (the third-greatest pair I've ever seen). I want to touch them almost as much as I want to keep talking to her (maybe a little more), but there are no circumstances under which she would let me do that.

Either she's trying to shake me loose, or we are in a speed-walking competition that I'm unaware of. She dashes between a couple of slow walkers and skirts along the outside of sidewalk scaffolding to avoid having to slow down for people.

Maybe I should give up. I don't know why I haven't yet. The universe is clearly trying to save me from myself. I bet if I looked for signs about parting ways, I would find them.

"Where are we heading?" I ask her when we come to a stop at a crosswalk. The haircut I'm supposed to be getting is going to have to wait. I'm pretty sure they let people with long hair go to college.

"*I* am heading uptown to my appointment and *you* are tagging along with me."

"Yes, I am," I say, ignoring her not-at-all-subtle emphasizing.

We cross the street and walk along quietly for a few minutes. The morning settles into itself. A few stores have propped open their doors. The weather's too cold for air-conditioning and too hot for closed doors. I'm sure my dad's done the same thing at our store.

We pass the extraordinarily well lit and extremely crowded window display of an electronics store. Every item in the display is tagged with a red ON SALE! sticker. There are hundreds of these stores all over the city. I can't understand how they stay in business.

"Who even shops in these?" I wonder out loud.

"People who like to haggle," she says.

Half a block later we pass another, virtually identical store and we both laugh.

I take out my phone. "So. You ready for these questions?"

"You are relentless," she says, not looking at me.

"Persistent," I correct her.

She slows down and looks over at me. "Do you really think asking me deep, philosophical questions is going to make us fall in love?" She puts air quotes (oh, how I dislike air quotes) around *deep* and *philosophical* and *fall in love*.

"Think of it as an experiment," I say. "What'd you say before about the scientific method?"

This gets me a small smile.

"Scientists shouldn't experiment on themselves," she counters.

"Not even for the greater good?" I ask. "For furthering mankind's knowledge of itself?"

That gets me a big laugh.

natasha

USING SCIENCE AGAINST ME is pretty smart.

Four Observable Facts: He's perfectly silly. And too optimistic. And too earnest. And pretty good at making me laugh.

"Number one's too hard," he says. "Let's start with question two: Would you like to be famous and how?"

"You first," I tell him.

"I'd be a famous poet in chief."

Of course he would. Observable Fact: He's a hopeless romantic.

"You'd be broke," I tell him.

"Broke with money but rich with words," he counters immediately.

"I'm going to vomit right here on the sidewalk." I say it too loudly and a woman in a suit gives us a wide berth.

"I'll clean you up," he says.

Really, he's too sincere by half. "What does a poet in chief even do?" I ask.

"Offers wise and poetic counsel. I'd be the person world leaders came to with nasty philosophical problems."

"That you solve by writing them a poem?" The skepticism in my voice cannot be missed.

"Or reading one," he says, with more unflappable sincerity.

I make some gagging sounds.

He bumps me lightly with his shoulder and then steadies me with his hand on my back. I like the feel of his hand so much that I speed up a little to avoid it.

"You can be cynical all you want, but many a life can be saved by poetry," he says.

I scour his face for a sign that he's joking, but no—he really does believe it. Which is sweet. Also stupid. But mostly sweet.

"What about you? What kind of fame do you want?" he asks.

This is an easy one. "I'd be a benevolent dictator."

He laughs. "Of any particular country?"

"Of the whole world," I say, and he laughs some more.

"All dictators think they're benevolent. Even the ones holding machetes."

"I'm pretty sure those ones know they're being greedy, murderous bastards."

"But you wouldn't be that?" he asks.

"Nope. Pure benevolence from me. I would decide what was good for everyone and do it."

"But what if what's good for one person isn't good for another?"

I shrug. "Can't please everyone. As my poet in chief, you could comfort the loser with a good poem."

"Touché," he says, smiling. He pulls out his phone again and begins thumbing through the questions. I take a quick look at my own phone. For a second I'm surprised by the crack in the screen, until I remember my fall from earlier. What a day I'm having. Again, I'm thinking about multiverses and wondering about the ones where both my phone and headphones are still intact.

There's a universe where I stayed home and packed like my mom wanted me to. My phone and headphones are fine, but I didn't meet Daniel.

There's a universe where I went to school and am safely sitting in English class instead of almost being hit by a car. Again, no Daniel.

In another Daniel-less universe, I *did* go to USCIS, but I didn't meet Daniel in the record store, so our chatting didn't have a chance to delay me. I arrived at the crosswalk before the BMW driver showed up, and there was no near-miss accident. My phone and headphones remain intact.

Of course, there is an infinite number of these universes, including one where I did meet Daniel but he wasn't able to save me at the crosswalk, and more than just my phone and headphones are broken.

I sigh and check the distance to Attorney Fitzgerald's office. Twelve more blocks. I wonder how much it will cost to fix my screen. But then, maybe I won't need to get it fixed. I'll probably need to get a new phone in Jamaica.

Daniel interrupts my thoughts, and I'm kind of grateful. I don't want to think about anything having to do with leaving.

"All right," he says. "Let's move on to number seven. What's your secret hunch about how you'll die?"

"Statistically speaking, a black woman living in the United States is most likely to die at the age of seventy-eight from heart disease."

We come to another crosswalk and he tugs me back from standing too close to the edge. His gesture and my response are so familiar, like we've done it many times before. He pinches my jacket at the elbow and tugs just slightly. I back up toward him and indulge his protectiveness.

"So the heart's gonna get you, then?" he asks. I forget for a moment that we're talking about death.

"Most likely," I say. "What about you?"

"Murder. Gas station or liquor store or someplace like that. Some guy with a gun will be robbing the place. I'll try to be a hero but do something stupid like knock over the soda can pyramid, and that'll freak robber guy out, and what would've been your average stick-'em-up will turn into a bloodbath. News at eleven."

I laugh at him. "So you're going to die an incompetent hero?"

"I'm going to die trying," he says, and we laugh together.

We cross the street. "This way," I tell him when he starts heading straight instead of right. "We need to go over to Eighth."

He pivots and grins at me like we're on an epic adventure.

"Hang on," he says, shrugging out of his jacket. It seems weirdly intimate to watch as he takes it off, so I watch two very old, very cranky guys argue over a single cab a few feet from us. There are at least three other free cabs in the immediate vicinity.

Observable Fact: People aren't logical.

"Will this fit in your backpack?" he asks, holding the jacket out to me. I know he's not asking me to wear it, like I'm his girlfriend or something. Still, carrying his jacket strikes me as even more intimate than watching him take it off.

"Are you sure?" I ask. "It'll get wrinkled."

"Doesn't matter," he says. He guides me off to the side so we're not blocking the other pedestrians, and suddenly we're standing pretty close. I don't remember noticing his shoulders before. Were they this broad a second ago? I pull my eyes away from his chest and up to his face, but that's not any better for my equilibrium. His eyes are even clearer and browner in the sunlight. They are kind of beautiful.

I slip my backpack off my shoulder and place it squarely between us so he has to back up a little.

He folds the jacket neatly and puts it inside.

His shirt is a crisp white, and the red tie stands out even more without his jacket on. I wonder what he looks like in regular clothes, and what regular clothes are for him. No doubt jeans and a T-shirt—the uniform of all American boys everywhere.

Is it the same for Jamaican boys?

My mood turns somber at the thought. I don't want to start over again. It was hard enough when we first moved to America. I don't want to have to learn the rituals and customs of a new high school. New friends. New cliques. New dress codes. New hangouts.

I scoot around him and start walking. "Asian American men are most likely to die of cancer," I say.

He frowns and double-steps to catch up. "Really? I don't like that. What kind?"

"I'm not sure."

"We should probably find out," he says.

He says *we* as if there's some future of us together where our respective mortalities will matter to each other.

"You really think you'll die of heart disease?" he asks. "Not something more epic?"

"Who cares about epic? Dead is dead."

He just stares at me, waiting for an answer. "Okay," I say. "I can't believe I'm about to tell you this. I secretly think I'm going to drown."

"Like in the open ocean, saving someone's life or something?"

"In the deep end of a hotel pool," I say.

He stops walking and pulls me off to the side again. A more considerate pedestrian there's never been. Most people just stop in the middle of the sidewalk. "Wait," he says. "You can't swim?"

I shrink my head down into my jacket. "No."

His eyes are searching my face and he's laughing at me without actually laughing. "But you're Jamaican. You grew up surrounded by water."

"Island heritage notwithstanding, I can't swim."

I can tell he wants to make fun of me, but he resists. "I'll teach you," he says.

"When?"

"Someday. Soon. Could you swim when you lived in Jamaica?" he asks.

"Yup, but then we got here, and instead of the ocean they had pools. I don't like chlorine."

"You know they have saltwater pools now."

"That ship has sailed," I say.

Now he does make fun of me. "What's your ship called? *Girl Who Grew Up on an Island, Which Is a Thing Surrounded on All Sides by Water, Can't Swim*? Because that would be a good name."

I laugh and thump him on the shoulder. He grabs my hand and holds my fingers. I try not to wish he could make good on his promise to teach me to swim.

daniel

I AM A SCHOLAR COMPILING the Book of Natasha. Here's what I know so far: She's a science geek. She's probably smarter than me. Her fingers are slightly longer than mine and feel good in my hands. She likes her music angsty. She's worried about something having to do with her mysterious appointment.

"Tell me again why you're wearing a suit?" she asks.

I groan long and loud and with feeling. "Let's talk about God instead."

"I get to ask questions too," she says.

We walk single file underneath more sidewalk scaffolding. (At any given moment approximately 99 [give or take] percent of Manhattan is under construction.)

"I applied to Yale. I have an interview with an alum later."

"Are you nervous?" she asks, when we're side by side again.

"I would be if I gave two shits."

"But you only give one shit?"

"Maybe half a shit," I say, laughing.

"So your parents are making you do it?"

A sudden yelling from the street grabs our attention, but it's only one cabdriver shouting at another.

"My parents are first-generation Korean immigrants," I say by way of explanation.

She slows her walking and looks over at me. "I don't know what that means," she says.

I shrug. "It means it doesn't matter what I want. I'm going to Yale. I'm going to be a doctor."

"And you don't want that?"

"I don't know what I want," I say.

From the look on her face, that was the worst thing I could say. She turns away from me and starts walking faster. "Well, you might as well be a doctor, then."

"What'd I do just now?" I ask, catching up to her.

She waves me off. "It's your life."

I feel like I'm close to failing a test. "Well, what do you want to be when you grow up?"

"A data scientist," she says, with no hesitation.

I open my mouth to ask WTF, but she fills me in with a practiced speech. I'm not the first person to have WTF'd her career choice.

"Data scientists analyze data, separate the noise from the signal, discern patterns, draw conclusions, and recommend actions based on the results."

"Are computers involved?"

"Yes, of course," she says. "There's a lot of data in this world."

"That's so practical. Have you always known what you wanted to be?" It's hard to keep the envy out of my voice.

She stops walking again. At this rate, we'll never get where she's going. "This isn't destiny. I chose this career. It didn't choose me. I'm not fated to be a data scientist. There's a career section in the library at school. I did research on growing fields in the sciences, and ta-da. No fate or destiny involved, just research."

"So it's not something you're passionate about?"

She shrugs and starts walking again. "It suits my personality," she says.

"Don't you want to do something you love?"

"Why?" she asks, like she genuinely doesn't understand the appeal of loving something.

"It's a long life to spend doing something you're only meh about," I insist. We scoot around a combination pretzel/hot dog cart that already has a line. It smells like sauerkraut and mustard (aka heaven).

She wrinkles her nose. "It's even longer if you spend it chasing dreams that can never, ever come true."

"Wait," I say. I put my hand on her arm to slow her down a little. "Who says they can't come true?"

This earns me a sideways glance. "Please. Do you know how many people want to be actors or writers or rock stars? A lot. Ninety-nine percent of them won't make it. Zero point nine percent of those left will make barely any money doing it. Only the last zero point one percent make it big. Everybody else just wastes their lives trying to be them."

"Are you secretly my father?" I ask.

"I sound like a fifty-year-old Korean man?"

"Without the accent."

"Well, he's just looking out for you. When you're a happy

doctor making lots of money, you'll thank him that you didn't become some starving artist hating your day job and dreaming pointlessly about making it big."

I wonder if she realizes how passionate she is about not being passionate.

She turns to look at me narrow-eyed. "Please don't tell me you're serious about the poetry thing."

"God forbid," I say with mock outrage.

We pass by a man holding a sign that says PLEASE HELP. DOWN ON MY LUCK. A cabbie on a mission honks long and loud at another cabbie, also on a mission.

"Are we really supposed to know what we want to do for the rest of our lives at the ripe old age of seventeen?"

"Don't you *want* to know?" she asks. She's definitely not a fan of uncertainty.

"I guess? I wish I could live ten lives at once."

She waves me off again. "Ugh. You just don't want to choose."

"That's not what I mean. I don't want to get stuck doing something that doesn't mean anything to me. This track I'm on? It goes on forever. Yale. Medical school. Residency. Marriage. Children. Retirement. Nursing home. Funeral home. Cemetery."

Maybe it's because of the importance of the day, maybe it's meeting her, but right now it's crucial to say exactly what I mean.

"We have big, beautiful brains. We invent things that fly. *Fly.* We write poetry. You probably hate poetry, but it's hard to argue with 'Shall I compare thee to a summer's day? Thou art more lovely and more temperate' in terms of sheer beauty. We are capable of big lives. A big history. Why settle? Why choose the practical thing, the mundane thing? We are born to dream and make the things we dream about."

It all comes out more passionately than I intend, but I mean every word.

Our eyes meet. There's something between us that wasn't there a minute ago.

I wait for her to say something flip, but she doesn't.

The universe stops and waits for us.

She opens her palm and she's going to take my hand. She's supposed to take my hand. We're meant to walk through this world together. I see it in her eyes. We are meant to be. I'm certain of this in a way I'm not certain about anything else.

But she doesn't take my hand. She walks on.

natasha

WE ARE HAVING A MOMENT I don't want to be having.

When they say the heart wants what it wants, they're talking about the poetic heart—the heart of love songs and soliloquies, the one that can break as if it were just-formed glass.

They're not talking about the real heart, the one that only needs healthy foods and aerobic exercise.

But the poetic heart is not to be trusted. It is fickle and will lead you astray. It will tell you that all you need is love and dreams. It will say nothing about food and water and shelter and money. It will tell you that this person, the one in front of you, the one who caught your eye for whatever reason, is the One. And he is. And she is. The One—for right now, until his heart or her heart decides on someone else or something else.

The poetic heart is not to be trusted with long-term decision-making.

I know all these things. I know them the way I know that Polaris, the North Star, is not actually the brightest star in the sky—it's the fiftieth.

And still here I am with Daniel in the middle of the sidewalk, on what is almost certainly my last day in America. My fickle, nonpractical, non-future-considering, nonsensical heart wants Daniel. It doesn't care that he's too earnest or that he doesn't know what he wants or that he's harboring dreams of being a poet, a profession that leads to heartbreak and the poorhouse.

I know there's no such thing as meant-to-be, and yet here I am wondering if maybe I've been wrong.

I close my open palm, which wants to touch him, and I walk on.

love

A Chemical History

ACCORDING TO SCIENTISTS, THERE ARE three stages of love: lust, attraction, and attachment. And, it turns out, each of the stages is orchestrated by chemicals—neurotransmitters—in the brain.

As you might expect, lust is ruled by testosterone and estrogen.

The second stage, attraction, is governed by dopamine and serotonin. When, for example, couples report feeling indescribably happy in each other's presence, that's dopamine, the pleasure hormone, doing its work.

Taking cocaine fosters the same level of euphoria. In fact, scientists who study both the brains of new lovers and cocaine addicts are hard-pressed to tell the difference.

The second chemical of the attraction phase is serotonin. When couples confess that they can't stop thinking about each other, it's because their serotonin level has dropped. People in love have the same low serotonin levels as people with OCD. The reason they can't stop thinking about each other is that they are literally obsessed.

Oxytocin and vasopressin control the third stage: attachment or long-term bonding. Oxytocin is released during orgasm and makes you feel closer to the person you've had sex with. It's also released during childbirth and helps bond mother to child. Vasopressin is released postcoitally.

Natasha knows these facts cold. Knowing them helped her get over Rob's betrayal. So she knows: love is just chemicals and coincidence.

So why does Daniel feel like something more?

daniel

THERE ARE EXACTLY NO ITEMS on the list of things I want to do less than go to my interview. And yet. It's almost eleven a.m., and if I'm going to go to this thing then I need to get gone.

Natasha and I have been walking along in silence ever since The Moment. I wish I could say it's a comfortable silence, but it isn't. I want to talk to her about it—The Moment—but who knows if she even felt it. No way does she believe in that stuff.

Midtown Manhattan is different from where we first met. More skyscrapers and fewer souvenir shops. The people act different too. They're not tourists out for pleasure or shopping. There's no excitement or gawking or smiling. These people work in these skyscrapers. I'm pretty sure my appointment is somewhere in this neighborhood.

We keep walking and not talking until we get to a giant concrete and glass monstrosity of a building. It amazes me that people spend their entire days inside places like this doing things they don't love for people they don't like. At least being a doctor will be better than that.

"This is where I'm going," she says.

"I can wait for you out here," I say, like a person who doesn't have an appointment that will determine his future in just over an hour.

"Daniel," she says, using the stern voice she's sure to use on our future children (she'll definitely be the disciplinarian). "You have an interview and I have this . . . thing. This is where we say goodbye."

She's right. I may not want the future my parents have planned for me, but I don't have any better ideas. If I stay here much longer, my train will derail from its track.

It occurs to me that maybe that's what I want. Maybe all the things I'm feeling for Natasha are just excuses to make it derail. After all, my parents would never approve. Not only is she not Korean, she is black. There's no future here.

That and the fact that my extreme like for her is clearly unrequited. And love is not love if it's not requited, right?

I should go.

I'm going to go.

I'm getting gone.

"You're right," I say.

She's surprised, and maybe even a little disappointed, but what difference does that make? She has to want this, and clearly she does not.

natasha

I WASN'T EXPECTING HIM to say that, and I didn't expect to feel disappointed, but I do. Why am I thinking about romance with a boy I'll never see again? My future gets decided in five minutes.

We're standing close enough to the building's sliding glass doors that the cool of the air-conditioning washes over my skin as people enter and exit.

He sticks out his hand for a shake but quickly pulls it back. "Sorry," he says, and blushes. He folds his arms across his chest.

"Well, I'm going," I say.

"You're going," he says, and then neither of us moves.

We stand there not saying anything for another few seconds until I remember I still have his jacket in my backpack. I take it out and watch as he shrugs it back on.

"In that suit, you look like you should work in this building," I say to him.

I mean it as a compliment, but he doesn't take it as one.

He tugs at his tie and grimaces. "Maybe I will one day."

"Well," I say after more staring-and-not-talking. "This is getting awkward."

"Should we just hug?"

"I thought you suits only shook hands." I'm trying to keep my tone light, but my vocal cords go all husky and weird.

He smiles and doesn't try to keep any of the sadness off his face. How can he be so okay with showing off his heart?

I have to look away from him. I don't want whatever is happening between us to happen, but it feels like trying to stop the weather from happening.

The doors open and the cool air washes over my skin again. I'm hot and cold at the same time. I open my arms for a hug at the same moment he does. We try to hug each other from the same side and end up bumping chests instead. We laugh awkwardly and stop moving.

"I'm going to go right," he says. "You go left."

"Okay," I say, and go left. He holds me, and since we're both about the same height my face brushes against his cheek, which is soft and smooth and warm. I let my head drop onto his shoulder and my body relaxes in his arms. For a minute, I let myself feel how tired I am. It's hard trying to hold on to a place that doesn't want you. But Daniel does want me. I feel it in the way he holds me tight.

I pull out of his arms and don't meet his eyes.

He decides not to say whatever he was going to say.

I get out my phone and check the time.

"Time to go," he says, before I can say it first.

I turn and walk into the cold building.

I think about him as I sign in with security. I think about him as I cross the lobby floor. I think about him in the elevator and down the long hallway and every moment until the moment that I have to stop thinking about him, when I enter the office.

The construction noises I heard over the phone earlier were actually due to construction, because the office is only halfway built. The walls are partly painted, and bare bulbs hang from the ceiling. Sawdust and paint splotches cover the tarped floor. Behind the desk, a woman sits with both hands resting on her office phone, as if she's willing it to ring. Despite her bright red lipstick and rose-rouged cheeks, she's very pale. Her hair is deep black and perfectly styled. Something about her doesn't seem quite real. She seems like she's playing a part—an extra from an old-school Disney cartoon or from a period movie set in the 1950s that called for secretaries. Her desk is neat, with color-coded stacks of files. There's a mug that says PARALEGALS DO IT CHEAPER.

She smiles a sad, trembling smile as I approach.

"Do I have the right place?" I ask out loud.

She stares at me mutely.

"Is this Attorney Fitzgerald's office?" I prompt.

"You're Natasha," she says.

She must be the person I spoke with earlier. I approach the desk.

"I have some bad news," she says. My stomach clenches. I'm not ready for what she's going to say. Is it over before it's even begun? Has my fate already been decided? Am I really being deported tonight?

A man in paint-splattered overalls walks in and starts drilling. Someone else I can't see begins hammering. She doesn't change her volume to adjust for the noise. I move even closer to the desk.

"Jeremy—Attorney Fitzgerald—was in a car accident an hour ago. He's still in the hospital. His wife says he's fine, just a few bruises. But he won't be back until late this afternoon."

Her voice sounds normal, but her eyes are anything but. She pulls the phone a little closer and looks at it instead of me.

"But we have an appointment now." My whine is uncharitable, but I can't help it. "I really need him to help me."

Now she does look at me, eyes wide and incredulous. "Didn't you hear what I said? He was hit by a car. He can't be here right now." She pushes a sheaf of forms at me and doesn't look at me again.

It takes me at least fifteen minutes to fill out the paperwork. On the first form, I answer several variations on the questions of whether I'm a communist, a criminal, or a terrorist and whether I would take up arms to defend the United States. I would not, but still I check the box that says yes.

Another form asks for details about what's happened in the deportation process so far.

The final form is a client questionnaire that asks me to give a full accounting of my time in the United States. I don't know what to say. I don't know what Attorney Fitzgerald is looking for. Does he want to know how we entered the country? How we hid? How it feels every time I write down my fake social security number on a school form? How every time I do, I picture my mom getting on that bus to Florida?

Does he want to know how it feels to be undocumented? Or how I keep waiting for someone to find out I don't belong here at all?

Probably not. He's looking for facts, not philosophy, so I write them down. We traveled to America on a tourist visa. When it came time for us to leave, we stayed. We have not left the country since. We have committed no crimes, except for my dad's DUI.

I hand her back the forms and she flips immediately to the client questionnaire. "You need more here," she says.

"Like what?"

"What does America mean to you? Why do you want to stay? How will you contribute to making America greater?"

"Is that really—"

"Anything Jeremy can use to humanize you will help," she says.

If people who were actually born here had to prove they were worthy enough to live in America, this would be a much less populated country.

She flips through my other forms as I write about what a hardworking, optimistic, patriotic citizen I would be. I write that America is my home in my heart, and how citizenship will legalize what I already feel. I belong here. In short, I am more sincere than I'm ever comfortable being. Daniel would be proud of me.

Daniel.

He's probably on a train on his way to his appointment. Will he do the proper thing and become a doctor after all? Will he think of me in the future and remember the girl he spent two hours with one day in New York? Will he wonder whatever happened to me? Maybe he'll do a Google search using only my first name and not get very far. More likely, though, he'll forget about me by this evening, as I will certainly forget about him.

The phone rings as I write, and she grabs it before it has a chance to ring twice.

"Oh my God, Jeremy. Are you all right?" She closes her eyes, cradles the phone with both hands, and presses it close to her face. "I wanted to come, but your wife said I should hold down the fort." Her eyes flick open when she says the word *wife*.

"Are you sure you're okay?" The more she listens, the brighter she becomes. Her face flushes and her eyes shine with happy tears.

She's so obviously in love with him I expect to see heart bubbles floating around the room. Are they having an affair?

"I wanted to come," she whispers again. After a series of murmured okays, she hangs up the phone. "He's all right." She beams. Her whole body is aglow with relief.

"That's great," I say.

She takes the forms from my hands. I wait as she reads through them.

"Would you like to hear some good news?" she asks.

Of course I would. I nod slowly.

"I've seen lots of cases like this, and I think you'll be okay."

I don't know what I was expecting her to say, but certainly not this.

"You really think he'll be able to help?" I can hear the hope and skepticism in my own voice.

"Jeremy never loses," she says, so proudly that she could be talking about herself.

But of course, that can't be true. Everyone loses something sometime. I should ask her to be more precise, to give me an exact win/loss ratio so I can decide how to feel.

"There's hope," she says simply.

Even though I hate poetry, a poem I read for English class pops into my head. *"Hope" is the thing with feathers.* I understand concretely what that means now. Something inside my chest wants to fly out, wants to sing and laugh and dance with relief.

I thank her and leave the office quickly, before I can ask her something that takes away this feeling. Usually I fall on the side of knowing the truth, even if the truth is bad. It's not the easiest way of being. Sometimes the truth can hurt more than you expect.

A few weeks ago my parents were arguing in their bedroom with the door closed. It was one of those rare occasions when my mom actually got angry with my dad to his face. Peter found me eavesdropping outside their door. After they were done arguing, I asked him if he wanted to know what I'd heard, but he didn't. He said he could tell that whatever I learned was bad, and he didn't really want any badness in his life just then. At the time I was annoyed with him. But later I thought maybe he'd been right. I wished I could unhear what I'd overheard.

Back in the hallway, I lean my forehead against the wall

and hesitate. I debate going back into the office to press her for more details but decide against it. What good will it do? I might as well wait for the official word from the lawyer. Besides, I'm tired of worrying. I know that what she said is not a guarantee. But I need to feel something other than resigned dread. Hope seems like a good substitute.

I consider calling my parents to tell them about this new development, but then I don't do that either. I have no new information to share. What would I say? A man I don't know has sent me to see another man I don't know. A paralegal, who is not a lawyer, whom I also don't know, says everything might be all right. What's the use in getting all our hopes up?

The person I really want to talk to is Daniel, but he's long gone to his interview.

I wish I'd been nicer to him.

I wish I'd gotten his phone number.

What if this immigration nonsense resolves itself? If I get to stay, how will I find him again? Because no matter how much I pretended it didn't exist, there was something between us. Something big.

hannah winter

A Fairy-Tale History, Part 1

HANNAH HAS ALWAYS THOUGHT OF herself as living in a fairy tale where she's not the star. She's neither the princess nor the fairy godmother. Neither the high, evil witch nor her familiar. Hannah is a minor character, illustrated for the first time on page twelve or thirteen. The cook, perhaps, presiding over crumpets and sugarplums. Or maybe she's the handmaiden, good-natured and just out of view.

It wasn't until she met and started working for Attorney Jeremy Fitzgerald that she imagined she could become the star. In him she recognized her One True Love. Her Happily-Ever-After. This despite the fact that he is a married man. Despite the fact that he's a father to two young children.

Hannah never believed he would love her back until the day he did just that.

That day is today.

attorney jeremy fitzgerald

A Fairy-Tale History, Part 1

JEREMY FITZGERALD was crossing the street when a drunk and distraught man—an insurance actuary—in a white BMW hit him at twenty miles per hour. The blow wasn't enough to kill him, but it was enough to make him consider his eventual death and his current life. It was enough to make him admit to himself that he was in love with his paralegal, Hannah Winter, and that he had been for some time now.

At some point later today, when he returns to his office, he will wordlessly take Hannah into his arms. He will hold her and wonder, very briefly, about the future that loving her will cost him.

daniel

Area Teenager Chooses Poorly

My mother, the pacifist, would kill me dead if she knew what I'd just done. I rescheduled my interview. For a girl. Not even a Korean girl, a black girl. A black girl I don't really know. A black girl I don't really know, who might not even like me.

The woman on the phone said my timing was perfect. She'd been about to call me to reschedule as well. The only appointment I could get is for late in the day, 6 p.m., so here I am in the lobby of the building where I left Natasha, reading the directory and keeping an eye out for her. Most of the tenants of this building are lawyers (J.D., Esq.) and accounting types (CPA, CFA, etc.). I've never seen so many degree abbreviations in my life. Daniel Jae Ho Bae, FB (Foolish Boy), DTF (Doomed to Failure).

What appointment could she possibly have in this building? Either she's an heiress with money to invest, or she's in trouble and needs a lawyer to help her.

Across the lobby, the elevator doors open and she walks out.

When I was rescheduling my appointment, a part of me wondered if I was being ridiculous. A girl I've just met isn't worth jeopardizing my future over. It was easier to have that thought when I wasn't looking at her, because now I can't remember why I hesitated at all.

Of course she's worth it. And I can't explain it.

Yes, she's pretty. The combination of her big hair and bright black eyes and full pink lips is undeniably cute. Also, she has the nicest legs that exist in the known world (I moved them up to number one from number three after careful study—I'm being objective here). So yes, I'm definitely attracted to her, but there's something else too, and I'm not just saying that because she has the nicest legs in the known universe. Objectively speaking.

I watch as she makes her way across the lobby. She's looking around, trying to find something or someone. Her shoulders literally sag when she doesn't find it. She's gotta be looking for me, right? Unless she met another potential love of her life in the thirty minutes she was away from me.

Outside, she does a slow 360 one way and then a slower 360 the other way. Whoever she's looking for is still not there.

natasha

HE'S NOT IN THE LOBBY, and he's not outside in the courtyard. I have to admit that he's not here and that I wanted him to be. My stomach feels a little hollow, like I'm hungry, but food is not what I want.

The day's gotten warmer. I take off my jacket, fold it over my forearm, and stand there trying to decide what to do next. I'm reluctant to leave, and reluctant to admit to myself that I don't want to leave. It's not that I think we were meant to be or anything ridiculous like that. But it would've been nice to spend the next few hours with him. It might've been nice to go on a date with him. I would've liked to know if he blushes when he kisses.

This is the last place I saw him. If I leave, then I have no chance of seeing him again. I wonder how his interview is going. Is he saying the right things, or is he letting all his doubt and existential angst shine through? The boy needs a life coach.

I'm about to go when something makes me take a final look around. I know it's not possible to feel a specific person's presence. More than likely my subconscious spotted him as I was walking through the lobby. People use poetic language to describe things they don't understand. Usually there's a scientific explanation if you only look for it.

Anyway, there he is.

He is here.

daniel

SHE'S WALKING TOWARD ME. A couple of hours ago I would've said that her face was expressionless, but I'm becoming a Natasha expert, and her face is only trying to be expressionless. If I had to guess, I would say that she's happy to see me.

"What happened to your interview?" she asks as soon as she's close enough.

No hug. No "I'm so happy to see you." Maybe I'm not such a Natasha expert after all.

Do I go with the facts or the truth (curiously, these are not always the same)? The fact is, I postponed. The truth is, I postponed so I could spend more time with her. I go with the truth:

"I postponed so I could spend more time with you."

"Are you insane? This is your life we're talking about."

"I didn't burn the building to the ground, Tash. I just moved it until later."

"Who is Tash?" she asks, but there's a smile at the corner of her lips.

"How did your thing go?" I point my chin in the direction

of the elevators. Her smile goes away. Note to self: Do not bring this up again.

"Fine. I have to come back at three-thirty."

I look at my phone: 11:35 a.m. "Looks like we have more time together," I say. I expect her to roll her eyes, but she doesn't. I take it as a small victory.

She shivers a little and rubs her hands down her forearms. I can see the goose bumps on her skin, and now I've learned another thing about her: she gets cold easily. I take her jacket and help her into it. She slides one arm in and then the other, and then shrugs to adjust the shoulders. I help her with the collar.

It's a small thing. I let my hand rest on the back of her neck, and she leans back into me just slightly. Her hair tickles my nose. It's a small thing, but it feels like something we've been doing for a long time now.

She turns, and I have to lift my hands so I don't touch her more intimately. Wherever we're going, we're not there yet.

"Are you sure you're not jeopardizing—" she begins.

"I don't actually care."

"You should care." She stops talking and looks up at me with restless eyes. "You did it for me?"

"Yes."

"What makes you so sure I'm worth it?"

"Instinct," I say. I don't know what it is about her that makes me fearless with the truth.

Her eyes widen and she shivers slightly. "You're impossible," she says.

"It's possible," I say.

She laughs, and her black eyes sparkle at me. "What should we do now?" she asks.

I need to get my hair cut and I need to get the pouch and deposit slips to my dad. I want to do neither of these things. What I want to do is find someplace cozy and cozy up with her. But. The pouch needs to be delivered. I ask her if she's up for a trip to Harlem and she agrees. Really, this is the absolute last thing I should be doing. If there are worse ideas than this, I don't know what they are. My dad's just going to freak her out. She's going to meet him and imagine that he's what I'll be like in fifty years, and then she'll go flying for the hills because that's what I would do in her place.

My dad's a weird guy. I say weird but what I mean is epically fucking strange. First, he doesn't really talk to anyone except customers. This includes me and Charlie. Unless berating counts as talking. If berating counts, then he's said more to Charlie this past summer and fall than he has in nineteen years. I may be exaggerating, but only slightly.

I don't know how I'm going to explain Natasha to him or Charlie. Well, Charlie I don't really care about, but my dad will notice her. He'll know something's up in the same way he always knows which customer is going to shoplift or who's good for an IOU and who's not.

Later tonight at dinner, he'll say something to my mom in Korean in the voice he uses to complain about Americans. I don't really want either of them involved in this yet. We're not ready for that kind of pressure.

Natasha says that all families are strange, and it's true. I'll have to ask her more about her family later after we do this thing. We descend into the subway.

"Get ready," I say.

natasha

HARLEM IS ONLY A TWENTY-FIVE-MINUTE subway ride from where we were, but it's like we've gone to a different country. The skyscrapers have been replaced by small, closely packed stores with bright awnings. The air smells brighter, less like a city and more like a neighborhood. Almost everyone on the street is black.

Daniel doesn't say anything as we walk along Martin Luther King Boulevard toward his parents' store. He slows down when we pass by an empty storefront with a huge FOR RENT sign and a pawnshop with a green awning. Finally we stop in front of a black hair care and beauty supply store.

It's called Black Hair Care. I've been into lots of these. "Go down the street to the beauty supply and pick up some relaxer for me," says my mother every two months or so.

It's a thing. Everyone knows it's a thing how all the black hair care places are owned by Koreans and what an injustice that is. I don't know why I didn't think of it when Daniel said they owned a store.

I can't see inside because the windows are covered with old, sun-faded posters of smiling and suited black women all with the same chemically treated hairstyle. Apparently—according to these posters, at least—only certain hairstyles are allowed to attend board meetings. Even my mom is guilty of this kind of sentiment. She wasn't happy when I decided to wear an Afro, saying that it isn't professional-looking. But I like my big Afro. I also liked when my hair was longer and relaxed. I'm happy to have choices. They're mine to make.

Next to me, Daniel is so nervous he's vibrating. I wonder if it's because I'm going to meet his dad, or because of the politics of his parents' owning this store. He faces me and tugs his tie from side to side, as if it's been too tight this whole time.

"So my dad's really—" He stops and starts again. "And my brother's really—"

His eyes are everywhere except on mine and his voice is strained, probably because he's trying to speak without breathing.

"Maybe you could just wait out here," he says, finally getting an entire sentence out.

At first I don't really think anything of it. I figure everyone's embarrassed by their family. I'm embarrassed about mine. Well, my father, at least. In Daniel's place, I'd do the same thing. My cheating ex, Rob, never met my father. It was just easier. No listening to my father's too-thick, fake American accent. No watching him try to find an opening so he can talk about himself and all his plans for the future and how he's going to be famous one day.

We're standing just in front of the store when two black teenage girls walk out laughing with each other. Another woman, also black, walks in.

It occurs to me that maybe he's not embarrassed about his family. Maybe he's embarrassed about me. Or maybe he's afraid his parents will be ashamed of me. I don't know why I didn't think of this before.

America's not really a melting pot. It's more like one of those divided metal plates with separate sections for starch, meat, and veggies. I'm looking at him and he's still not looking at me. Suddenly we're having a moment I didn't expect.

hair

An African American History

IN FIFTEENTH-CENTURY AFRICAN CIVILIZATIONS, hairstyles were markers of identity. Hairstyle could indicate everything from tribe or family background to religion to social status. Elaborate hairstyles designated power and wealth. A subdued style could be a sign that you were in a state of mourning. More than that, hair could have spiritual importance. Because it's on your head—the highest part of your body and closest to the skies—many Africans viewed it as a passageway for spirits to the soul, a way to interact with God.

That history was erased with the dawn of slavery. On slave ships, newly captured Africans were forcibly shaved in a profound act of dehumanization, an act that effectively severed the link between hair and cultural identity.

Postslavery, African American hair took on complex associations. "Good" hair was seen as anything closer to European standards of beauty. Good hair was straight and smooth. Curly, textured hair, the natural hair of many African Americans, was seen as bad. Straight hair was beautiful. Tightly curled hair was ugly. In the early 1900s, Madam C. J. Walker, an African

American, became a millionaire by inventing and marketing hair care products to black women. Most famously, she improved on the design of the "hot comb," a device for straightening hair. In the 1960s, George E. Johnson marketed the "relaxer," a chemical product used to straighten otherwise curly African American hair. According to some estimates, the black hair care industry is worth more than one billion dollars annually.

Since postslavery days and through to modern times, debate has raged in the African American community. What does it mean to wear your hair natural versus straightened? Is straightening your hair a form of self-hatred? Does it mean you think your hair in its natural state is not beautiful? If you wear your hair naturally, are you making a political statement, claiming black power? The way African American women wear their hair has often been about much more than vanity. It's been about more than just an individual's notion of her own beauty.

When Natasha decides to wear hers in an Afro, it's not because she's aware of all this history. She does it despite Patricia Kingsley's assertions that Afros make women look militant and unprofessional. Those assertions are rooted in fear—fear that her daughter will be harmed by a society that still so often fears blackness. Patricia also doesn't raise her other objection: Natasha's new hairstyle feels like a rejection. She's been relaxing her own hair all her life. She'd relaxed Natasha's since she was ten years old. These days when Patricia looks at her daughter, she doesn't see as much of herself reflected back as before, and it hurts. But of course, all teenagers do this. All teenagers separate from their parents. To grow up is to grow apart.

It takes three years for Natasha's natural hair to grow in fully. She doesn't do it to make a political statement. In fact, she liked having her hair straight. In the future, she may make it straight again. She does it because she wants to try something new.

She does it simply because it looks beautiful.

daniel

Area Boy Is as Big an Asshole as His Brother

"Maybe you could just wait out here," I said, like I'm ashamed of her, like I'm trying to keep her hidden. My regret is instantaneous. No waiting for a few minutes to realize the full impact of my words. Nope. Nope. Nope. Immediate and all-consuming.

And once they're out, I can't believe I said them. Is this what I'm made of? Nothing?

I'm a bigger asshole than Charlie.

I can't look at her. Her eyes are on my face and I can't look at her. I want that time machine. I want the last minute back.

I fucked up.

If it's going to be Daniel and Natasha, then dealing with my dad's racism is only the beginning. But she and I are just at the beginning, and I just don't want to have to deal with him right now. I want to do the easy thing, not the right thing. I want to fall in love, with an emphasis on the *falling* part.

No obstacles in the way, please. No one needs to get bruised up falling in love. I just want to fall the way everybody else gets to.

natasha

I'LL BE FINE.

I'll be fine waiting here. I understand. Really I do. But there's part of me, the part that doesn't believe in God or true love, that really wants him to prove me wrong about not believing in those things. I want him to choose me. Even though it's way too early in the history of us. Even though it's not what I would do. I want him to be as noble as he first seemed to be, but of course he's not. Nobody is. So I let him off his own hook.

"Don't worry so much," I say. "I'll wait."

daniel

WHEN YOU'RE BORN, THEY (God or little aliens or whoever) should send you into the world with a bunch of free passes. A Do-Over, a Rain Check, a Take-Backsie, a Get Out of Jail Free Card. I would use my Do-Over now.

I look up at her and realize she knows exactly what I'm going through. She'll understand if I just go inside and hand over the pouch and come back outside. Then we can just continue on our way and I won't have to have any "Who was that girl?" conversations later with my dad. No "Once you go black" cracks from Charlie. This little weirdness will be a small hiccup on our road to greatness, to epic coupledom.

But I can't do it. I can't leave her out here. Partly because it's the right thing to do. But mostly because she and I are not really at the beginning.

"Can I try that again?" I ask, deploying my Do-Over.

She smiles so big that I know that whatever happens will be worth it.

natasha

A BELL CHIMES AS SOON as we enter. It's like every other beauty supply store I've ever been in. It's small and crammed with rows of metal shelves overflowing with plastic bottles promising that their secret formula is best for your hair, skin, etc.

The cash register is right across from the entrance, so I see his father right away. Immediately I know where Daniel gets his good looks. His dad is older and balding, but he has the same sharp bone structure and perfectly symmetrical face that make Daniel so attractive. He's busy ringing up a customer and doesn't acknowledge Daniel at all, though I'm sure he saw us both. The customer is a boy around my age, black with short purple hair, three lip rings, one nose ring, an eyebrow ring, and too many earrings to count. I want to see what he's buying, but it's already bagged.

Daniel pulls the pouch from his suit pocket and starts to walk over. His dad gives him a brief glance. I'm not sure what was communicated, but Daniel stops moving and sighs.

"You need to go to the bathroom or anything?" he asks. "There's one in the back."

I shake my head. He strangles the pouch with his hands.

"Well, this is it. This is the store."

"Want to show me around?" I ask to help distract him.

"Not much to see. First three aisles are for hair. Shampoo, conditioner, extensions, dyes, lots of chemical things I don't understand. Aisle three is makeup. Aisle four is equipment."

He glances at his dad, but he's still busy.

"Do you need something?" he asks.

I touch my hair. "No, I—"

"I didn't mean a product. We have a fridge in the back with soda and stuff."

"Sure," I say. I like the idea of seeing behind the scenes.

We walk down the hair dye aisle. All the boxes feature broadly smiling women with the most perfectly colored and styled hair. It's not hair dye being sold in these bottles, it's happiness.

I stop in front of a group of boxes with brightly colored dyes and pick up a pink one. There's a very small, secret, impractical part of me that's always wanted pink hair.

It takes Daniel a few seconds to realize that I've stopped walking.

"Pink?" he asks, when he sees the box in my hand.

I wiggle it at him. "Why not?"

"Doesn't seem like your style."

Of course he's completely right, but I hate that he thinks so. Am I too predictable and boring? I think back to the boy I saw when we entered the store. I bet he keeps everyone guessing.

"Shows how much you know," I say, and pat my hair. His eyes follow my hand, and now I'm really self-conscious and hoping he's not going to ask to touch my hair or a bunch of dumb questions about it. Not that I don't want him to touch my hair, because I do—just not as a curiosity.

"I think you would look beautiful with a giant pink Afro," he says.

Sincerity is sexy, and my cynical heart notices.

"The whole thing wouldn't be pink. Maybe just the ends."

He reaches for the box, so now we're both holding it and facing each other in an aisle that really only has enough space for one.

"It would look like strawberry frosting," he says. With his other hand he pulls a few strands of my hair through his fingers, and I find that I don't mind, not one little bit.

"Oh, look. My. Little. Brother is here," says a voice from the end of the aisle. Daniel jerks his hand from my hair. We both let go of the dye at the same time, and the box clatters to the floor. Daniel bends to pick it up. I turn to face our interloper.

He's taller and broader than Daniel. On his face, the family bone structure seems even sharper. He rests the broom he was holding against a shelf and saunters down the aisle toward us. His wide, dark eyes are filled with curiosity and a kind of mischievous glee.

I'm not sure I like him.

Daniel stands up and hands the dye back to me.

"What's up, Charlie?" he asks.

"The. Sky. Is. Up. Little brother," says Charlie. I get the feeling he's been using that phrase that same way for all their lives.

He's looking at me as he says it, and his face is more sneer than smile.

"Who. Is. This?" he asks, still only looking at me.

Next to me, Daniel takes a deep breath and readies himself to say something, but I jump in.

"I'm Natasha." He stares at me as if there must be more to say. "A friend of your brother's," I continue.

"Oh, I thought maybe he'd caught a shoplifting customer." His face is a parody of innocence. "We get a lot of those in a store like this." His eyes are laughing and mean. "I'm sure you understand."

I definitely don't like him.

"Jesus Christ, Charlie," Daniel says. He takes a step toward Charlie but I grab his hand. He stops and links his fingers with mine and squeezes.

Charlie makes a big show of looking down at our joined hands and then back up at us.

"Is this what I think it is? Is it looooove, Little. Brother?" He claps his hands together with a loud smack and does a laughing two-step dance.

"This. Is. Great. Yes. You know what this means, don't you? All the heat will be off me. When the 'rents find out about this, I'll be a Boy Scout again. Fuck academic probation."

He's laughing loudly now and rubbing his palms together, like a villain detailing his plans for world domination.

"Wow. You're an asshole," I say, unable to help myself.

He smiles as if I've paid him a compliment. But the smile doesn't last long.

He looks at our hands again and then at Daniel. "You're such a punk," he says. "Where are you gonna go with this?"

I squeeze Daniel's hand tighter and pull it to my side. I want to prove Charlie wrong. "Do your thing and let's get out of here," I say.

He nods, and we turn away—and walk right into his father. I pull my hand from his at the same time he's letting mine go, but it's too late. His father's already seen us.

daniel

Giant Bag of Dicks Masquerades as Teenage Boy, Fools Exactly No One

Charlie is a giant bag of dicks that I'd like to light on fire. I want to hit him in his perfectly smug face. It's not a new emotion for me, since I've wanted to do it since I was ten, but this time he's finally gone too far. I'm thinking how good it will feel to break my hand on his face, but I'm also focused on the feel of Natasha's hand in mine.

I need to get her out of here before my family derails my life just as it's getting started.

"What are you doing?" my father asks in Korean.

I decide to ignore the question he's really asking. Instead, I hold out the pouch for him to take.

"Mom said I had to bring you this." I say it in English so Natasha doesn't think we're talking about her.

Charlie sidles up next me. "Want me to help translate for your *friend*?" he asks.

He overemphasizes *friend*. Because being a dick on fire is Charlie's raison d'être.

My dad gives him a hard look. "I thought you don't understand Korean," he says to Charlie.

Charlie shrugs. "I get by." Not even my dad's disapproval can stop him from enjoying himself at my expense.

"Is that why you fail out of Harvard? You only get by?" This part he says in Korean because the last thing my dad would want to do is air our dirty laundry in front of a *miguk saram.* An American.

Charlie doesn't give a crap and translates anyway, but he's smiling a little less. "Don't worry," he says to Natasha. "He's not talking about you. Not yet. He's just calling me stupid."

Dad's face goes completely blank, so I know he's really angry now. Charlie's got him trapped. Anything he says Charlie will translate, and my dad's sense of propriety can't allow that to happen. Instead, he turns into Deferential Store Owner like I've seen him do a million times to a million customers.

"You want something before you leave?" he asks Natasha. He clasps his hands, half bends at the waist, and smiles his best customer-service smile.

"No, thank you, Mr.—" She stops because she doesn't know my last name.

My dad doesn't answer.

"Yes. Yes. You friend of Daniel's. Take anything you want." This is an accident in progress, but I don't know how to stop it. He pats at his pockets until he finds his glasses and peers at the bottles on the shelf.

"Not this aisle," he mutters. "Come with me."

Maybe if we just go along this will all be over quickly. Natasha and I follow him helplessly while Charlie laughs.

My dad finds what he's looking for one aisle over. "Here.

Relaxer for your hair." He pulls a big black and white tub from a shelf and hands it to Natasha.

"Relaxer," he says again. "Make your hair not so big."

How was I born into this family and how can I get out of it? Charlie laughs long and loud.

I start to say that she doesn't need anything, but Natasha interrupts. "Thank you, Mr.—"

"Bae," I say, because she should know my last name.

"Mr. Bae. I don't need any—"

"Hair too big," he says again.

"I like it big," she says.

"Better get a different boyfriend, then," says Charlie. He waggles his eyebrows to make sure we all get his innuendo. I'm surprised he doesn't follow it up with a hand gesture just to be absolutely clear. My surprise doesn't last, because he holds his thumb and forefinger apart by an inch.

"Good joke, Charlie," I say. "Yes, my penis is only an inch long." I don't bother to look at my father's face.

Natasha turns to me and her mouth actually drops open. She's definitely reconsidering her recent life choices. I practically fling the pouch at my father. Things cannot get any worse, so I reach for her hand despite the fact that my father is standing right there. Mercifully, she lets me take it.

"Thank you, come again," booms Charlie when we're almost out the door. He's like a pig in shit. Or just the shit.

I flip him off and ignore the vast disapproval coming from my father, because there'll be time for that later.

natasha

I'M LAUGHING EVEN THOUGH I know I shouldn't. That was the most perfectly awful experience. Poor Daniel.

Observable Fact: Families are the worst.

We're almost all the way back to the subway station before he finally stops tugging me along. He slaps a palm against the back of his neck and hangs his head.

"I'm sorry," he says, so quietly that I more lip-read it than hear it.

I'm trying to keep my laughter suppressed, because he looks like someone died, but I'm having a hard time. The image of his dad trying to shove the tub of relaxer at me rises in my mind and the laughter just bubbles out of me. Once I start, I can't stop. I clutch my stomach as hysterics take me over. Daniel just stares at me. His frown is so deep it might become permanent.

"That was terrible," I say, finally calm. "I don't think that could've gone any worse. Racist dad. Racist *and* sexist older brother."

Daniel rubs the spot on his neck and frowns some more.

"And the store! I mean, the ancient posters of those women, and your dad critiquing my hair, and your brother making a small penis joke."

By the time I'm done listing all the things that were awful, I'm laughing again. It takes him a few more seconds, but finally he smiles too, and I'm glad for it.

"I'm glad you think this is funny," he says.

"Come on," I say. "Tragedy is funny."

"Are we in a tragedy?" he asks, smiling broadly now.

"Of course. Isn't that what life is? We all die at the end."

"I guess so," he says. He steps closer, takes my hand, and places it on his chest.

I study my nails. I study my cuticles. Anything to avoid looking up into those brown eyes of his. His heart thrums beneath my fingers.

Finally I look up and he covers my hand with his.

"I'm sorry," he says. "I'm sorry about my family."

I nod, because the feel of his heartbeat is doing funny things to my vocal cords.

"I'm sorry about everything, about the whole history of the world and all its racism and the unfairness of all of it."

"What are you even saying? It's not your fault. You can't apologize for racism."

"I can and I do."

Jesus. Save me from the nice and sincere boys who feel things too deeply. I still think what happened is funny in its perfect awfulness, but I understand his shame too. It's hard to come from someplace or someone you're not proud of.

"You're not your dad," I say, but he doesn't believe me. I understand his fear. Who are we if not a product of our parents and their histories?

hair

A Korean American History

DANIEL'S FAMILY DID NOT ENTER the black hair care business by chance. When Dae Hyun and Min Soo moved to New York City, there was an entire community of fellow South Korean immigrants waiting to help them. Dae Hyun's cousin gave them a loan and advised them to open a black hair care store. His cousin had a similar store, as did many other immigrants in his new community. The stores were thriving.

The dominance of South Koreans in the black hair care industry also did not happen by chance. It began in the 1960s with the rise in popularity of wigs made with South Korean hair in the African American community. The wigs were so popular that the South Korean government banned the export of raw hair from its shores. This ensured that wigs featuring South Korean hair could *only* be made in South Korea. At the same time, the U.S. government banned the import of wigs that contained hair from China. Those two actions effectively solidified the dominance of South Korea in the wig market. The wig business naturally evolved to the more general black hair care business.

It's estimated that South Korean businesses control between sixty and eighty percent of that market, including distribution, retail, and, increasingly, manufacturing. Be it for cultural reasons or for racial ones, this dominance in distribution makes it nearly impossible for any other group to gain a foothold in the industry. South Korean distributors primarily distribute to South Korean retailers, effectively shutting everyone else out of the market.

Dae Hyun is not aware of any of this history. What he knows is this: America is the land of opportunity. His children will have more than he once did.

daniel

I WANT TO THANK HER for not hating me. After that experience in my parents' store, who could blame her? Also, she didn't need to react to my family as peacefully as she did. If she'd yelled at both my brother and my dad, I would've understood. It's a miracle (water-into-wine variety) that she's still willing to hang out with me, and I'm more than grateful for it.

Instead of saying all that, I ask her if she wants to get some lunch. We're back at the subway entrance, and all I want to do is get as far away from the store as possible. If the D line went to the moon, I'd buy a ticket.

"I'm starving," I say.

She rolls her eyes. "Starving, really? You have a penchant for exaggeration."

"It's to offset your precision."

"Do you have a place in mind?" she asks.

I suggest my favorite restaurant in Koreatown and she agrees.

We find side-by-side seats on the train and settle in. It'll take forty minutes to get all the way back downtown.

I take out my phone to find more questions. "Ready for more?" I ask her.

She slides closer to me so our shoulders are pressed together, and peers down at my phone. She's so close her hair tickles my nose. I can't help it. I take what I think is a discreet sniff of her hair that is not discreet at all.

She scoots away from me, eyes wide and mortified. "Did you just smell me?" she asks. She touches the section of hair where my nose just was.

I don't know what to say. If I admit it, I'm creepy and weird. If I deny it, I'm a liar *and* creepy and weird. She pulls the strands that she's touching across her nose and sniffs at it herself. Now I need to make sure that she doesn't think I think her hair smells bad.

"No. I mean, yes. Yes, I smelled it."

I stop talking because her eyes have gone wider than eyes should be able to go.

"And?" she prompts.

It takes me a second to work out what she's asking. "It smells good. You know sometimes in spring when it rains just for like five minutes and then the sun comes out right away and the water's evaporating and the air is still damp? It smells like that. Really good."

I make my mouth close even though it just wants to keep talking. I look back down at my phone and wait, hoping she'll come close again.

natasha

HE THINKS MY HAIR SMELLS like spring rain. I'm really trying to remain stoic and unaffected. I remind myself that I don't like poetic language. I don't like poetry. I don't even like people who like poetry.

But I'm not dead inside either.

daniel

SHE COMES CLOSE AGAIN and I barrel ahead, because apparently that's who I am with this girl. Maybe part of falling in love with someone else is also falling in love with yourself. I like who I am with her. I like that I say what's on my mind. I like that I barrel ahead despite the obstacles she raises. Normally I would give up, but not today.

I raise my voice over the clacking of the train against the tracks. "Right. On to section two." I look up from my phone. "Ready for this? We're leveling up on the intimacy."

She frowns at me but still nods. I read the questions aloud and she chooses number twenty-four: How do you feel about your relationship with your mother (and father)?

"You have to go first," she says.

"Well. You met my dad." I don't even know where to begin with this question. Of course I love him, but you can love someone and still have a not-so-great relationship with them. I wonder how much of our non-relationship is because of typical father versus teenage boy stuff (a ten o'clock curfew, really?) and how much of it is cultural (Korean Korean versus Korean American). I don't know if it's even possible to separate the two.

Sometimes I feel like we're on opposite sides of a soundproofed glass wall. We can see each other but we can't hear each other.

"So you feel bad, then?" she teases.

I laugh because it's such a simple and concise way to describe something so complicated. The train brakes suddenly and jostles us even closer together. She doesn't move away.

"And your mom?" she asks.

"Pretty good," I say, and realize that I mean it. "She's kind of like me. She paints. She's artistic." Funny, I've never thought of us being the same in this way before. "Now your turn."

She looks at me. "Remind me again why I agreed to this?"

"Want to stop?" I ask, even though I know she'll say no. She's the kind of person who finishes what she starts. "I'll make it easy on you. You can just give me a thumbs-up or thumbs-down, okay?"

She nods.

"Mom?" I ask

Thumbs-up.

"Way up?"

"Let's not go overboard. I'm seventeen and she's my mom," she says.

"Dad?"

Thumbs-down.

"Way down?" I ask.

"Way, way, way down."

natasha

"IT'S HARD TO LOVE SOMEONE who doesn't love you back," I tell him. He opens his mouth and then closes it again. He wants to tell me that of course my father loves me. All parents love their children, he wants to say. But that's not true. Nothing is ever universal. *Most* parents love their children. It's true that my mother loves me. Here's another thing that's also true: I am my father's greatest regret.

How do I know?

He said so himself.

samuel kingsley

A History of Regret, Part 2

SAMUEL KINGSLEY WAS CERTAIN BEING famous was his destiny. Surely God wouldn't have gifted him with all this talent with no place to display it.

And then Patricia came along. Surely God wouldn't have given him a beautiful wife and children if he didn't mean to provide for them.

Samuel remembers the moment he met her. They were still in Jamaica, in Montego Bay. It'd been raining outside, one of those tropical storms that start as suddenly as they stop. He'd ducked into a clothing store for shelter so he wouldn't be soaked for his audition.

She was the store manager, so the first time he saw her she was wearing a name tag and looking very official. Her hair was short and curly and she had the biggest, prettiest, shyest eyes he'd ever seen. He never could resist a shy girl—all that caution and mystery.

He'd quoted Bob Marley and Robert Frost. He'd sung. Patricia never stood a chance against the force of his charm. His audition time came and went, but he didn't care. He couldn't get enough of those eyes that widened so dramatically at the slightest flirtation.

Still, a part of him had said to stay away. Some prescient part of him saw the two paths diverging in the yellow wood. Maybe if he'd chosen the other path, if he'd left the store instead of stayed, it would've made all the difference.

daniel

"KOREAN FOOD? BEST FOOD. Healthy. Good for you," I say to Natasha, imitating my mom. It's something she says every time we go out to dinner. Charlie always suggests we go to an American place, but Mom and Dad always take us to Korean, even though we eat Korean food at home every day. I don't mind because it turns out I agree with my mom. Korean food? Best food.

Natasha and I don't have much time left before her appointment, and I'm beginning to doubt that I can make her fall in love with me in the next couple of hours. But I can at least make her want to see me again tomorrow.

We walk into my favorite *soon dubu* joint to greetings of *"Annyeonghaseyo"* from the staff. I love this place, and their seafood stew is almost as good as my mom's. It's not fancy at all, just small wooden tables in the center surrounded by booths on the perimeter. It's not crowded right now, so we manage to snag a booth.

Natasha asks me to order for her. "I'll eat whatever you tell me to," she says.

I ring the little bell attached to the table and a waitress

appears almost instantly. I order two seafood *soon dubu, kalbi,* and *pa jun.*

"There's a bell?" she asks after the waitress leaves.

"Awesome, right? We're a practical people," I say, only half kidding. "Takes all the mystery out of food service. When will my waiter appear? When will I get the check?"

"Do American restaurants know about this? Because we should tell them. Bells should be mandatory."

I laugh and agree, but then she takes it back.

"No, I changed my mind. Can you imagine some jerk just leaning on the bell demanding ketchup?"

The *panchan,* complimentary side dishes, arrive almost immediately. A part of me braces to have to explain to her what she's eating. Once, a friend of a friend made a *What's in this food? Is it dog?* joke. I felt like shit but still I laughed. It's one of those moments that makes me want that Do-Over Card.

Natasha, though, doesn't ask any questions about the food.

The waitress comes over and hands us both chopsticks.

"Oh, can I have a fork, please?" Natasha asks.

The waitress gives her a disapproving look and turns to me. "Teach girlfriend how to use chopsticks," she says, and walks away.

Natasha looks at me with wide eyes. "Does that mean she's not going to bring me a fork?"

I laugh and shake my head. "What the hell?"

"I guess you should teach me how to use chopsticks," she says.

"Don't worry about her," I say. "Some people aren't happy until everything is done their way."

She shrugs. "Every culture is like that. The Americans, the French, the Jamaicans, the Koreans. Everyone thinks their way is the best way."

"Us Koreans might actually be right, though," I say, grinning.

The waitress returns and places the soup and two uncooked eggs in front of us. She tosses paper-clad spoons into the center of the table.

"What's this called?" Natasha asks, when the waitress is out of earshot.

"Soon dubu," I say.

She watches me crack my egg into the soup and bury it under cubes of steaming tofu and shrimp and clams so it will cook. She does the same and doesn't make a comment about whether it's safe to eat.

"This is delicious," she says, sipping a spoonful. She practically wiggles with pleasure.

"How come you call yourself Korean?" she asks after a few more sips. "Weren't you born here?"

"Doesn't matter. People always ask where I'm from. I used to say here, but then they ask where are you *really* from, and then I say Korea. Sometimes I say North Korea and that my parents and I escaped from a water dungeon filled with piranhas where Kim Jong-un was holding us prisoner."

She doesn't smile like I expect her to. She just asks me why I do that.

"Because it doesn't matter what I say. People take one look at me and believe what they want."

"That sucks," she says, scooping up some kimchi and popping it into her mouth. I could watch her eat all day.

"I'm used to it. My parents think I'm not Korean enough. Everybody else thinks I'm not American enough."

"That really sucks." She moves on from the kimchi to bean sprouts. "I don't think you should say you're from Korea, though."

"Why not?"

"Because it's not true. You're from here."

I love how simple this is for her. I love that her solution to everything is to tell the truth. I struggle with my identity and she tells me just to say what's true.

"It's not up to you to help other people fit you into a box," she says.

"Do people do it to you?"

"Yeah, except I'm really not from here, remember? We moved here when I was eight. I had an accent. The first time I saw snow, I was in homeroom and I was so amazed I stood up to stare at it."

"Oh no."

"Oh yes," she says.

"Did the other kids—"

"It wasn't pretty." She mock-shivers at the memory. "Want to hear something even worse? My first spelling quiz the teacher marked that I spelled *favorite* wrong because I included the *u*."

"That *is* wrong."

"Nope." She waves her spoon at me. "The correct English spelling includes the *u*. So sayeth the Queen of England. Look it up, American boy. Anyway, I was such a little nerd that I went home and brought her the dictionary and got my points back."

"You didn't."

"I did," she says, smiling.

"You really wanted those points."

"Those points were mine." She giggles then, which is not a thing I thought she did. Of course, I've only known her for a few hours, so obviously I don't know everything about her yet. I love this part of getting to know someone. How every new piece of information, every new expression, seems magical. I can't imagine this becoming old and boring. I can't imagine not wanting to hear what she has to say.

"Stop doing that," she says.

"What?"

"Staring at me."

"Okay," I say. I unearth my egg and see that it's cooked perfectly to a soft boil. "Let's eat them together," I tell her. "It's the best part."

She scoops hers out, and now we're both sitting there egg in spoon, spoon in hand.

"On three. One. Two. Three."

We pop the eggs into our mouths. I watch as her eyes widen. I know the moment the yolk bursts in her mouth. She closes her eyes like this is the most delicious thing she's ever tasted. She said not to stare but I'm staring. I love the way she seems to feel things with her entire body. I wonder why a girl who is so obviously passionate is so adamantly against passion.

the waitress

A History of Love

LEARN HOW TO USE CHOPSTICKS.

Teach girlfriend how to use chopsticks.

My son, he did the same thing. He date white girl. My husband? He don't accept it. At first, I agree with him. We don't speak to our son for a year after he told us. I thought: We don't talk to him. Make him see reason, come to senses.

We don't talk and I miss him. I miss my little boy and his American jokes and the way he pinch my cheeks and tell me I'm the prettiest of all the *omma*s. My son, who was never embarrassed of me when all the other boys get too American.

We don't talk to him for over a year. Finally when he call I think this is it. He finally understand. White girl will never understand us, never be Korean. But only call to say he's getting married. He wants us to come to wedding. I hear in his voice how much he loves her. I hear how he loves her more than me. I hear that if I don't go to his wedding, I will lose my only son. My only son, who loves me.

But Daddy say no. My son begged us to come and I say no until he stop begging.

He got married. I saw pictures on the Facebook.

They have first son. I saw pictures on the Facebook.

They have another child. A girl this time.

My *sohn-jah,* and I only know them from computer.

Now when these boys come in here with these girls who don't look like their *omma*s, I get angry. This country try to take everything from you. Your language, your food, your children.

Learn how to use chopsticks.

This country can't have everything.

natasha

JUST UNDER TWO HOURS to go before my appointment, and Daniel really wants to go to *norebang,* which is the Korean word for karaoke. *Karaoke* is itself the Japanese word for embarrassing oneself by singing in front of a room filled with strangers who are only there to laugh at you.

"It's not like the American version," he insists when I balk. "This is much more civilized."

By *civilized,* he means that you embarrass yourself in a small, private room in front of only your friends instead. His favorite *norebang* place is coincidentally right next door to where we've just had lunch. It's owned and operated by the same people, so we don't even have to go outside because there's an entrance inside the restaurant.

Daniel chooses one of the smallest rooms, but it's still big. They're clearly meant to accommodate parties of six or eight instead of just two. The room is dimly lit, and plush red leather couches line most of the perimeter. A large square coffee table sits just in front of the couches. On it there's a microphone, a complicated-looking remote, and a thick book that has *Song*

Menu written on the cover in three languages. Next to the door there's a large TV where the lyrics will appear. A disco ball hangs from the ceiling.

Bev would love this place. First, she has kind of an obsession with disco balls. She has four hanging from the ceiling of her room and a disco ball lamp/clock contraption. Second, she's got a great voice and will take any excuse to use it in front of groups of people. I check my phone for more texts from her, but there's nothing. She's just busy, I tell myself. She hasn't forgotten about me already. I'm still here.

Daniel closes the door. "I can't believe you've never been to *norebang*," he says.

"Shocking, I know," I say back.

With the door closed, the room feels small and intimate.

He gives me a look like he's thinking the same thing.

"Let's get some dessert," he says, and presses a button on the wall for service. The same waitress from the restaurant appears to take our order. She doesn't bother to look at me. Daniel orders us *patbingsoo*, which turns out to be shaved ice with fruit, small, soft rice cakes, and sweet red beans.

"Like it?" he asks. It's important to him that I do.

I finish it in six spoonfuls. What's not to like? It's sweet and cold and delicious.

He beams at me and I beam back.

Observable Fact: I like making him happy.

Observable Fact: I don't know when that happened.

He grabs the song menu from the table and flips to the

English section. While he agonizes over song choice, I watch the K-pop videos playing on the television. They're candy-colored and infectious.

"Just choose a song," I tell him when the third video starts.

"This is *norebang*," he says. "You don't just choose a song. A song chooses you."

"Tell me you're kidding," I say.

He winks at me and begins loosening his tie. "Yes, I'm kidding, but pipe down. I'm trying to find something to properly impress you with my vocal stylings."

He unbuttons the top button of his shirt. I watch his hands as he pulls the tie off over his head. It's not like he's taking his clothes off. It's not like he's getting undressed right here in front of me. But it feels like he is. I can't see anything scandalous, just a quick glimpse of the skin at his throat. He pulls the rubber band from his hair and tosses it to the table. His hair is just long enough to fall into his face, and he brushes it behind his ears absentmindedly. I can't help staring. It feels like I've been waiting for him to do this all day.

Observable fact: He is pretty hot with his hair down.

Observable fact: He's pretty hot with his hair up too.

I pull my eyes away and stare at the air conditioner on the wall instead. I'm considering adjusting the temperature down.

He rolls up his sleeves, which makes me laugh. He's acting like we're about to engage in serious physical labor. I'm trying not to notice the long, smooth lines of his forearms, but my eyes keep traveling over them.

"Are you a good singer?" I ask.

He looks at me with mock solemnity, but his dancing eyes give him away.

"Not gonna lie," he says. "I am good. Italian-opera-singer good." He grabs the remote to key in his song choice. "Are you?" he asks.

I don't answer. He'll find out soon enough. In fact, my singing will definitely cure him of the crush he has on me.

Observable Fact: I am the worst singer on earth.

He stands up and walks to the open area in front of the television. Apparently, he's going to need space to maneuver. He adjusts his stance until his feet are planted wide, bows his head so that his hair obscures his face, and holds the microphone up in the air in one hand—classic rock star pose. It's "Take a Chance on Me" by ABBA. He puts a hand over his heart and croons the first verse. À la the song title, it's all about taking chances, specifically me taking a chance on him.

By the second verse, he's warmed up and throwing me cheesy pop star looks with eyebrow raises, penetrating stares, and pouty lips. According to the lyrics, we can do so many fun things as long as we're together. The fun things include dancing, walking, talking, and listening to music. Strangely, there's no mention of kissing. He pantomimes each activity like some sort of deranged mime, and I can't stop laughing.

Verse three has him down on his knees in front of me. There's something in the lyrics about feeling all alone when pretty birds have flown that I don't quite understand. Am I the bird? Is he? Why are there birds?

For the rest of the song he's back up on his feet, gripping the microphone with both hands and singing with abandon. My hysterical laughter doesn't faze him. Also, he wasn't kidding about being a good singer. He's excellent. He even does his own backing vocals, which consists of him singing "take a chance" over and over again.

And it's not like he's trying to be sexy. It's just funny. So funny that it becomes sexy. I didn't know funny could do that. I notice the way his dress shirt stretches across his chest as he does his disco moves. I notice how long his fingers are when he runs his hands through his hair dramatically. I notice how nice and firm his butt looks in his suit pants.

Observable Fact: I have a thing for butts.

Given my crappy day, none of this should be working on me. But it definitely is. It's his complete lack of self-consciousness. He doesn't care if he's making a fool of himself. His only goal is to make me laugh.

It's a long song, and he's hot and sweaty by the end of it. After he's done, he watches the monitor until a candy-pink cartoon microphone dances across the screen and holds up a sign: 99%. The screen fills with confetti.

I groan. "You didn't say there would be grades."

He throws me a triumphant grin and collapses on the seat right next to me. Our forearms brush and separate and brush again. I feel ridiculous for noticing it, but I do notice it.

He moves away to retrieve the microphone and hand it to me.

"Bring it," he says.

daniel

I WISH I'D THOUGHT ABOUT doing *norebang* earlier. Being alone with her in a dimly lit room is a little bit of heaven (disco heaven). She's flipping through the song book and making noises about being a terrible singer. I'm staring at her, getting my fix in, because she's too distracted to tell me to quit doing it.

I can't decide what part of her face is my favorite. Right now it might be her lips. She's holding the bottom one in her teeth in what I think is her the-agony-of-too-many-choices face.

Finally she chooses. Instead of picking up the remote, she bends over the table to reach it and enter the code. Her dress pulls up a little and I can see the back of her thighs. They have little crease marks from the couch. I want to wrap my hand around them and smooth the marks with my thumb.

She turns to look at me and I can't even pretend I wasn't staring. I don't want to. I want her and I want her to know that I want her. She doesn't look away from me. Her lips part (they really are the nicest lips in the known universe) and she touches her tongue to her bottom one.

I'm going to get up and I'm going to kiss her. No force on

earth can stop me, except that her song starts and crushes the moment with melancholy.

I recognize the opening chords. It's "Fell on Black Days" by Soundgarden. The song starts with the band's lead singer, Chris Cornell, telling us that everything he's feared has come to life. It goes all the way downhill from there until we get to the chorus, where we learn one billion times (give or take) that he's fallen on black days. It is (objectively speaking) one of the most depressing songs ever written.

Nevertheless, Natasha loves it. She strangles the mike with both hands and squeezes her eyes shut. Her singing is earnest and heartfelt and completely awful.

It's not good.

At all.

I'm pretty sure she's tone-deaf. Any note she does hit is purely coincidental. She sways awkwardly from side to side with her eyes closed. She doesn't need to read the lyrics because she knows this song by heart.

By the time she gets to the final chorus, she's forgotten about me totally. Her awkwardness melts away. The singing is still not good, but she's got one hand over her heart and she's belting a lyric about not knowing her fate with real emotion in her voice.

Mercifully, it ends. It's a cure for happiness, that song. She peeks at me. I've never seen her look shy. She bites her bottom lip again and scrunches up her face. She's adorable.

"I love that song," she says.

"It's a little morose, isn't it?" I tease.

"A little angst never hurt anyone."

"You're the least angst-ridden person I've ever met."

"Not true," she says. "I'm just good at pretending."

I don't think she meant to admit that to me. I don't think she likes to show her soft spots. She turns away and puts the mike down on the table.

But I'm not letting her get away from this moment. I grab her hand and pull her toward me. She doesn't resist, and I don't stop pulling until the full lengths of our bodies are touching. I don't stop pulling until she's in my breathing space.

"That was the worst singing ever," I say.

Her eyes are shining. "I told you I was bad," she says.

"You didn't."

"In my head I did."

"Am I in your head?" I ask her.

She's so close that I can feel the slight heat from her blush.

I put my hand on her waist and bury my fingers in her hair. Anything can happen in the breath of space between us. I wait for her, for her eyes to say yes, and then I kiss her. Her lips are like soft pillows and I sink into them. We start out chaste, just lips touching, tasting, but soon we can't get enough. She parts her lips and our tongues tangle and retreat and tangle again. I'm hard everywhere but it feels too good, too *right* to be embarrassed about. She's making little moaning sounds that make me want to kiss her even more.

I don't care what she says about love and chemicals. This will not fade away. This is more than chemistry. She pulls away, and her eyes are shimmering black stars looking into mine.

"Come back," I say, and kiss her like there's no tomorrow.

natasha

I CAN'T STOP. I DON'T want to stop. My body absolutely does not care what my brain thinks. I feel his kiss everywhere. The tips of my hair. The center of my belly. The backs of my knees. I want to pull him into me, and I want to melt into him.

We move backward and the back of my legs bump into the couch. He guides me down until he's half on top of me but with one leg still on the ground.

I need to keep kissing. My body is hectic. I can't get enough. I can't get close enough. Something chaotic and insistent builds inside me. I'm arching off the couch to get closer to him than I already am. His hand squeezes my waist and travels up to my chest. He brushes lightly over my breast. I wrap my arms around his neck and then thread my fingers into his hair. Finally. I've wanted to do that all day.

Observable Fact: I don't believe in magic.

Observable Fact: We *are* magic.

daniel

HOLY...

natasha

. . . SHIT.

daniel

WE CANNOT HAVE SEX in the *norebang*.

We.

Can.

Not.

But I'm going to go ahead and admit that I want to. If I don't stop kissing her I'm going to ask her to, and I don't want her to think I'm the kind of guy who would ask a girl he's just met to have sex in the *norebang* after their first (quasi) date, even though I'm totally that kind of guy because Jesus Christ, I really do want to have sex with her right now right here in the *norebang*.

natasha

MY HANDS CANNOT STOP touching him. They slide themselves out of his hair and down to the hard, shifting muscles of his back. Of their own volition they slide over his butt.

As I suspected, it is spectacular. Firm and round and perfectly proportioned. It's the kind of butt that requires holding. He should never wear pants.

I palm and squeeze it and it feels even better than I'd expected.

He pushes himself up, arms on either side of my head, and smiles at me. "It's not a melon, you know."

"I like it," I say, and squeeze again.

"It's yours," he tells me.

"Have you ever considered wearing chaps?" I ask.

"Absolutely not," he says, laughing and blushing.

I really like making him blush.

He lowers himself and kisses me again. It feels like there's no part of me that's not being kissed right now. I drag my hands away from his butt and up to his shoulders to slow us down. If I kiss him anymore, it's just going to make it harder on me later.

So.

No more kissing.

daniel

I FEEL THE HESITATION in her lips, and to be honest, I'm a little freaked out by how intense this is too. I push myself up and pull her up to seated. I palm the back of her neck and rest my forehead against hers. We're both breathing too fast, too ragged. I knew we had chemistry, but I didn't expect this.

We're kindling amid lightning strikes. A lit match and dry wood. Fire Danger signs and a forest waiting to be burned.

Of all the ways today could've gone, I couldn't have predicted this. But now I'm sure that everything that's happened today has been leading me to her and us to this moment and this moment to the rest of our lives.

Even Charlie's academic probation from Harvard feels like it's part of the plan to get us to this point. If not for Charlie and his fuck-up, my mom wouldn't have said what she did this morning.

If she hadn't, I wouldn't have left so early for the haircut that I have not gotten yet.

I wouldn't have gotten on the 7 train with the theological conductor looking for God.

If not for him, I wouldn't have left the subway to walk, and I wouldn't have seen Natasha having her religious musical experience. If not for the conductor's talk of God, I wouldn't have noticed her DEUS EX MACHINA jacket.

If not for that jacket, I wouldn't have followed her into the record store.

If not for her thieving ex-boyfriend, I wouldn't have spoken to her.

Even the jerk in the BMW deserves some credit. If he hadn't run that red, I wouldn't have gotten a second chance with her.

All of it, everything, was leading us back here.

When we're both breathing normally again, I kiss the tip of her nose.

"Told you," I say, and kiss it again.

"Nose fetishist," she says, and then: "What did you tell me?"

I punctuate my words with nose kisses.

"We."

Kiss.

"Are."

Kiss.

"Meant."

Kiss.

"To."

Kiss.

"Be."

Kiss.

She pulls away. Her eyes have been replaced by storm clouds, and she untangles her limbs from mine. It's hard to let her go, like pulling magnets apart. Did I freak her out with my talk of fate? She scoots over on the couch and puts way too much space between us. I don't want to let the moment go. A few seconds ago I thought it would last forever.

"Want to sing another one?" I ask. My voice rattles and I clear my throat. I look over at the TV. We didn't get a chance to see her score before we started kissing. It's 89%, which is terrible. It's pretty hard to get less than 90% in *norebang*.

She glances over at the TV too but doesn't say anything. I can't fathom what's happening in her head. Why's she resisting this thing between us? She touches her hair, pulls on a strand and lets it go, pulls on another and lets it go.

"I'm sorry," she says.

I slide over and close the distance she put between us. Her hands are clasped in her lap.

"What are you sorry for?" I ask.

"For running hot and cold."

"You weren't so cold just a minute ago," I say, making the absolute lamest joke (along with puns, innuendos are the lowest form of humor) I could possibly make in this moment. I even waggle my eyebrows and then wait for her reaction. This could go either way.

A smile overtakes her face. Those storm clouds in her eyes don't stand a chance. "Wow," she says, her voice warm around her smile. "You sure have a way with words."

"And the ladies," I say, hamming it up even more. I'll make a fool of myself just to make her laugh.

She laughs some more and leans back on the couch. "You sure you're qualified to be a poet? That was the worst line I've ever heard."

"You were expecting something—"

"More poetic," she says.

"Are you kidding? Most poems are about sex."

She's skeptical. "Do you have actual data to back that up? I wanna see some numbers."

"Scientist!" I accuse.

"Poet!" she retorts.

We both smile, delighted and not trying to hide our delight from each other.

"Most poems I've seen are about love or sex or the stars. You poets are obsessed with stars. Falling stars. Shooting stars. Dying stars."

"Stars are important," I say, laughing.

"Sure, but why not more poems about the sun? The sun is also a star, and it's our most important one. That alone should be worth a poem or two."

"Done. I will only write poems about the sun from now on," I declare.

"Good," she says.

"Seriously, though? I think most poems are about sex. Robert Herrick wrote a poem called 'To the Virgins, to Make Much of Time.'"

She pulls her legs up to lotus position on the couch and doubles over with laughter. "He did not."

"He did," I say. "He was basically telling virgins to lose their virginity as soon as possible just in case they died. God forbid you should die a virgin."

Her laughter fades. "Maybe he was just saying that we should live in the moment. As if today is all we have."

She's serious again, and sad, and I don't know why. She rests the back of her neck against the sofa and looks up at the disco ball.

"Tell me about your dad," I say.

"I don't really want to talk about him."

"I know, but tell me anyway. Why do you say he doesn't love you?"

She picks her head up to look at me. "You're relentless," she says, and flops her head back again.

"Persistent," I say.

"I dunno how to say it. My dad's primary emotion is regret. It's like he made some giant mistake in his past, like he took a wrong turn, and instead of ending up wherever he was supposed to be, he ended up in this life with me and mom and my brother instead."

Her voice wobbles while she's saying it, but she doesn't cry. I reach out and take her hand and we both watch the TV screen. Her dancing score's been replaced by a soundless ad for Atlantic City casinos.

"My mom makes these beautiful paintings," I say to her. "Really incredible."

I can still picture the tears in her eyes when my dad gave

her the present. She'd said, "*Yeobo,* you didn't have to do that."

"It's something only for you," he said. "You used to paint all the time."

I was so surprised by that. I thought I knew everything about my mom—about both of them, really—but here was this secret history I didn't know about. I asked her why she stopped and she waved her hand in the air like she was wiping the years away.

"Long time ago," she said.

I kiss Natasha's hand and then confess: "Sometimes I think maybe she made a wrong turn having us."

"Yes, but does *she* think that?"

"I don't know," I say. And then: "But if I had to guess, I would say I think she's happy with the way her life turned out."

"That's good," she says. "Can you imagine living your whole life thinking you made a mistake?" She actually shudders as she's saying it.

I raise her hand to my lips and kiss it. Her breathing changes. I tug her forward, wanting to kiss her, but she stops me.

"Tell me why you want to be a poet," she says.

I lean back and rub my thumb over her knuckles. "I don't know. I mean, I don't even know if it's what I want for a career or anything. I don't get how I'm supposed to know that already. All I know is I like to do it. I really like to do it. I have thoughts and I need to write them down, and when I write them down they come out as poems. It's the best I ever feel about myself besides—"

I stop talking, not wanting to freak her out again.

She raises her head from the sofa. "Besides what?" Her eyes are bright. She wants to know the answer.

"Besides you. You make me feel good about myself too."

She pulls her hand out of mine. I think she's going into retreat mode again, but no. She leans forward and kisses me instead.

natasha

I KISS HIM TO GET him to stop talking. If he keeps talking I will love him, and I don't want to love him. I really don't. As strategies go, it's not my finest. Kissing is just another way of talking except without the words.

daniel

ONE DAY I WILL WRITE AN ODE about kissing. I will call it "Ode to a Kiss."

It will be epic.

natasha

WE'D PROBABLY STILL BE KISSING if our cranky waitress hadn't returned to demand to know if we wanted anything
else to eat. We didn't, and it was time to go anyway. I still want
to take him to the Museum of Natural History, my favorite
place in New York. I tell him that and we walk outside.

After the dark of the *norebang,* the sun seems too bright.
And not just the sun—everything seems too much. The city is
much too loud and much too crowded.

For a few seconds, I'm disoriented by the businesses stacked
high on top of each other with Korean signage until I remember that we're in Koreatown. This section of the city is supposed
to look like Seoul. I wonder if it does. I squint against the
sun and contemplate going back inside. I'm not ready for the
rowdy, bustling reality of New York to reassert itself yet.

That's the thought that brings me to my senses: Reality. *This*
is reality. The smell of rubber and exhaust, the sound of too
many cars going nowhere, the taste of ozone in the air. This is
reality. In the *norebang* we could pretend, but not out here. It's
one of the things I like most about New York City. It deflects
any attempts you make to lie to yourself.

We turn to each other at the same time. We're holding hands, but even that feels like pretend now. I tug my hand from his to adjust my backpack. He waits for me to give it back but I'm not quite ready yet.

daniel

Area Boy Incapable of Leaving Well Enough Alone

We're sitting side by side on the train, and even though it keeps jostling us together, I can feel her slipping away. No one is seated across from us; we watch each other in the window. My eyes slide to her face as she looks away. Her eyes slide to mine as I do the same. Her backpack's in her lap and she's hugging it to her chest like it might get up and walk away at any second.

I could reach out and take her hand, force the issue, but I want her to be the one to do it this time. I want her to acknowledge this thing between us out loud. I can't leave well enough alone. I want her to say the words. *We're meant to be.* Something. Anything. I need to hear them. To know that I'm not alone in this.

I should let it go.

I am going to let it go.

"What are you so afraid of?" I ask, not letting it go at all.

natasha

I HATE PRETENSE, BUT HERE I AM pretending. "What are you talking about?" I say to his reflection in the subway window instead of to him.

daniel

I ALMOST BELIEVE THAT SHE doesn't know what I'm talking about. Our eyes meet in the window like it's the only place we can look at each other.

"We're meant to be," I insist. It comes out all wrong—bossy and scolding and pleading all at the same time. "I know you feel it too."

She doesn't say a word, just gets up and goes to stand by the train doors. If anger were like heat, I'd be able to see the waves radiating from her body.

Part of me wants to go to her and apologize. Part of me wants to demand to know just what her problem is anyway. I make myself remain seated for the two stops left until the train finally screeches into the Eighty-First Street station.

The doors open. She pushes her way through the crowd and runs up the stairs. As soon as we're at the top, she shunts us to the side and swings around to face me.

"Don't you tell me what to feel," she whisper-shouts. She's going to say something else but decides against it. Instead, she walks away from me.

She's frustrated, but now I am too. I catch up with her.

"What's your problem?" I actually throw my hands up in the air as I say it.

I don't want to be fighting with her. Central Park is just across the street. The trees are lush and beautiful in their fall colors. I want to wander through the park with her and write poems in my notebook. I want her to make fun of me for writing poems in my notebook. I want her to educate me on the how and why the leaves change color. I'm sure she knows the exact science of it.

She swings her backpack onto both shoulders and crosses her arms in front of her body. "Meant-to-be doesn't exist," she says.

I don't want to have a philosophical discussion, so I concede. "Okay, but if it did, then—"

She cuts me off. "No. Enough. It just doesn't. And even if it did, we are definitely not."

"How can you say that?" I know I'm being unreasonable and irrational and probably lots of other things I shouldn't be. This is not something you can fight with another person about.

You can't persuade someone to love you.

A small breeze rustles the leaves around us. It's colder now than it's been all day.

"Because it's true. We're not meant to be, Daniel. I'm an undocumented immigrant. I'm being deported. Today is my last day in America. Tomorrow I'll be gone."

Maybe there's another way to interpret her words. My brain picks out the most important ones and rearranges them, hoping for a different meaning. I even try to compose a quick poem, but the words won't cooperate. They just sit there, too heavy for me to pick up.

Last.

Undocumented.

America.

Gone.

natasha

ORDINARILY SOMETHING like this—fighting in public—would embarrass me, but I barely even notice anyone except Daniel. If I'm honest with myself, it's been like this all day.

He presses his forehead into his hands and his hair forms a curtain around his face. I don't know what I'm supposed to say or do now. I want to take the words back. I want to keep pretending. It's my fault that things went so far. I should've told him from the beginning, but I didn't think we'd get to this point. I didn't think I would feel this much.

daniel

"I POSTPONED MY APPOINTMENT because of you." My voice is so quiet that I don't know if I mean for her to hear me, but she does.

Her eyes widen. She starts to say three different things before settling on: "Wait. This is my fault?"

I'm definitely accusing her of something. I'm not sure what. A bike courier hops onto the sidewalk a little too close to us. Someone yells at him to use the street. I want to yell at him too. Follow the rules, I want to say.

"You could've warned me," I say. "You could've told me you were leaving."

"I did warn you," she says, defensive now.

"Not enough. You didn't say you'd be living in another country in less than twenty-four hours."

"I didn't know that we'd—"

I interrupt her. "You knew when we met what was going on with you."

"It wasn't your business then."

"And it is now?" Even though the situation is hopeless, just hearing her say it's my business now gives me some hope.

"I tried to warn you," she insists again.

"Not hard enough. Here's how you do it. You open your mouth and you say the truth. None of this crap about not believing in love and poetry. 'Daniel, I'm leaving,' you say. 'Daniel, don't fall in love with me,' you say."

"I did say those things." She's not yelling, but she's not being quiet either.

A very fashionable toddler in a peacoat gives us wide eyes and tugs on her father's hand. A tyranny of tourists (complete with guidebooks) checks us out like we're on display.

I lower my voice. "Yes, but I didn't think you meant them."

"Whose fault is that?" she demands.

I don't have anything to say to that, and we just stare at each other.

"You can't really be falling for me," she says, quieter now. Her voice is somewhere between distress and disbelief.

Again I don't have anything to say. Even I'm surprised by how much I've been feeling for her all day. The thing about falling is you don't have any control on your way down.

I try to calm the air between us. "Why can't I be falling for you?" I ask.

She tugs hard on the straps of her backpack. "Because that's stupid. I told you not to—"

And now I've had enough. My heart's been on my sleeve all day, and it's pretty bruised up now.

"Just great. You don't feel anything? Was I kissing myself back there?"

"You think a few kisses mean forever?"

"I think *those* kisses did."

She closes her eyes. When she opens them again, I think I see pity there. "Daniel—" she begins.

I cut her off. I don't want pity. "No. Whatever. I don't want to hear it. I get it. You don't feel the same. You're leaving. Have a nice life."

I take all of two steps before she says, "You're just like my father."

"I don't even know your father," I say while putting my jacket on. It feels tighter somehow.

She folds her arms across her chest. "Doesn't matter. You're just like him. Selfish."

"I am not." Now I'm defensive.

"Yes you are. You think the entire world revolves around you. Your feelings. Your dreams."

I throw my hands up. "There is nothing wrong with having dreams. I may be a stupid dreamer, but at least I have them."

"Why is that a virtue?" she demands. "All you dreamer types think the universe exists just for you and your passion."

"Better than not having any at all."

She narrows her eyes at me, ready to debate. "Really? Why?"

I can't believe I have to explain this. "That's what we're put on earth to do."

"No," she says, shaking her head. "We're put here to evolve and survive. That's it."

I knew she'd bring science into it. She can't really believe that. "You don't believe that," I say.

"You don't know me well enough to say that," she says. "Besides, dreaming is a luxury and not everyone has it."

"Yes, but *you* do. You're afraid of becoming your dad. You don't want to choose the wrong thing, so you don't choose anything at all." I know there's a better way for me to tell her this, but I'm not feeling like my best self right now.

"I already know what I want to be," she says.

I can't stop myself from scoffing. "A data scientist or whatever? That's not a passion. It's just a job. Having dreams never killed anybody."

"Not true," she says. "How can you be this naïve?"

"Well, I'd rather be naïve than whatever it is you are. You only see things that are right in front of your face."

"Better than seeing things that aren't there."

And now we're at an impasse.

The sun hides behind a cloud and a cool breeze blows over us from across Central Park. We watch each other for a little while. She looks different out of the sunlight. I imagine I do too. She thinks I'm naïve. More than that, she thinks I'm ridiculous.

Maybe it's better to end things this way. Better to have a tragic and sudden end than to have a long, drawn-out one where we realize that we're just too different, and that love alone is not enough to bind us.

I think all these things. I believe none of them.

The wind picks up again. It stirs her hair a little. I can picture it with pink tips so clearly. I would've liked to see it.

natasha

"YOU SHOULD GO," I TELL HIM.

"So that's it?" he asks.

I'm glad he's being a jerk. It makes things easier. "Are you thinking at all about me? *I wonder how Natasha's feeling. How did she get to be an undocumented immigrant? Does she want to go live in a country she doesn't know at all? Is she completely devastated by what's happening to her life?*"

I read guilt on his face. He takes a step toward me, but I back up.

He stops moving.

"You're just waiting for someone to save you. Don't want to be a doctor? Don't be a doctor, then."

"It's not that simple," he says quietly.

I narrow my eyes at him. "To quote you from five minutes ago. Here's how you do it: You open your mouth and say what's true. 'Mom and Dad? I don't want to be a doctor,' you say. 'I want to be a poet because I am stupid and don't know better,' you say."

"You know it's not that easy," he says, even quieter than before.

I tug on the straps on my backpack. It's time to go. We're just delaying the inevitable. "You know what I hate?" I ask. "I really hate poetry."

"Yeah, I know," he says.

"Shut up. I hate it, but I read something once by a poet named Warsan Shire. It says that you can't make a home out of human beings, and that someone should've told you that."

I expect him to tell me that the sentiment is not true. I even want him to, but he doesn't say anything.

"Your brother was right. There's no place for this to go. Besides, you don't love me, Daniel. You're just looking for someone to save you. Save yourself."

daniel

Area Teen Convinced That His Life Is Complete and Utter Shit

How I want her to be right. How I want not to be falling in love with her at all.

I watch her walk away, and I don't stop her or follow her. What an absolute idiot I've been. I've been acting like some mystical, crystal-worshiping dummy. Of course this is what's happening now. All this nonsensical talk about *fate* and *destiny* and *meant-to-be*.

Natasha's right. Life is just a series of dumb decisions and in-decisions and coincidences that we choose to ascribe meaning to. School cafeteria out of your favorite pastry today? It must be because the universe is trying to keep you on your diet.

Thanks, Universe!

You missed your train? Maybe the train's going to explode in the tunnel, or Patient Zero for some horrible bird flu (water-fowl, goose, pterodactyl) is on that train, and thank goodness you weren't on it after all.

Thanks, Universe!

No one bothers to follow up with destiny, though. The cafeteria just forgot there was another box in the back, and you got a slice of cake from your friend anyway. You fumed while waiting for another train, but one came along eventually. No one died on the train you missed. No one so much as sneezed.

We tell ourselves there are reasons for the things that happen, but we're just telling ourselves stories. We make them up. They don't mean anything.

fate

A History

FATE HAS ALWAYS BEEN the realm of the gods, though even the gods are subject to it.

In ancient Greek mythology, the Three Sisters of Fate spin out a person's destiny within three nights of their birth. Imagine your newborn child in his nursery. It's dark and soft and warm, somewhere between two and four a.m., one of those hours that belong exclusively to the newly born or the dying.

The first sister—Clotho—appears next to you. She's a maiden, young and smooth. In her hands she holds a spindle, and on it she spins the threads of your child's life.

Next to her is Lachesis, older and more matronly than her sister. In her hands, she holds the rod used to measure the thread of life. The length and destiny of your child's life is in her hands.

Finally we have Atropos—old, haggardly. Inevitable. In her hands she holds the terrible shears she'll use to cut the thread of your child's life. She determines the time and manner of his or her death.

Imagine the awesome and awful sight of these three sisters

pressed together, presiding over his crib, determining his future.

In modern times, the sisters have largely disappeared from the collective consciousness, but the idea of Fate hasn't. Why do we still believe? Does it make tragedy more bearable to believe that we ourselves had no hand in it, that we couldn't have prevented it? It was always ever thus.

Things happen for a reason, says Natasha's mother. What she means is Fate has a Reason and, though you may not know it, there's a certain comfort in knowing that there's a Plan.

Natasha is different. She believes in determinism—cause and effect. One action leads to another leads to another. Your actions determine your fate. In this way she's not unlike Daniel's dad.

Daniel lives in the nebulous space in between. Maybe he wasn't meant to meet Natasha today. Maybe it was random chance after all.

But.

Once they met, the rest of it, the love between them, was inevitable.

natasha

I'M NOT GOING TO LET this thing with Daniel stop me from going to the museum. This is one of my favorite areas of the city. The buildings here aren't quite as tall as those in Midtown. It's nice being able to see patches of uninterrupted sky.

Ten minutes later, I'm in the museum in my favorite section— the Hall of Meteorites. Most people head right through this room to the gemstone one next door, with its flashy precious and semiprecious rocks. But I like this one. I like how dark and cool and spare it is. I like that there's hardly ever anyone here.

All around the room, vertical cases with shining spotlights display small sections of meteorites. The cases have names like Jewels from Space, Building Planets, and Origins of the Solar System.

I head right over to my favorite of all the meteorites— Ahnighito. It's actually just a section of the much larger Cape New York meteor. Ahnighito is thirty-four tons of iron and is the largest meteorite on display in any museum. I step up to the platform that it sits on and trail my hands across it. The surface is metal-cold and pockmarked from thousands of tiny impacts. I close my eyes, let my fingers dip in and out of the divots. It's hard to believe that this hunk of iron is from outer space. Harder still to believe that it contains the origins of the solar system. This room is my church, and standing on this platform is my pillar. Touching this rock is the closest I ever come to believing in God.

This is where I would've taken Daniel. I would've told him to write poetry about space rocks and impact craters. The sheer number of actions and reactions it's taken to form our solar system, our galaxy, our universe, is astonishing. The number of things that had to go exactly right is overwhelming.

Compared to that, what is falling in love? A series of small coincidences that we say means everything because we want to believe that our tiny lives matter on a galactic scale. But falling in love doesn't even begin to compare to the formation of the universe.

It's not even close.

daniel

"Symmetries"
A Poem by Daniel Jae Ho Bae

I will
stay on my
side. And you will
stay on an-
other

natasha

MY FATHER AND I WERE close once. In Jamaica, and even after we moved here, we were inseparable. Most times it felt like me and my dad—the Dreamers—against my mom and my brother—the Non-Dreamers.

He and I watched cricket together. I was his audience when he ran lines for auditions. When he was finally a famous Broadway actor, he would get me all the best parts for little girls, he'd say. I listened to his stories about how our life would be after he became famous. I listened long after my mom and brother had stopped listening.

Things started to change about four years ago, when I was thirteen. My mom got sick of living in a one-bedroom apartment. All her friends in Jamaica lived in their own houses. She got sick of my dad working in the same job for basically the same pay. She got sick of hearing what would happen when his ship came in. She never said anything to him, though, only to me.

You children too big to be sleeping in the living room now. You need you privacy.

I never going to have a real kitchen and a real fridge. Is time for him to give up that foolishness now.

And then he lost his job. I don't know if he was fired or laid off. My mom said once that she thought he quit, but she couldn't prove it.

On the day it happened he said: "Maybe is a blessing in disguise. Give me more time to pursue me acting."

I don't know who he was talking to, but no one responded.

Now that he wasn't working, he said he would audition for roles. But he hardly ever did. There was always an excuse:

Me not right for that part.

Them not going to like me accent, man.

Me getting too old now. Acting is a young man game.

When my mom got home from work in the evening, my father told her he was trying. But my brother and I knew better.

I still remember the first time we saw him disappear into a play. Peter and I had walked home from school. We knew something strange was up because the front door was hanging open. Our father was in the living room—our bedroom. I don't know if he didn't hear us come in, but he didn't react. He was holding a book in his hand. Later I realized it was actually a play—*A Raisin in the Sun*.

He was wearing a white button-up shirt and slacks and reciting the lines. I'm not sure why he was even holding the play because he already had it memorized. I still remember parts of the monologue. The character said something about seeing his future stretched out in front of him and how it—the future—was just a looming empty space.

When my father finally noticed us watching, he scolded us

for sneaking up on him. At first I thought he was just embarrassed. No one likes being caught unawares. Later, though, I realized it was more than that. He was ashamed, as if we'd caught him cheating or stealing.

After that he and I didn't do much of anything together anymore. He stopped watching cricket. He turned down all my offers to help him memorize lines. His side of my parents' bedroom grew more cluttered with stacks of used and yellowed paperbacks of famous plays. He knew all the roles, not just the leads but the bit parts as well.

Eventually he stopped with all pretense of auditioning or looking for a job. My mom gave up the pretense that we'd ever own a house or even find an apartment with more than one bedroom. She took extra shifts at work to make ends meet. Last summer, I got a job at McDonald's instead of volunteering at New York Methodist hospital like I used to.

It's been over three years of this. We come home from school to find him locked in his bedroom, running lines with no one. His favorite parts are the long, dramatic monologues. He is Macbeth and Walter Lee Younger. He complains bitterly about this or that actor and his lack of skill. He heaps praise on those he judges to be good.

Two months ago, through no fault of his own, he got a part. Someone he'd met years ago during one of his auditions was staging a production of *A Raisin in the Sun*. When he told my mom, the first thing she asked was "How much you getting paid?"

Not *Congratulations*. Not *I'm so proud of you*. Not *Which part?* or *When is it?* or *Are you so excited?* Just *How much you getting paid?*

She looked at him with flat eyes when she said it. Unimpressed eyes. Tired eyes that had just come off two shifts in a row.

I think we were all a little shocked. She'd even shocked herself. Yes, she'd been frustrated with him for years, but that one moment showed us all how far apart they really were now. Even Peter, who sides with my mother in all things, flinched a little.

Still. You couldn't fault her. Not really. My father had been dreaming his life away for years. He lived in those plays instead of the real world. He still does. My mother didn't have time for dreaming anymore.

Neither do I.

samuel kingsley

A History of Regret, Part 3

HE'S A LITTLE AFRAID OF NATASHA, to be honest. The things she's interested in now? Chemistry and physics and math. Where did they come from? Sometimes when he looks at her doing her homework at the kitchen table, he thinks she belongs to someone else. Her world is bigger than him and the things he taught her to be interested in. He doesn't know when she outgrew him.

One night after she and Peter had gone to bed, he went to the kitchen for water. She'd left her math book and homework on the table. Samuel doesn't know what overcame him, but he turned on the light, sat down, and flipped through the book. It looked like hieroglyphics, like some ancient language left by a time and a people he could never hope to understand. It filled him with a kind of dread. He sat there for a long time, running his fingers over the symbols, wishing his skin were porous enough to let all the knowledge and history of the world in.

After that night, every time he looked at her he had the vague sense that someone had come in when he wasn't looking and snatched his sweet little girl away.

Sometimes, though, he still catches a glimpse of the old Natasha. She'll give him a look like she used to when she was younger. It's a look that wants something from him. A look that wants him to be more, do more, and love more. He resents it. Sometimes he resents her. Hasn't he done enough already? She's his first child. He's already given up all his dreams for her.

daniel

I DON'T KNOW WHAT TO DO with myself now. I'm supposed to be blowing with the wind, but there's no wind anymore. I want to get a hobo outfit and a sandwich board and scrawl *What now, Universe?* across it. Now might be a good time to admit that the universe is not paying attention, though.

It's fair to say that I hate everything and everyone.

The universe is an asshole, just like Charlie.

Charlie.

That sack of shit.

Charlie, who told my would-be girlfriend that we didn't stand a chance. Charlie, who accused her of being a shoplifter. Charlie, who told her I had a small dick. Charlie, who I've wanted to punch in the face for eleven years now.

Maybe this is the wind. My hate for Charlie.

No time like the present.

I've got nothing left to lose today.

natasha

THE PARALEGAL IS A LITTLE more rumpled when I see her this time. A lock of her hair is out of place and falls into her eyes. Her eyes are glitter under the fluorescent lights, and her bright red lipstick is gone. She looks like she's been kissed.

I check my phone to make sure I'm not too early or late, but I'm right on time.

"Welcome back, Ms. Kingsley. Follow me, please."

She stands and begins walking. "Jeremy—I mean, Mr. Fitz—I mean, Attorney Fitzgerald is just through here."

She knocks quietly at the only door and waits, eyes even brighter than before.

The door swings open.

I might as well not be standing there, because Attorney Fitzgerald doesn't see me at all. He looks at his paralegal in a way that makes me want to apologize for intruding. She's looking at him in the same way.

I clear my throat very loudly.

Finally he drags his eyes away from her. "Thank you, Ms. Winter," he says. He might as well be declaring his love.

I follow him. He sits down at his desk and presses his fingers against his temples. He's got a small bandage just above his eyebrow and another around his wrist. He looks like an older and more harried version of the picture on his website. The only things that are the same are that he's white, and his eyes are bright green.

"Sit sit sit sit," he says, all in one breath. "Sorry for the delay. I had a little accident this morning, but now we don't have much time, so please, tell me how this all came to pass."

I'm not sure where to begin. Should I tell this lawyer the entire history? What should I include? I feel like I need to go back in time to explain it all.

Should I tell him about my father's aborted dreams? Should I tell him that I think dreams never die even when they're dead? Should I tell him that I suspect my father lives a better life in his head? In that life, he's renowned and respected. His kids look up to him. His wife wears diamonds and is the envy of men and women alike.

I would like to live in that world too.

I don't know where to begin, so I start with the night he ruined our lives.

natasha kingsley

A Daughter's History

THE THEATER WAS EVEN SMALLER than Peter and I expected. The sign said MAXIMUM CAPACITY: 40 PEOPLE. Tickets were fifteen dollars each, with the proceeds going to cover the rental of the space for two hours on a Wednesday night. The actors weren't given complimentary tickets for friends and family, so he had to buy three for us.

My father loves ritual and ceremony but has very few things to be ritualistic or ceremonial about. Now he had this play, and these tickets. He couldn't help himself. First he went out and picked up Chinese takeout—General Tso's chicken and shrimp fried rice for everyone.

He sat us all down at the very small table in our kitchen. We never eat at the table, because it's cramped with more than two people sitting at it. That night, though, he insisted we eat together as a family. He even served us himself, which is a thing that had never happened before. To my mom he said, "See? I got paper plates so you don't have a bunch of dishes to wash up later." He said it with a perfect American accent.

My mom didn't respond. We should've taken that as a sign.

As soon as we were done eating, he stood and held a plain white envelope up in the air like it was a trophy.

"Let's see what we have for dessert," he said. He made, and held, eye contact with each of us in turn. I watched as my mom cut her eyes away from him before he moved on to Peter and then to me.

"My family. Please do me the very great honor of coming to see me perform the role of Walter Lee Younger in the Village Troupe's production of *A Raisin in the Sun*."

Then he opened the envelope slowly, like he was at the Academy Awards announcing the Best Actor category. He took out the tickets and handed one to each of us. He looked so proud. More than that, he looked so *present*. For a few minutes, he wasn't lost in his head, or a play, or some dream fantasy. He was right there with us, and he didn't want to be somewhere else. I'd forgotten what that was like. He has this gaze that can make you feel *seen*.

There was a time when my father thought the world of me, and I really missed it right then. More than that, though? I missed the days when I thought the world of him, and thought he could do no wrong. I used to believe that all it took to make him happy was us, his family. There are pictures of me from when I was three wearing a MY DAD IS THE COOLEST T-shirt. On it there was a father penguin and a daughter penguin holding hands, surrounded by icy blue hearts.

I wish I still felt that way. Growing up and seeing your

parents' flaws is like losing your religion. I don't believe in God anymore. I don't believe in my father either.

My mother kissed her teeth when he gave her the ticket. She might as well have slapped him. "You and you foolishness," she said, and stood up. "You can keep you ticket. I not going anywhere."

She walked out of the kitchen. We listened as she walked the twenty steps to the bathroom and slammed the door with all her might.

None of us knew what to say. Peter slumped in his chair and hung his head so you couldn't find his face under his dreadlocks. I just looked at the space where she'd been. My father's eyes disappeared behind his dreaming veil. In his typical denial-of-reality way, he said:

"Don't worry 'bout you mother. She don't mean it, man."

But she did mean it. She didn't go with us. Even Peter couldn't convince her. She said the ticket price was a waste of her hard-earned money.

On the night of the show, Peter and I took the subway alone to the theater. My father had gone ahead to get ready. We sat in the first row and didn't mention the empty seat next to us.

I want to be able to say now that he was not good. That his talents were only mediocre. Mediocre would explain all the years of rejection. It would explain why he gave up and retreated from real life and into his head. And I don't know if I can see my father clearly. Maybe I'm still seeing with my old, hero-worship eyes, but what I saw was this:

He was excellent.

He was transcendent.

He belonged on that stage more than he's ever belonged with us.

daniel

Area Teen Pretty Sure Day Can't Get Worse, Is Wrong About That

My dad's with a customer when I walk in. His eyes tell me that he will have many things to say to me later.

I might as well give us some more to talk about.

It's just after the lunch rush, so the store's pretty empty. There's only one other customer—a woman looking at blow dryers.

I don't see Charlie cleaning or restocking any of the shelves, so I figure he must be slacking off in the stockroom in the back.

I'm not even nervous. I don't give a shit if he beats my face in, so long as I say what I have to say first. I drop my jacket outside the stockroom door and turn the handle, but it's locked. There's no reason for it to be locked with him in it. He's probably jacking off in there.

He pulls the door open before I can pound on it. Instead of his usual sneer, his face is a combination of tired and defensive. He must've thought it was my dad trying to get in.

As soon as he sees it's just me, his face goes into full superior asshole smirk. He makes a show of looking over my shoulder and around me.

"Where's your girlfriend?" He says *girlfriend* like it's a joke, the way you would say a word like *booger*.

I stand there looking at him, trying to figure out not *how* we're related, but *why*. He pushes past me, deliberately bumping into my shoulder.

"She dump you already?" he asks, after taking a quick look down a couple of aisles to verify that she's really not here. His shit-eating grin is firmly in place.

He's baiting me, I know. I know it, and still—I'm letting the hook pierce me like some dumb fish that's been hooked a billion times before and still hasn't figured it out yet that hooks are the enemy.

"Fuck you, Charlie," I say.

That catches him off guard. He stops smiling and takes a good look at me. My tie and jacket are missing. My shirt's untucked. I don't look like someone who has the Most Important Interview of His Life in a couple of hours. I look like someone who wants to get into a fight.

He puffs himself up like a blowfish. He's always been so proud of the two years and two inches that he has on me. It's just him and me back here, and that makes him bold.

"Why. Are. You. Here. Little. Brother?" he asks. He steps closer, so that we're toe to toe, and pushes his face closer to mine.

He expects me to back down.

I don't back down.

"I came to ask you a question."

He pulls his face back just a little. "Sure, I'd fuck her," he says. "Is that what happened? She want me instead of you?"

The thing about being a fish on a hook is the more you try to get off, the more trapped you are. The hook just buries itself deeper and you bleed a little more. You can't get off the hook. You can only go through it. Said another way: the hook has to go through you, and it's gonna hurt like a motherfucker.

"Why are you like this?" I ask him.

If I've surprised him, he doesn't show it. He just goes on with his usual shittiness. "Like what? Bigger, stronger, smarter, better?"

"No. Why are you an asshole to me? What'd I do to you?"

This time he can't hide his surprise. He pulls out of my space, even takes a step back.

"Whatever. That what you came here for? To whine about me being mean to you?" He looks me up and down again. "You look like shit. Don't you have to try to get into Second-Best School today?"

"I don't care about that. I don't even want to go." I say it quietly, but it still feels good to say it at all.

"Speak. Up. Little. Brother. I didn't hear you."

"I don't want to go," I say louder, before realizing that my dad left his position at the register and is now close enough to hear me. He starts to say something, but then the doorbell chimes. He pivots away.

I turn back to Charlie. "I've been trying to figure it out for years. Maybe I did something to you when we were younger and I don't remember."

He snorts. "What could you do to me? You're too pathetic."

"So you're just an asshole?" I ask. "Just the way you're made?"

"I'm stronger. And smarter. And better than you."

"If you're so smart, what are you doing back here, Charlie? Is it big fish, small pond syndrome? Were you just a tiny douche bag fish at Harvard?"

He clenches his fists. "Watch your mouth."

My guess is good. More than good, even.

"I'm right, aren't I? You're not the best there. Turns out you're not the best here either. How does it feel to be Second-Best Son?"

I'm the one with the hook now. His face is red and he's puffing himself back up. He gets right in my face. If he clenches his jaw any more it will break.

"You want to know why I don't like you? Because you're just like them." He points his chin in the direction of our dad. "You and your Korean food and your Korean friends and studying Korean in school. It's pathetic. Don't you get it, Little Brother? You're just like everybody else."

Wait. What?

"You hate me because I have Korean friends?"

"Korean is *all* you are," he spits out. "We're not even from the goddamn country."

And I get it. I really do. Some days it's hard to *be* in America. Some days I feel like I'm halfway to the moon, trapped between the Earth and it.

The fight leaves me. I'm just sorry for him now, and that's exactly the worst thing I can do to him. He sees the pity on my face. It enrages him. He grabs me by the collar.

"Fuck you. You think because you grew your hair out and you like poetry anybody's gonna treat you any different? You think because you bring some black girl in here? Or should I call her African American, or maybe just—"

But I don't let him get the word out. I thought I would have to work myself up to it, but I don't have to.

I punch him right in the fucking face.

My fist catches him around the eye socket area, so my knuckles hit mostly bone. It hurts me more than it has any right to, given that I'm the one supposedly delivering this beatdown. He stumbles back but doesn't fall flat like people do in the movies.

This is, frankly, disappointing. Still, the look on his face is worth all the I'm-sure-they're-broken bones in my hand. I definitely hurt him. What I mean is: I caused him physical pain, as was my intention. I wanted him to know that I, his Little Brother, could dish it out and not just take it. Now he knows I can hurt him, and that I'm done putting up with his crap.

I don't do enough damage, though. I watch his expression turn from pain to surprise to rage. He comes at me with his extra two inches and his extra twenty pounds of muscle.

First he punches me in the stomach. I swear it's like his fist goes through my stomach and out through my spinal cord. I double over and think that maybe I'll just stay in this position, but he's not having it. He pulls me up by my collar. I try to block my face with my hands because I know that's where he's going, but the stomach punch makes me slow.

His fist smashes into the side of my mouth. My lip splits open on the inside from bashing into my teeth. It splits open on the outside because the bastard hit me while wearing some giant-ass secret society ring. That's gonna leave a mark (possibly forever).

He's still got my collar in his fist, ready to deliver another blow, but I'm ready for him. I block my face with my hands and bring my knee right up into his balls—hard, but not hard enough to prevent him from having future little demon spawn children.

I'm nice like that.

He's down on the ground, clutching the family jewels that he wishes were not Korean, and I'm holding my jaw, trying to figure out if I still have all my teeth, when my dad comes over to us.

"Museun iriya?" he says. Which loosely translates to "WHAT'S GOING ON HERE?"

natasha

ATTORNEY FITZGERALD'S FINGERS are steepled and his eyes are fixed on mine. He leans forward in his chair slightly. I can't decide if he's listening, or if he just wants to look like he's listening.

How many stories like mine has he heard over the years? I'm amazed that he's not telling me to get to the point. I finish telling him everything about the night in question:

The actors took three bows. They would've taken a fourth if the audience members hadn't started filing out.

Afterward, Peter and I stayed in our seats, waiting for our father to come back out to get us. We waited for thirty minutes before he showed up. I don't think it was because he knew we were waiting. He appeared through the thick red curtains and walked to the center of the stage. He stood there for a full minute, just staring out into the now-empty theater.

I don't believe in souls, but his soul was on his face. I've never seen him happier. I'm certain he will never be that happy again.

Peter broke the spell because I couldn't bring myself to do it.

"You ready, Pops?" he shouted.

My father looked down at us with his faraway eyes. When

he looks at us like that I'm not sure if it's him who's missing, or us.

Peter got uncomfortable, the way he always does when my father does that. "Pops? You ready, man?"

When my father finally spoke, he had no trace of a Jamaican accent and no Jamaican diction at all. He sounded like a stranger.

"You children go on ahead. I will see you later."

I speed through the rest of the story. My father spends the rest of that evening drinking with his new actor friends. He drinks too much. On his way home, he rams his car into a parked police car. In his drunkenness he tells the police officer the whole history of our coming to America. I imagine he monologued for this audience of one. He tells the policeman we're undocumented immigrants, and that America never gave him a fair shot. The officer arrests him and calls Immigration and Customs Enforcement.

Attorney Fitzgerald's brows are furrowed. "But why would your father do that?" he asks.

It's a question I know the answer to.

samuel kingsley

A Father's History

CHARACTERS
Patricia Kingsley, 43
Samuel Kingsley, 45

ACT TWO
SCENE THREE

Interior bedroom. A single queen-sized bed with headboard dominates the space. Perhaps a picture frame or two. The floor on Samuel's side of the bed is overflowing with books. Stage right we see an opening to a hallway. Samuel and Patricia's teenage daughter is listening, but neither Samuel nor Patricia knows it. It's not clear that they would care if they did.

PATRICIA: Lawd have mercy, Kingsley.

She is seated on the edge of her bed. Her face is in her hands. Her speech is muffled.

SAMUEL: It don't mean nothing, man. We going to get a good lawyer.

Samuel Kingsley is standing on his side of the room. He is hunched with his face in shadow. A spotlight shines brightly on the single sheet of paper he holds in his left hand.

PATRICIA: And how we a go pay for a lawyer, Kingsley?

SAMUEL: Lawd, Patsy. We figure it out, man.

Patricia takes her face out of her hands and looks at her husband as if she's seeing him for the first time.

PATRICIA: You remember the day we did meet?

Samuel slowly crumples the paper in his hand. He continues to do this throughout the scene.

PATRICIA: You don't remember, Kingsley? How you came into the store, then you kept coming back day after day? That was so funny. One day you buy something and the next day you return it until you wear me down.

SAMUEL: Wasn't no wearing down, Patsy. It was courting.

PATRICIA: You remember all the promises you make me, Kingsley?

SAMUEL: Patsy—

PATRICIA: You say all me dreams would come true. We going have children and money and big house. You say me happiness more important than you own. You remember that, Kingsley?

She rises from the bed and the spotlight follows her as she moves.

SAMUEL: Patsy—

PATRICIA: Let me tell you something. I didn't believe you when we started out. But after a time I change my mind. You a good actor, Kingsley, because you make me believe all the pretty things you say to me.

The paper in Samuel's hand is fully crumpled now. The spotlight moves to his face and he's no longer hunched. He is angry.

SAMUEL: You know what me tired of hearing about? Me tired of your dreams. What 'bout mine?

If it wasn't for you and children them, I would have all the things I want. You complain 'bout house and kitchen and extra bedroom. But what 'bout me? I don't have any of the thing them that I want. I don't get to use my God-given talent.

I rue the day I walk into that store. If it wasn't for you and the children, my life would be betta. I would be doing the thing God put me on this earth to do. I don't want hear nothing more 'bout your dreams. Them not nothing compared to mine.

natasha

BUT I DON'T TELL ATTORNEY Fitzgerald that part—about how my father's wife and children are his greatest regret because we got in the way of the life he dreamed for himself.

Instead, I say, "A few weeks after he was arrested we got the Notice to Appear letter from Homeland Security."

He looks over one of the forms I filled out earlier for the paralegal and gets a yellow legal pad out of his desk drawer.

"So then you went to the Master Calendar Hearing. Did you bring a lawyer with you?"

"Only my parents went," I tell him. "And they didn't bring a lawyer." My mom and I talked about it a lot before the appointment. Should we hire a lawyer we couldn't really afford, or wait to see what happened at the hearing? We'd read online that you didn't really need a lawyer for the first appointment. At that point my father was still insisting that everything would miraculously work itself out. I don't know. Maybe we wanted to believe that was true.

Attorney Fitzgerald shakes his head and jots something down on his legal pad. "So at the hearing, the judge tells them they can accept Voluntary Removal or file for Cancellation of

Removal." He looks down at my forms. "Your younger brother is a U.S. citizen?"

"Yes," I say, watching as he notes that down too. Peter was born almost exactly nine months after we moved here. My parents were still happy with each other then.

My father didn't accept the Voluntary Removal at that hearing. That night, my mom and I researched Cancellation of Removal. In order to qualify, my dad needed to have lived in the United States for at least ten years, have shown good moral character, and be able to prove that being deported would cause an extreme hardship on a spouse, parent, or child who was a U.S. citizen. We thought Peter's citizenship was going to be our saving grace. We hired the cheapest lawyer we could find and went to the Merits Hearing armed with this new strategy. But as it turns out, it's very difficult to prove "extreme hardship." Going back to Jamaica will not put Peter's life in danger, and no one cares about the psychological danger of uprooting a child from his home, not even Peter himself.

"And at the Merits Hearing the judge denies your case and your father accepts the Voluntary Removal." Attorney Fitzgerald says it flatly, like the outcome was inevitable.

I nod instead of answering out loud. I'm not sure I'll be able to talk without crying. Any hope I had is slipping away.

I'd argued that we should appeal the judge's decision, but our lawyer advised against it. She said we had no case and that we were out of options. She suggested we leave voluntarily so we wouldn't have a deportation on our records. That way we'd have a hope of returning one day.

Fitzgerald puts his pen down and leans back in his chair. "Why did you go to USCIS today? It's not even their jurisdiction."

I have to clear the tears pooling in my throat before I can answer. "I didn't know what else to do." The truth is, despite the fact that I don't believe in miracles, I was hoping for one.

He's silent for a long time.

Finally I can't take any more. "It's okay," I say. "I know I'm out of options. I don't even know why I came here."

I make a move to get up, but he waves me back down. He steeples his fingers again and looks around the office. I follow his eyes to the unpacked boxes lining the wall just to his right. Behind him, a folding ladder rests against an empty bookshelf.

"We're just moving in," he says. "The construction guys were supposed to be done weeks ago, but you know what they say about plans." He smiles and touches the bandage on his forehead.

"Are you okay, Mr. Fitz—"

"I'm fine," he says, rubbing at the bandage.

He picks up a framed picture from his desk and looks at it. "This is the only thing I've unpacked so far." He turns the picture so I can see it. It's him with his wife and two children. They seem happy.

I smile politely.

He puts it back down and looks at me. "You're never out of options, Ms. Kingsley."

It takes me a second to realize that he's back to talking about

232

my case. I lean forward in my seat. "Are you saying you can fix this?"

"I'm one of the best immigration lawyers in this city," he says.

"But how?" I ask. I lay my hands on his desk, press my fingers against the wood.

"Let me go see a judge friend of mine. He'll be able to get the Voluntary Removal reversed so at least you don't have to leave tonight. After that we can file an appeal with the BIA—the Board of Immigration Appeals."

He checks his watch. "Just give me a couple of hours."

I open my mouth to ask for more facts and specifics. I find them reassuring. The poem comes back to me. *"Hope" is the thing with feathers.* I close my mouth. For the second time today I'm letting go of the details. Maybe I don't need them. It would be so nice to let someone else take over this burden for a little while.

"Hope" is the thing with feathers. I feel it fluttering in my heart.

daniel

MY DAD LOOKS AT ME from head to toe, and I feel like the second-rate slacker he's always taken me for. I will always be Second Son to him, no matter what Charlie does. I must look even worse than when I first came in. The top button of my shirt is missing from where Charlie grabbed me. There's even a bloodstain on it from my busted lip. I'm sweaty, and my hair is sticking to the side of my face. Premium Yale material right here.

He gives me an order. "Get some ice for your lip and come back out here."

Charlie's next. "You hit your little brother? That what you learn from America? To hit your family?"

I almost want to stay and hear where this goes, but my fat lip is getting fatter. I go into the back room and grab a can of Coke and press it against my lip.

I've never liked this room. It's too small and always clogged with half-opened boxes of product. There are no chairs, so I sit on the floor with my back against the door so no one can get in. I need five minutes before dealing with my life again.

My lip throbs in time to my heartbeat. I wonder if I need

stitches. I press the can closer and wait to feel (or not feel) the numbness.

This is what I get for letting the Fates guide me—beat up, girlfriend-less, future-less. Why did I postpone my interview? Worse, why did I let Natasha walk away?

Maybe she was right. I'm just looking for someone to save me. I'm looking for someone to take me off the track my life is on, because I don't know how to do it myself. I'm looking to get overwhelmed by *love* and *meant-to-be* and *destiny* so that the decisions about my future will be out of my hands. It won't be me defying my parents. It will be Fate.

The Coke can does the trick. I can't feel my lip anymore. Good thing Natasha's not here, because my kissing days are over, at least for today. And with her, there's no tomorrow.

Not that she'd ever let me kiss her again.

From the other side of the door, my dad orders me to come out. I put the can back in the fridge and tuck my shirt in.

I open the door to find him standing there alone. He leans in close to me. "I have a question for you," he says. "Why do you think it matters what you want?"

The way he asks, it's like he's genuinely confused by the emotion. What is this *desire* and *wanting* that you speak of? He's confused by why they matter at all.

"Who cares what you *want*? The only thing that matters is what is good for you. Your mother and I *only* care about what is good for you. You go to school, you become a doctor, you be successful. Then you never have to work in a store like this. Then you have money and respect, and all the things you want will come. You find a nice girl and have children and you have the American Dream. Why would you throw your future away for temporary things that you only want right now?"

It's the most my father has ever said to me at once. He's not even angry as he says it. He talks like he's trying to teach me something basic. One plus one equals two, son.

Ever since he bought the oil paints for *omma*, I've wanted to have a conversation like this with him. I've wanted to know why he wants the things he wants for us. Why it's so important to him. I want to ask him if he thinks *omma*'s life would've been better if she'd kept painting. I want to know if he's sad that she gave it up for him and for us.

Maybe this moment right now between my dad and me is the meaning of today. Maybe I can begin to understand him. Maybe he can begin to understand me.

"*Appa*—" I begin, but he holds his hand up to silence me and keeps it there. The air around us is still and metallic. He looks at me and through me and past me to some other time.

"No," he says. "You let me finish. Maybe I make it too easy for you boys. Maybe this is my fault. You don't know your history. You don't know what poor can do. I don't tell you because I think things are better that way. Better not to know. Maybe I am wrong."

I'm so close. I'm at the edge of knowing him. We're at the edge of knowing each other.

I'm going to tell him that I don't want the things for myself that he wants for me. I'm going to tell him that I'll be okay anyway.

"*Appa*—" I begin again, but again his hand goes through the air. Again I am silenced. He knows what I'm going to say, and he doesn't want to hear it.

My father is shaped by the memory of things I will never know.

"Enough. You don't go to Yale and become a doctor, then you find a job and pay for college yourself."

He walks back to the front of the store.

I'll admit that there's something refreshing about having it all laid out for me like this. Future or No Future.

My suit jacket is still crumpled by the door. I grab it and put it on. The lapel almost covers the bloodstain.

I look around for Charlie, but he's nowhere to be found.

I walk to the door. My dad's behind the cash register, staring off at nothing. I'm about to leave when he says the final thing, the thing he's been waiting to say.

"I saw the way you look at that girl," he says. "But that can never be."

"I think you're wrong," I tell him.

"Doesn't matter what you think. You do the right thing."

We make and hold eye contact. It's the holding of eye contact that tells me he's not sure what I'm going to do.

Neither am I.

dae hyun bae

A Dad's History

DAE HYUN BAE OPENS AND CLOSES the cash register. Opens and closes it again. Maybe it really is his fault that his sons are the way they are. He's told them nothing about his past. He does it because he's a father who loves his sons fiercely, and it's his way of protecting them. He thinks of poverty as a kind of contagion, and he doesn't want them to hear about it lest they catch it.

He opens the register and packs the large bills into the deposit pouch. Charlie and Daniel think money and happiness are not related. They don't know what poor is. They don't know that poverty is a sharp knife carving away at you. They don't know what it does to a body. To a mind.

When Dae Hyun was thirteen and still living in South Korea, his father began grooming him to take over the family's meager crab fishing business. The business barely made any money. Every season was a fight for survival. And every season they survived, but just barely. For most of his childhood, there was never any doubt in Dae Hyun's mind that he would eventually take over the business. He was the eldest of three sons. It was his place. Family is destiny.

He can still remember the day that sparked a small rebellion in his mind. For the first time, his father had taken him out on the fishing boat. Dae Hyun hated it. Trapped in the cold mesh-metal baskets, the crabs formed a furious, writhing column of desperation. They scrabbled and clawed their way over each other, trying to get to the top and to escape.

Even now, the memory of that first day still crops up at unexpected times. Dae Hyun wishes he could forget it. He'd imagined that coming to America would wipe it clean. But the memory always comes back. Those crabs never gave up. They fought until they died. They would've done anything to escape.

natasha

IT'S HARD TO KNOW HOW to feel now. I don't really trust what's happened, or maybe I just haven't had enough time to process it.

I check my phone. Bev's finally texted. She loves, loves, loves Berkeley. She says she thinks she's destined to go there. Also, California boys are cute in a different way from New York boys. The last text asks how I am, with a string of broken heart emojis. I decide to call and tell her what Attorney Fitzgerald said, but she doesn't pick up.

call me, I text.

I push my way through the revolving doors and out into the courtyard, and then I just stop moving. A handful of people are having lunch on the benches next to the fountain. Separate groups of fast walkers in suits go in and out of the building. A line of black town cars idles at the curb while their drivers smoke and chat with each other.

How can this be the same day? How can all these people be going about their lives totally oblivious to what's been happening to mine? Sometimes your world shakes so hard, it's difficult to imagine that everyone else isn't feeling it too.

That's how I felt when we first got the deportation notice. It's also how I felt when I figured out that Rob was cheating on me.

I take out my phone again and look up Rob's number before remembering I deleted it. My brain holds on to numbers, though, and I dial his from memory. I don't realize why I'm calling until I'm actually on the phone with him.

"Heyyyyyyyy, Nat," he drawls. He doesn't even have the grace to sound surprised.

"My name's not Nat," I say. Now that I have him on the phone, I'm not sure I want him on the phone.

"Not cool what you and your new dude did today." His voice is deep and slow and lazy, like it's always been. Funny how things that once seemed so charming can become dull and annoying. We think we want all the time in the world with the people we love, but maybe what we need is the opposite. Just a finite amount of time, so we still think the other person is interesting. Maybe we don't need acts two and three. Maybe love is best in act one.

I ignore his scolding, and the urge to point out that *he* was the one shoplifting, and therefore *he* was the uncool one. "I have a question," I say.

"Go for it," he says.

"Why did you cheat on me?"

Something falls to the floor on his end and he stammers the beginning of three different answers.

"Calm down," I say. "I'm not calling to fight with you and I definitely don't want to get back together. I just want to know.

241

Why didn't you just break up with me? Why cheat?"

"I don't know," he says, managing to stumble over three simple words.

"Come on," I urge. "There's gotta be a reason."

He's quiet, thinking. "I really don't know."

I stay silent.

"You're great," he says. "And Kelly's great. I didn't want to hurt your feelings and I didn't want to hurt her feelings." He sounds sincere, and I don't know what to do with that.

"But you must've liked her better to cheat, right?"

"No. I just wanted both of you."

"That's it?" I ask. "You didn't want to choose?"

"That's it," he says, as if that's enough.

This answer is so wholly lame, so unbelievably unsatisfying, that I almost hang up. Daniel would never feel this way. His heart chooses.

"One more question. Do you believe in true love and all that stuff?"

"No. You know me better than that. You don't believe in it either," he reminds me.

Don't I? "Okay. Thanks." I'm about to hang up, but he stops me.

"Can I at least tell you that I'm sorry?" he asks.

"Go ahead."

"I'm sorry."

"Okay," I say. "Don't cheat on Kelly."

"I won't," he says. I think he means it while he's saying it.

I should call my parents and tell them about Attorney

242

Fitzgerald, but they're not who I want to tell right now. Daniel. I need to find him and tell him.

Rob says I don't believe in true love. And he's right. I don't. But I might want to.

daniel

I LEAVE THE STORE. A violinist is standing on a milk crate in front of the pawnshop right next door. She's pale and scrawny and bedraggled in a poetic sort of way, like something out of *David Copperfield*. Unlike her, the violin is pristine. I listen for a few seconds but don't know if she's any good. I know there's an objective way to judge these things. Is she playing all the right notes in the right order and in tune?

But there's another way to judge too: does this music being played right here, right now, matter to someone?

I decide it matters to me. I jog back to where she is and drop a dollar into her hat. There's a sign next to the hat that I don't read. I don't really want to know her story. I just want the music and the moment.

My dad said Natasha and I can never work out. And maybe he's right, but not for the reasons he thinks. What an idiot I've been. I should be with her right now, even if today is all we have. Especially if today is all we have.

We live in the Age of the Cell Phone, but I do not have her cell phone number. I don't even know her last name. Like an idiot, I Google "Natasha Facebook New York City" and get

5,780,000 hits. I click through maybe a hundred links, and while the Natashas are all quite lovely, none of them is *my* Natasha. Who knew that her name was so flipping popular?

It's 4:15 p.m. and the streets are starting to fill up again with evening commuters heading for the subways. Like me, they look worse for wear. I jog on the curb to prevent pedestrians on the sidewalk from slowing me down.

I don't have a plan except to find her again. The only thing to do is to go to her Last Known Location—the lawyer's office on Fifty-Second—and hope that Fate is on my side and she's still there.

natasha

A COUPLE, BOTH WITH BRIGHT blue Mohawks, is arguing in front of the Fifty-Second Street subway entrance. They're doing that weird whisper-hiss thing that couples do when they fight in public. I can't hear what they're saying, but their gestures say it all. She's outraged at him. He's exasperated with her. They're definitely not at the beginning of their relationship. They both look too weary for that. You can see their long history just in the way they lean toward each other. Is this the last fight they'll ever have? Is this the one that ends it all?

I look back at them after I pass. Once upon a time I'm sure they were in love. Maybe they still are, but you can't tell from looking.

daniel

I DESCEND INTO THE SUBWAY and say a prayer to the subway gods (yes, multiple gods) that the train ride will be free of electrical issues and religiously challenged conductors.

What if I'm too late? What if she's already gone? What if stopping to give a dollar to that violinist started a chain of events that causes me to miss her?

We pull into the station. Directly across the platform, the downtown train pulls in at the same time. Our doors close, but the train doesn't move.

On the platform, a group of about twenty people in brightly colored skintight bodysuits materializes. They look like tropical birds against the dark gray of the subway. They line up and then freeze in place, waiting for something to set them off.

It's a flash mob. The train across the platform doesn't move either. One of the dancers, a guy in electric blue with an enormous package, presses play on a boom box.

At first it just seems like chaos, each person dancing to their own tune, but then I realize they're just offset by a few seconds. It's like singing in a round except they're dancing. They start out with ballet and move on to disco, and then break-dancing, before the subway cops catch on. The dancers scatter and my fellow passengers applaud wildly.

We pull away, but now the atmosphere in the train is completely changed. People are smiling at each other and saying how cool that was. It's at least thirty seconds before everyone puts back on his or her protective I'm-on-a-train-filled-with-strangers face. I wonder if that was the dancers' intention—to get us all to connect just for a moment.

natasha

I'M SITTING WITH MY BACK to the platform, so I don't really see how it starts. The only way I know something unusual is happening is that the entire train car seems to be looking at something behind me. I turn around and find that there's a flash mob dancing on the platform. They're all wearing very bright clothing and disco dancing.

Only in New York City, I think, and take out my phone to snap a few pictures. My fellow passengers cheer and clap. One guy even starts doing his own moves.

The dance doesn't last long, because three subway cops break it up. A few *boos* go up before everyone resumes being impatient about the train not moving.

Normally I would've wondered what the point of those people was. Don't they have jobs or something better to do? If Daniel were here, he'd say that maybe this is the thing they're supposed to be doing. Maybe the whole point of the dancers is just to bring a little wonder into our lives. And isn't that just as valid a purpose as any?

daniel

I DART OUT of the Fifty-Second Street subway and almost run into a couple making out like nobody's business. Even without the blue hair, they'd be hard to miss because they're basically fused together from head to toe. They need a room, and stat. Seriously. It's like they're having an emergency make-out session right here on the sidewalk. They've each got the other's ass firmly in hand. Mutual ass grabbage.

A pinched-face man makes a disapproving clucking sound as he walks by. A little boy gawks at them with a wide-open mouth. His dad covers his eyes.

Watching them makes me unreasonably happy. I guess the cliché is true. People in love want everyone else to be in love. I hope their relationship lasts forever.

natasha

I MAKE THE RIGHT onto MLK Boulevard and walk toward
Daniel's store. At the shop next door to his, a girl is standing on
a milk crate, playing violin. She's white, with long black hair
that hasn't been washed in a long time. Her face is too thin—
not fashionable thin, but hungry thin. She's such a sad, strange
sight that I have to stop.

The sign next to her tip hat reads PLEASE HELP. NEED $$$ TO BUY
VIOLIN BACK FROM LOAN SHARK. A thick black arrow on the sign
points to the pawnshop. I can't imagine how life led her to this
place, but I take out a dollar and throw it into her hat, bringing
her total to two dollars.

The door to the pawnshop opens, and an enormous white
guy in a white tracksuit comes out and over to us. He is all
jowls and scowls.

"Time's up," he says, holding out his giant hand to her.

She stops playing immediately and hops down from the
crate. She gathers the money from the hat and gives it to him.
She even gives him the hat.

Tracksuit pockets the money and puts the hat on his head.

"How much is left?" she asks.

He takes a small notebook and pencil out of his pocket and writes something down. "One fifty-one and twenty-three cents." He snaps his fingers at her for the violin.

She hugs the violin to her chest before relinquishing it.

"I'll be back tomorrow. You promise not to sell it?" she asks.

He grunts an assent. "You show up, I don't sell it," he concedes.

"I promise to be here," she says.

"Promises don't mean shit," he says, and walks away.

She looks at the storefront for a long time. I can't tell from her face whether she agrees with him.

daniel

EVEN IF NATASHA WERE STILL here, I wouldn't know where to go in the glass monstrosity of a building. I stare at the directory, trying to divine her location. I know she went to see a lawyer, but the directory is not very specific. For instance, it doesn't say *Attorney So-and-So, Immigration Lawyer to Seventeen-Year-Old Jamaican Girls Named Natasha*. I ransack my mind and come up with nothing.

I take out my phone to check the time. Just over an hour until my Date with Destiny. It occurs to me that I should check the new address the receptionist gave me earlier. If it's too far away, I'll have the perfect excuse to ditch it.

According to Google Maps, though, I'm already there. Either Google is having an existential crisis, or I am. I look at the address again and then back up at the directory.

No shit. My interview *is* in this building.

I am already where I'm supposed to be.

natasha

I PUSH THE DOOR OPEN, and the bell chimes with happy optimism. I am not that optimistic about my chances here. But I have to try.

I expect to see Daniel's dad behind the counter, but Charlie's there instead. He's typing something on his phone and barely glances up. I wonder who I'd have more luck with—Charlie or his dad. I don't have a choice, though, because his dad is nowhere in sight.

I walk up to the counter. "Hey," I say.

He keeps typing away for a few seconds before banging the phone down on the counter. Probably not the best way to greet a potential customer.

"What can I help you with?" he asks, when he finally looks up.

I'm shocked to see that his eye socket is red and swollen. It will be bruised black-and-blue by morning. He raises his hand and touches his eye self-consciously. His knuckles are bruised too.

It takes him a second to recognize me. "Wait. Aren't you Daniel's little girlfriend?"

He must practice sneering in the mirror. He's excellent at it.

"Yes," I say.

He looks past me, searching for Daniel. "Where is that little shit?"

"I'm not sure. I was hoping—" I begin.

He cuts me off and gives me a slow, wide smile. I think he's trying to be sexy. I can see how, if you didn't know him at all, it would work. But I do know him a little, and the smile makes me want to punch him in the other eye.

"Come back for the better brother, I see."

He winks the bad eye and then flinches in pain.

Observable Fact: I don't believe in karma.

But I might start.

"Do you have his cell phone number?" I ask.

He leans back in his chair and picks up his phone from the counter. "You two get into a fight or something?"

As much as I don't want to tell him anything, I have to keep this cordial.

"Something like that," I say. "Do you have it?"

He flips his phone end over end. "You got a Korean boy fetish or what?"

He's smirking, but his eyes are watching me steadily. At first I think he's just goading me—but then I realize it's a serious question. He cares about the answer. I'm not sure if he even knows how much he cares.

"Why does it have to be a fetish?" I ask. "Why can't I just like your brother?"

He scoffs. "Please. What's to like? Guys like him are a dime a dozen."

And then I realize what Charlie's problem with Daniel is. He hates that Daniel doesn't hate himself. For all his uncertainties, Daniel is still more comfortable in his skin than Charlie will ever be in his.

I feel sorry for him, but I don't let it show. "Please help me."

"Tell me why I should." He's not smiling or sneering or smirking at all anymore. He has all the power and we both know it. I don't know him well enough to appeal to the good part of him. I'm not even sure if there *is* a good part of him.

"Think how much trouble I'll cause for your brother," I say. "He's in love with me. He won't give me up no matter what your parents say or do. You can just sit back and enjoy the show."

He throws his head back and laughs. He really is not a good person. I mean, he might have some good parts. I think most people do. But Charlie's bad parts outweigh the good ones. I'm sure there are good reasons he is the way he is, but then I decide that the reasons don't matter.

Some people exist in your life to make it better. Some people exist to make it worse.

Still, though, he does a good thing for his brother: he gives me the number.

daniel

MY PHONE RINGS, and I almost drop it like it's possessed.
I don't recognize the number, but answer anyway.

"Hello?"

"Is this Daniel?"

"Natasha?" I ask, even though I know it's her.

"Yes, it's me." Her voice smiles. "Your brother gave me your
number."

Now I begin to suspect it's a practical joke by my asshole
brother. No way would he ever do something so kind.

"Who is this?" I demand.

"Daniel, it's me. It's really me."

"He gave you my number?"

"Maybe he's not so bad after all," she says.

"Not a chance," I say back, and we both laugh.

I found her.

Well, she found me.

I can't believe it.

"Where are you?"

"I just left your store. Where are you?"

"I'm at your lawyer's office building."

"What? Why?"

"It's the only place I could think to find you."

"You've been looking for me?" Her voice is shy.

"Will you forgive me for being such a jerk earlier?"

"It's okay. I should've told you."

"It wasn't my business."

"Yes it was," she says.

It's not the three words I want to hear from her, but it's damn close.

natasha

HE'S SITTING ON ONE OF THE BENCHES that face the fountain and writing in his notebook. I knew I'd be happy to see him, but I didn't expect to feel gleeful. I have to stop myself from jumping up and down and clapping my hands and maybe doing a twirl.

Gleeful.

Which is not like me.

So I don't do it.

But the smile on my face needs to be measured in miles instead of inches.

I slide onto the bench and bump his shoulder with mine. He pulls the notebook up to his face, covering his mouth, and then turns to face me. His eyes are wide and dancing. I don't think anyone's ever been as happy to see anyone as Daniel is to see me.

"Hey," he says from behind the notebook.

I reach out to lower the book, but he shifts his body back from me.

"What's wrong?" I ask.

"I might have gotten into a small fight," he says.

"You got into a *small* fight and now I can't see your face?"

"I just wanted to warn you first."

I reach out again. This time he lets me lower the book. The right side of his lip is swollen and bruised. He looks like he's been in a boxing match.

"You fought with your brother," I say, making the connection.

"He had it coming." He keeps his face neutral, downplaying his feelings for my benefit.

"I didn't think poets fought."

"Are you kidding? We're the worst." He smiles at me, but then flinches in pain. "I'm fine," he says, watching my face. "It looks worse than it is."

"Why did you fight?" I ask.

"It doesn't matter."

"Yes it does—"

"No it doesn't." His lips are firm and straight. Whatever happened, he's not going to tell me.

"Was it about me?" I ask, even though I know the answer.

He nods.

I decide to let it go. It's enough to know that he thinks I'm worth fighting for.

"I was pretty mad at you before," I say. I need to say it before we go any further.

"I know. I'm sorry. I just couldn't believe it."

"That I didn't tell you?" I ask.

"No. That after all the things that had to happen to get us to meet today, something else was gonna tear us apart."

"You really are hopeless."

"It's possible," he says.

I rest my head on his shoulder and tell him about going to the museum and Ahnighito and all the things that had to go right for our solar system, galaxy, and universe to form. I tell him compared to that, falling in love just seems like small coincidences. He doesn't agree, and I'm glad for it. I reach out again and touch his lip. He captures my hand and turns his face in to my palm and kisses the center. I've never really understood the phrase *they have chemistry* before now. After all, everything is chemistry. Everything is combination and reaction.

The atoms in my body align themselves with the atoms in his. It's the way I knew he was still in the lobby earlier today.

He kisses the center of my palm again, and I sigh. Touching him is order and chaos, like being assembled and disassembled at the same time.

"You said you had good news," he says. I read the hope on his wide-open face. What if it hadn't worked out? How would we have survived being torn apart? Because it feels impossible now, the idea that we don't belong together. But then, I think, of course we would've survived. Separation is not fatal.

Still, I'm glad we don't have to find out. "The lawyer says he thinks he can figure it out. He thinks I'll get to stay," I say.

"How sure is he?" he asks. Surprisingly, he's more skeptical than I am.

"Don't worry. He seemed pretty sure," I say, and let my happy tears fall. For once, I'm not embarrassed to be crying.

"You see?" he says. "We're meant to be. Let's go celebrate."

He pulls me in close. I tug the tie out of his hair and run my fingers through it. He buries his hands in mine and leans in to kiss me, but I put my finger against his lips to stop him. "Hold that kiss," I say.

It occurs to me that there's one call I want to make. It's a silly impulse, but Daniel's almost got me believing in meant-to-be.

This entire chain of events was started by the security guard who delayed me this morning. If it weren't for her fondling my stuff, then I wouldn't have been late. There'd have been no Lester Barnes, no Attorney Fitzgerald. No Daniel.

I dig around my backpack and pull out Lester Barnes's business card. My call goes straight to voice mail. I leave a rambling message thanking him for helping me and asking him to thank the security guard for me.

"She has long brown hair and sad eyes and she touches everyone's stuff," I say as a way to describe her. Just before I hang up, I remember her name. "I think her name is Irene. Please tell her thanks for me."

Daniel gives me a quizzical look.

"I'll explain later," I tell him, and scoot my way back into his arms. "Back to *norebang*?" I ask against his lips. My heart is trying to escape my body through my chest.

"No," he says. "I have a better idea."

daniel

"WANT TO KNOW SOMETHING CRAZY?" I ask as I lead her back into the building. "My interview appointment is here too."

"No way," she says, and stops walking briefly.

I grin at her, dying to know how her scientific brain is going to deal with this epic level of coincidence. "What are the odds?"

She laughs at me. "Enjoying yourself, are you?"

"You see? I've been right all day. We were meant to meet. If we hadn't met earlier, maybe we would've met now." My logic is completely refutable but she doesn't refute me. Instead, she slips her hand into mine and smiles. I may make a believer out of her yet.

My plan is to get us to the roof so that we can make out in privacy. We sign in for my appointment at the security desk. The guard directs us to the elevator banks. The one we get on must be the local, because it stops at practically every floor. Suited people get on and off, talking loudly about Very Important Things. Despite what Natasha said earlier, I can never work in a building like this. Finally we get to the top floor. We get off, find a stairwell, and walk up one flight and straight into a locked gray door with a NO ROOF ACCESS sign.

I refuse to believe it. Clearly the roof is just behind these doors. I turn the handle, hoping for a miracle, but it's locked.

I rest my forehead against the sign. "Open sesame," I say to the door.

Magically, it opens.

"What the hell?" I stumble forward, right into the same security guard from the lobby. Unlike us, he must've taken an express elevator.

"You kids aren't allowed up here," he grunts. He smells like cigarette smoke.

I pull Natasha through the doorway with me. "We just wanted to see the view," I say, in my most-respectful-with-just-a-hint-of-pleading-but-non-whining voice.

He raises skeptical eyebrows and starts to say something, but a coughing fit overtakes him until he's hunched over and thumping his heart with his fist.

"Are you okay?" Natasha asks. He's only bent slightly now, both hands on his thighs. Natasha puts a hand on his shoulder.

"Got this cough," he says between coughs.

"Well, you shouldn't smoke," she tells him.

He straightens and wipes his eyes. "You sound like my wife."

"She's right," she says, not missing a beat.

I try to give her a look that says *don't argue with the old security guard with the lung problem, otherwise he won't let us stay up here and make out,* but even if she interpreted my facial expression correctly, she ignores me.

"I used to be a candy striper in a pulmonary ward. That cough does not sound good."

We both stare at her. I, because I'm picturing her in a candy striper outfit and then picturing her out of it. I'm pretty sure this is going to be my new nighttime fantasy.

I don't know why he's staring at her. Hopefully not for the same reason.

"Give them to me," she says, holding out her hand for his pack of cigarettes. "You need to stop smoking." I don't know how she manages to sound so genuinely concerned and bossy at the same time.

He pulls the pack out of his jacket pocket. "You think I haven't tried?" he asks.

I look at him again. He's too old to be doing this job. He looks like he should be retired and spoiling his grandkids somewhere in Florida.

Natasha keeps holding out her hand until he hands over the pack.

"Be careful of this one," he says to me, smiling.

"Yes, sir."

He puts his jacket on. "How do you know I won't just go get some more?" he asks her.

"I guess I don't," she says, shrugging.

He looks at her for a long moment. "Life doesn't always go the way you plan," he says.

I can see that she doesn't believe him. He can see it too, but he lets it go.

"Stay away from the edge," he says, winking at both of us. "Have a good time."

joe

A Planned History

THE GIRL REMINDED HIM a little of his Beth. Direct but sweet. That, more than anything, is why he let them stay up on the roof. He knows perfectly well that the only view they'll be looking at is each other. No harm in that, he thinks.

He and his Beth were the same way. And not just at the beginning of their marriage, but all throughout. They won the lottery with each other, they liked to say.

Beth died last year. Six months after they'd both retired. In fact, the cancer diagnosis came the day after retirement. They had so many plans. Alaskan cruise to see the aurora borealis (hers). Venice to drink grappa and see the canals (his).

That's the thing that gets to Joe even now. All the plans they'd made. All the saving. All the waiting around for the perfect time.

And for what? For nothing.

The girl is right, of course. He shouldn't smoke. After he lost Beth, he took himself out of retirement and took up smoking again. What did it matter if he worked himself to death? What did it matter if he smoked himself to death? There was nothing left to live for, nothing left to plan for.

He takes one last look at the girl and the boy before closing the door. They're looking at each other like there's nowhere else they'd rather be. He and his Beth were like that once.

Maybe he will give up smoking after all. Maybe he'll make some new plans.

natasha

DANIEL WALKS TO THE EDGE of the roof and looks out at the city. His hair is loose and blowing in the breeze and he's got his poet face on. The non-bruised side of his face smiles.

I go to him and slip my hand into his. "Aren't you gonna write something down, poet boy?" I tease.

He smiles wider, but doesn't turn to look at me. "It looks so different from up here, doesn't it?" he asks.

What does he see when he looks out? I see miles of rooftops, most of them empty. A few of them are populated with long-abandoned things—nonworking HVAC units, broken office furniture. Some have gardens, and I wonder who tends them.

Daniel takes out his notebook now, and I move a little closer to the edge.

Before these buildings were buildings, they were just the skeletons of them. Before they were skeletons, they were crossbeams and girders. Metal and glass and concrete. And before that, they were construction plans. Before that, architectural plans. And before that, just an idea someone had for the making of a city.

Daniel puts away his notebook and pulls me back from the edge. He puts his hands on my waist.

"What do you even write in there?" I ask.

"Plans," he says. His eyes are merry and staring at my lips and I'm having trouble thinking. I take a little step back but he follows, like we're dancing.

"I—Jesus. Have you been this sexy the whole day?" I ask.

He laughs and blushes. "I'm glad you think I'm sexy." His eyes are still on my lips.

"Is it gonna hurt if I kiss you?" I ask him.

"It'll be a good pain." He puts his other hand on my waist like he's anchoring us. My heart just will not settle down. Kissing him can't be as good as I remember. When we had our first kiss, I thought I was kissing him for the last time. I'm sure that made it more intense. This kiss will be more normal. No fireworks and chaos, just two people who like each other a lot, kissing.

I get on my tiptoes and move in even closer. Finally his eyes meet mine. He moves his hand from my waist and places it over my heart. It beats under his palm like it's beating *for* him.

Our lips touch, and I try to keep my eyes open for as long as possible. I try not to succumb to the crazy entropy of this thing between us. I don't understand it. Why this person? Why Daniel and not any of the boys before? What if we hadn't met? Would I have had a perfectly ordinary day and not know that I was missing something?

I wrap my arms around his neck and lean into him, but I can't get close enough. The restless, chaotic feeling is back. I want things that I can name, and some things that I can't. I want this one moment to last forever, but I don't want to miss all the other moments to come. I want our entire future together, but I want it here and now.

I'm slightly overwhelmed and break the kiss. "Go. Over. There," I say, and punctuate each word with a kiss. I point to a spot far away from me, out of kissing range.

"Here?" he asks taking a single step back.

"At least five more."

He grins at me, but complies.

"All our kisses aren't going to be like that, are they?" I ask him.

"Like what?"

"You know. Insane."

"I love how direct you are," he says.

"Really? My mom says I go too far."

"Maybe. I still love it, though."

I lower my eyes and don't respond. "How much time until your interview?" I ask.

"Forty minutes."

"Got any more of those love questions for me?"

"You're not in love with me yet?" His voice is filled with mock incredulity.

"Nope," I say, and smile at him.

"Don't worry," he says. "We've got time."

daniel

IT FEELS LIKE A MIRACLE that we get to sit here on this rooftop, like we're part of a secret sky city. The sun is slowly retreating across the buildings, but it's not dark yet. It will be soon, but for now there's only an idea of darkness.

Natasha and I are sitting cross-legged against the wall next to the stairwell door. We're holding hands, and she's resting her head on my shoulder. Her hair is soft against the side of my face.

"Are you ready for the dinner guest question yet?" I ask.

"You mean who I'd invite?"

"Yup."

"Ugh, no. You go first," she says.

"Easy," I say. "God."

She raises her head from my shoulder to look at me. "You really believe in God?"

"I do."

"One guy? In the sky? With superpowers?" Her disbelief isn't mocking, just investigative.

"Not exactly like that," I say.

"What, then?"

I squeeze her hand. "You know the way we feel right now? This connection between us that we don't understand and we don't want to let go of? That's God."

"Holy hell," she exclaims. "You poet boys are dangerous."

She pulls my hand into her lap and holds it with both of hers.

I tilt my head back and watch the sky, trying to pick shapes out of the clouds. "Here's what I think," I say. "I think we're all connected, everyone on earth."

She runs her fingertips over my knuckles. "Even the bad people?"

"Yes. But everyone has at least a little good in them."

"Not true," she says.

"Okay," I concede. "But everyone has done at least one good thing in their lifetime. Do you agree with that?"

She thinks it over and then slowly nods.

I go on. "I think all the good parts of us are connected on some level. The part that shares the last double chocolate chip cookie or donates to charity or gives a dollar to a street musician or becomes a candy striper or cries at Apple commercials or says I love you or I forgive you. I think that's God. God is the connection of the very best parts of us."

"And you think that connection has a consciousness?" she asks.

"Yeah, and we call it God."

She laughs a quiet laugh. "Are you always so—"

"Erudite?" I ask, interrupting.

She laughs louder now. "I was gonna say cheesy."

"Yes. I'm known far and wide for my cheesiness."

"I'm kidding," she says, bumping her shoulder into mine. "I really like that you've thought about it."

And I have too. This is not the first time I've had these thoughts, but it's the first time I've really been able to articulate them. Something about being with her makes me my best self.

I pull her hand to my lips and kiss her fingers. "What about you?" I ask. "You don't believe in God?"

"I like your idea of it. I definitely don't believe in the fire and brimstone one."

"But you believe in something?"

She frowns, uncertain. "I really don't know. I guess I'm more interested in *why* people feel like they have to believe in God. Why can't it just be science? Science is wondrous. The night sky? Amazing. The inside of a human cell? Incredible. Something that tells us we're born bad and that people use to justify all their petty prejudices and awfulness? I dunno. I guess I believe in science. Science is enough."

"Huh," I say. Sunlight reflects off the buildings, and the air around us takes on an orange tinge. I feel cocooned even in this wide-open space.

She says, "Did you know that the universe is approximately twenty-seven percent dark matter?"

I did not know that, but of course she does.

"What is dark matter?"

Delight is the only word for the look on her face. She tugs

her hand out of mine, rubs her palms together, and settles in to explain.

"Well, scientists aren't exactly sure, but it's the difference between an object's mass and the mass calculated by its gravitational effect." She raises her eyebrows expectantly, as if she's said something profound and earth-shattering.

I am profoundly un-earth-shattered.

She sighs. Dramatically.

"Poets," she mutters, but with a smile. "Those two masses should be the same." She raises an explanatory finger. "They *should* be the same, but they're not, for very large bodies like planets."

"Oh, that's interesting," I say, really meaning it.

"Isn't it?" She's beaming at me and I'm really a goner for this girl. "Also, it turns out the visible mass of a galaxy doesn't have enough gravity to explain why it doesn't fly apart."

I shake my head to let her know I don't understand.

She goes on. "If we calculate the gravitational forces of all the objects we can detect, it's not enough to keep galaxies and stars in orbit around each other. There has to be more matter that we can't see. Dark matter."

"Okay, I get it," I say.

She gives me skeptical eyes.

"No, really," I say. "I get it. Dark matter is twenty-seven percent of the universe, you said?"

"Approximately."

"And it's the reason why objects don't hurtle themselves off into deep dark space? It's what keeps us bound together?"

274

Her skepticism turns into suspicion. "What is your addled poet brain getting at?"

"You're gonna hate me."

"Maybe," she agrees.

"Dark matter *is* love. It's the attracting force."

"Oh God Jesus no. Yuck. Blech. You're the worst."

"Oh, I am good," I say, laughing hard.

"The absolute worst," she says, but she leans in and laughs hard along with me.

"I'm totally right," I say, triumphant. I recapture her hand.

She groans again, but I can tell she's thinking about it. Maybe she doesn't disagree as much as she thinks she does.

I scroll through the questions on my phone. "Okay, I have another one. Complete the following sentence: We're both in this room feeling . . ."

"Like I have to pee," she says, smiling.

"You really hate talking about serious things, don't you?"

"Have you ever had to pee really bad?" she asks. "It's a serious thing. You could cause serious damage to your bladder by—"

"Do you really have to pee?" I ask.

"No."

"Answer the question," I tell her. I'm not letting her joke her way out of this one.

"You first," she says, sighing.

"Happy, horny, and hopeful."

"Alliteration. Nice."

"Your turn, and you have to be sincere," I tell her.

She sticks her tongue out at me. "Confused. Scared."

I pull her hand into my lap. "Why are you scared?"

"It's been a long day. This morning I thought I was being deported. I've been gearing myself up for that for two months. Now it looks like I'll get to stay."

She turns to look at me. "And then there's you. I didn't know you this morning, and now I don't really remember not knowing you. It's all a little much. I feel out of control."

"Why is that so bad?" I ask.

"I like to see things coming. I like to plan ahead."

And I get it. I really do. We are programmed to plan ahead. It's part of our rhythm. The sun rises every day and defers to the moon every night. "Like the security guard said, though—planning doesn't always work."

"Do you think that's true? I think mostly you can plan. Mostly things don't just come out of nowhere and bowl you over."

"Probably the dinosaurs thought that too, and look what happened to them," I tease.

Her smile is so broad that I have to touch her face. She turns her face in to my palm and kisses it. "Extinction-level events notwithstanding, I think you can plan ahead," she says.

"I bowled you over," I remind her, and she doesn't deny it.

"Anyway," I say. "So far you only have two things—confused and scared."

"All right, all right. I'll give you what you want and say 'happy.' "

I sigh dramatically. "You could've said that one first."

"I like suspense," she says.

"No you don't."

"You're right. I hate suspense."

"Happy because of me?" I ask.

"And not being deported. But mostly you."

She pulls our joined hands to her lips and kisses mine. I could stay here forever interrupting our talking with kissing, interrupting our kissing with talking.

"When are we doing the staring-into-each-other's-eyes thing?" I ask.

She rolls the very eyes that I want to stare into. "Later. After your interview," she says.

"Don't be scared," I tease.

"What's to be scared of? All you'll see is iris and pupil."

"The eyes are the windows to the soul," I counter.

"Stuff and nonsense," she says.

I check the time on my phone unnecessarily. I know it's almost time for my interview, but I want to linger out here in sky city some more. "Let's get in a couple more questions," I say. "Lightning round. What's your most treasured memory?"

"The first time I got to eat ice cream in a cone instead of in a cup," she says with no hesitation.

"How old were you?"

"Four. Chocolate ice cream while wearing an all-white Easter Sunday dress."

"Whose idea was that?" I ask.

"My father's," she says, smiling. "He used to think I was the greatest thing ever."

"And he doesn't anymore?"

"No," she says.

I wait for her to continue, but she moves on: "What's your memory?"

"We took a family trip to Disney World when I was seven. Charlie really wanted to go on Space Mountain, but my mom thought it'd be too scary for me and she wouldn't let him go by himself. And neither of my parents wanted to go."

She tightens her grip on my hands, which is cute since I clearly survived the experience. "So what happened?"

"I convinced my mom that I really wasn't scared. I told her I'd been looking forward to the ride since forever."

"But you weren't?" she asks.

"No. I was scared shitless. I just did it for Charlie."

She bumps my shoulder and teases. "I already like you. You don't have to convince me that you're a saint."

"That's the thing. I wasn't being saintly. I think I knew our relationship wasn't going to last. I was just trying to convince him I was worth it. It worked too. He told me I was brave and he let me finish all his popcorn."

I tilt my head back and look up at the clouds. They're barely moving across the sky.

"Do you think it's funny that both of our favorite memories are about the people we like the least now?" I ask.

"Maybe that's why we dislike them," she says. "The distance between who they were and who they are is so wide, we have no hope of getting them back."

"Maybe," I say. "You know what the worst part of that story is?"

"What?"

"I hate roller coasters to this day because of that trip."

She laughs, and I laugh with her.

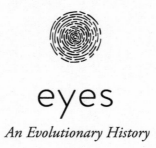

eyes

An Evolutionary History

SCIENTISTS THEORIZE that the first "eyes" were nothing more than a pigmented, light-sensitive spot on the skin of some ancient creature. That spot gave it the ability to sense light from dark—an advantage, since darkness could indicate that a predator was close enough to block out light. Because of this, they survived more, reproduced more, and passed this ability down to their offspring. Random mutations created a deepening depression in the light-sensitive spot. This depression led to slightly better vision and, therefore, more survival. Over time, that light-sensitive spot evolved to become the human eye.

How did we go from eyes as a survival mechanism to the idea of love at first sight? Or the idea that eyes are the windows to the soul? Or to the cliché of lovers staring endlessly into each other's eyes?

Studies have shown that the pupils of people who are attracted to each other dilate from the presence of dopamine. Other studies suggest that threads in the eye can indicate personality tendencies, and that maybe eyes are a kind of window to the soul after all.

And what about the lovers who spend hours staring into each other's eyes? Is it a display of trust? *I will let you in close and trust you not to hurt me while I'm in this vulnerable position.* And if trust is one of the foundations of love, perhaps the staring is a way to build or reinforce it. Or maybe it's simpler than that.

A simple search for connection.

To see.

To be seen.

daniel

ATTORNEY FITZGERALD'S DOOR is at the end of a long, gray, and mostly featureless hallway. I try (and fail) not to take this as a sign about my future. There's no name on the door, just a number. No one answers when I knock. Maybe he's left for the day already? Because that would be ideal. Then it wouldn't be my fault that I didn't get to go to Yale and become a doctor. Never mind that I'm ten minutes late because of all the kissing. I regret nothing.

I turn the handle and walk right into a sobbing woman. She's not even crying into her hands to hide her face like people usually do. She's standing in the middle of the room taking huge gulps of air with tears streaming down her face. Her mascara is streaked across her cheeks and her eyes are puffy and red, like she's been crying for a long time.

When she realizes that I'm standing there, she stops crying and wipes her face with the back of her hands. The wiping makes it worse, so now mascara is across her nose too.

"Are you okay?" I ask, asking the dumbest question I can think of. Clearly she's not okay.

"I'm fine," she says. She chews on her bottom lip and

tries to smooth her hair, but again, she makes the problem worse.

"You're Daniel Bae," she says. "You're here for the admission interview."

I take a step toward her. "Can I get you a glass of water or a tissue or something?" I spy an empty box of Kleenex on her desk next to a PARALEGALS DO IT CHEAPER mug.

"I'm completely fine. He's just through there," she says, pointing to a door behind her.

"Are you sure you're—" I begin, but she cuts me off.

"I have to go now. Tell him that he's the most wonderful person I've ever met but that I have to go."

I say "Okay," even though I won't be telling him any of that. Also, it's a pretty small office. He's probably already heard her declaration.

She walks back to her desk and picks up the PARALEGALS mug. "And tell him that I want to stay, but I can't. It's better for both of us."

Then she starts crying again. And now I can feel my own eyes welling up with tears. Not cool.

She stops crying abruptly and stares at me. "Are you crying?" she asks.

I wipe my eyes. "It's just a stupid thing that happens to me. I start crying when I see other people crying."

"That's really sweet." Now that it's not drowning in tears, her voice is kind of musical.

"It's kind of a pain in the ass, actually."

"Language," she says, frowning.

"Sorry." What kind of person objects to an innocent word like *ass*?

She accepts my *sorry* with a slight nod. "We just moved into this office, and now I'll never see it again." She sniffles and then wipes her nose. "If I'd known how this would end, I would never have started."

"Everyone wants to be able to predict the future," I say. Her eyes fill with tears again even as she's nodding her agreement.

"When I was a little girl, fairy tales were my favorite books because even before you opened them, you knew how they were going to end. Happily ever after." She glances at the closed door behind her, closes her eyes, and opens them again. "In the fairy tales, the princess never does the wrong thing."

The office door behind me opens. I turn, curious to see what the most wonderful person in the world looks like. Except for the bandage over his right eye, he looks pretty normal.

"Daniel Bae?" he asks, looking only at me. His eyes don't flit over to her for even a second.

I hold out my hand for a shake. "Mr. Fitzgerald. It's nice to meet you."

He doesn't shake my hand. "You're late," he says, and walks back into his office.

I turn to say goodbye to the secretary, but she's already gone.

natasha

I TAKE MY PHONE OUT of my backpack. Still no return call or text from Bev. Maybe she's on another tour. I remember she said she wanted to make it to University of California, San Francisco, too.

I should call my mom. Probably I should've called her at many points today. She's called three more times while Daniel and I were on the roof.

I text her: *coming home soon.*

The phone buzzes back at me almost immediately. I guess she's been waiting for word from me.

been trying to reach u for 2 hours.

sorry! I text back.

She always has to have the last word, so I wait for the inevitable reply:

so no news then? hope u didn't get u hopes up.

I toss the phone into my backpack without answering.

Sometimes I think my mom's worst fear is being disappointed. She combats this by trying her hardest never to get her hopes up, and urging everyone else to do the same.

It doesn't always work. Once she brought home a casting-call flyer for an Off-Off-Off-Broadway play for my father. I don't know where she found it or even what the role was. He took it from her and even said thank you, but I'm pretty sure he never called the number.

I decide to wait for the final call from Attorney Fitzgerald before saying anything to her. My mom's already dealt with too much disappointment.

The trouble with getting your hopes too far up is: it's a long way down.

samuel kingsley

A History of Regret, Part 4

SOME PEOPLE ARE BORN FOR greatness. God give a lucky few of us some talent and then put us on earth to make use of it.

Only two times in my life I get to use mine. Two months ago when I did *A Raisin in the Sun* in Manhattan, and ten years ago when I did it in Montego Bay.

There's just something about me and that play that was meant to be. In Jamaica, the *Daily* called my performance *miraculous*. I got a standing ovation.

Me. Not the other actors. Me alone.

Is a funny thing. That play send me to America, and now it sending me back to Jamaica.

Patricia ask me how me could tell the cop all our business. *Him not no preacher,* she say. *It not no confession,* she say. I tell her I was just drunk and coming off the stage high. The highest thing you can do is the thing God put you on this earth to do.

I tell her I didn't mean to do it. And is true what I tell her, but the opposite true too. Maybe I do it on purpose. This not no confession. I just saying that the thought is there in my mind. Maybe I do it on purpose. We couldn't even fill all the seats in the place.

America done with me and I done with it. More than anything, that night remind me. In Jamaica I got a standing ovation. In America I can't get an audience.

I don't know. Maybe I do it on purpose. You can get lost in you own mind, like you gone to another country. All you thoughts in another language and you can't read the signs even though they everywhere all around you.

daniel

THE FIRST THING I SEE on his desk is a file with Natasha's name on it. *Natasha Kingsley,* it says. It has to be her, right? How many Natasha Kingsleys could there be? Not only are our meetings in the same building, but also her lawyer and my interviewer are the same person? The odds have to be astronomical, right? I can't wait to see the look on her face when I tell her.

I look up at him and then around the office for other signs. "Are you an immigration lawyer?" I ask.

He looks up from what I presume is my application. "I am. Why?"

"I think I know one of your clients," I say, and pick up the file.

He snatches it away from me. "Don't touch that. It's privileged." He pulls it as far away from me as possible.

I grin at Fitzgerald and he frowns back at me. "Yeah, sorry," I say. "It's just you saved my life."

"What are you talking about?" He flexes his right wrist and I notice that his hand is bandaged. Now I remember that his paralegal said he'd been in a car accident.

I point at the file. "I just met her—Natasha—today."

He's still frowning at me, not getting it. "When I met her she was being deported, but then she met with you and you did your lawyer magic, and now she's going to stay."

He rests the bandaged hand on his desk. "And how did that save *your* life?"

"She's the One," I say.

He frowns. "Didn't you say you just met her today?"

"Yup." I can't do anything about the big smile on my face.

"And she's the One?" He doesn't actually put air quotes around "the One," but I can hear them in his voice. Vocal air quotes (not better than actual air quotes).

He steeples his fingers and stares at me for a good long while. "Why are you here?" he asks.

Is this a trick question? "For my admission interview?"

He looks me over pointedly. "No, really. Why are you here in my office right now? You obviously don't care about this interview. You show up here looking like you've been in a brawl. It's a serious question. Why did you come here?"

There's no way to answer this but honestly. "My parents made me."

"How old are you?"

"Seventeen."

He looks down at my file. "It says here that you're interested in the pre-med track. Are you?"

"Not really," I say.

"Not really or no?" Lawyers like certainty.

"No."

"Now we're getting somewhere," he says. "Do you want to go to Yale?"

"I don't even know if I want to go to college."

He leans forward in his chair. I feel like I'm being cross-examined. "And what's your big dream?"

"To be a poet."

"Oh good," he says. "Something practical."

"Believe it or not, I've heard that one before."

He leans in even more. "I'll ask you again. Why are you here?"

"I have to be."

"No you don't," he fires back. "You can just get up and walk out that door."

"I owe it to my parents."

"Why?"

"You wouldn't understand."

"Try me."

I sigh (long-suffering variety). "My parents are immigrants. They moved to this country for a better life. They work all the time so my brother and I can have the American Dream. Nowhere in the American Dream does it say you can skip college and become a starving artist."

"It says whatever you want it to."

I snort. "Not in my family it doesn't. If I don't do this, I get cut off. No funds for college. No nothing."

This confession at least stops his rapid-fire questioning. He leans back in his chair. "Would they really do that?" he asks.

I know the answer, but I can't make myself say it right away. I think about my dad's face earlier this afternoon. He's so determined that Charlie and I have a better life than he did. He'll do anything to guarantee it.

"Yes," I say. "He would." But not because he's evil. And not because he's a Stereotypical Korean Parent. But because he can't see past his own history to let us have ours.

A lot of people are like that.

Fitzgerald whistles low. "So I guess you have to be sure the poetry thing is worth it."

Now I'm the one leaning in. "Haven't you ever done something only because you're obligated to? Just because you made a promise?"

His eyes drift away from mine. For whatever reason, this question changes the dynamic between us. It feels like we're in the same boat.

"Meeting your obligations is the definition of adulthood, kid. If you're going to make mistakes and break promises, now's the time."

He stops talking, flexes his wrist, and grimaces. "Get your screwing up done now, when the consequences aren't so bad. Trust me. It gets harder to do it later."

Sometimes people tell you things by not telling you things. I glance at his left hand and see his wedding ring.

"Is that what happened to you?" I ask.

He unsteeples his fingers and twists the ring around his finger. "I'm a married man with two kids."

"And you're having an affair with your paralegal."

He rubs at the bandage above his eye. "It just started today." He looks over to his closed door, as if he's hoping she'll be standing right there. "Ended today too," he says quietly.

I didn't actually expect him to admit it, and now I'm not sure what to say.

"You think I'm a bad guy," he says.

"I think you're my interviewer," I answer. Maybe it's better for us to just get this interview back on course.

He covers his eyes with his hands. "I met her too late. I've always had lousy timing."

I don't know what to tell him. Not that he's looking to me for advice. Ordinarily I would say follow your heart. But he's a married man. *His* heart is not the only one involved.

"So what are you gonna do? Let her go?" I ask.

He looks at me for a long time, thinking. "You're going to have to do the same," he says finally.

He pulls Natasha's file from under his elbow. "I couldn't do it. I thought I could, but I couldn't."

"Do what?" I ask.

"Stop her deportation."

He's going to have to spell it out for me, because I'm not processing what he's saying. "Your Natasha is getting deported tonight after all. I couldn't stop it from happening. The judge wouldn't overturn the Voluntary Removal."

I don't know what a Voluntary Removal is, but all I can think is that there's a mistake. It's definitely a mistake. Now I'm hoping it really is a different Natasha Kingsley.

"I'm sorry, kid," he says. He slides the file across to me, as if my looking at it is somehow going to help. I flip it open. It's some sort of official form. All I see is her name: Natasha Katherine Kingsley. I didn't know her middle name. Katherine. It suits her.

I shut the file and slide it back to him. "There has to be something you can do."

The finger steeple is back and he shrugs. "I've tried everything already."

The shrug pisses me off. This is not a small thing. This isn't *Oh, you missed your appointment. Come again tomorrow.* This is Natasha's life. And mine.

I stand up. "You didn't try hard enough," I accuse him. I'm willing to bet the affair with his secretary has something to do with this. I bet he's spent the day breaking promises to his wife and children. And to Natasha too.

"Look, I know you're upset." His voice is even, like he's trying to calm me down.

But I don't want to be calm. I press my hands into his desk and lean forward. "There has to be something you can do. It's not her fault her dad is such a fuck-up."

He slides his chair back from the desk. "Sorry. Homeland Security doesn't like it if you overstay your visa."

"But she was just a kid. She didn't have a choice. It's not like she could've said *Mom, Dad, our visa is expired. We should go back to Jamaica now.*"

"Doesn't matter. The law has to draw a line somewhere. Their last appeal was denied. The only hope was the judge. If they leave tonight, then there's a slight chance she can reapply for a visa in a few years."

"But America is her home," I shout. "It doesn't matter where she was born." I don't say the rest of it, which is that she belongs with me.

"I wish there was something I could do," he says. He touches the bandage above his eye again and seems genuinely sorry. Maybe I'm wrong about him. Maybe he really did try.

"I'm planning on calling her after you and I are done here," he says.

After we're done. I've completely forgotten that this meeting is supposed to be about me getting into Yale. "You're just going to call her and tell her over the phone?"

"Does it matter how she hears it?" he asks, frowning.

"Of course it matters." I don't want her to hear the worst news of her life over the phone from someone she barely knows. "I'll do it," I say. "I'll tell her."

He shakes his head. "I can't let you do that. It's my job."

I just sit there not knowing what to do. My lip throbs. The spot on my ribs where Charlie punched me hurts. The place in my heart where Natasha is hurts.

"I'm sorry, kid," he says again.

"What if she doesn't get on the plane? What if she just stays?" I am desperate. Breaking the law seems a small price to pay to get her to stay.

Another head shake. "I don't recommend that. As a lawyer or otherwise."

I have to get to her and tell her first. I don't want her to be alone when she hears the news.

I walk out of his office and into the empty reception area. The paralegal didn't come back.

He follows me. "So that's it?" he asks. "No more interview?"

I don't stop walking. "You said it yourself. I don't really care about Yale."

He puts a hand on my arm so I have to turn and face him. "Look, I know I said you should get your screwing up done now while you're still a kid, but Yale's a big deal. Going there could open a lot of doors for you. It did for me."

And maybe he's right. Maybe I'm being shortsighted.

I look around his office. How long will it take for the construction to be done? I wonder. How long will it take for him to hire a new paralegal?

I jut my chin in the direction of her desk. "You did all the things you were supposed to, and you're still not happy."

He rubs again at the bandage above his eye and doesn't look over at the desk. He's tired, but not the kind of tired that sleeping can fix.

I tell him, "If I don't go now, I'll always regret it."

"What's another half an hour to finish this interview?" he insists.

Does he really need me to tell him that all the seconds matter? That our own universe exploded into existence in the space of a breath?

"Time counts, Mr. Fitzgerald," I tell him.

Finally he turns away from me and looks at the empty desk.

"But you know that already," I say.

jeremy fitzgerald

A Fairy-Tale History, Part 2

JEREMY FITZGERALD DIDN'T TELL DANIEL the
truth. The reason he wasn't able to stop Natasha's deportation
is that he missed the court appointment with the judge who
could've reversed the Voluntary Removal. He missed it because
he's in love with Hannah Winter, and instead of going to see
the judge, he spent the afternoon at a hotel with her.

Alone in his partially built office, Jeremy will think of Daniel
Bae constantly for the next week. He will remember what
Daniel said about time counting. He'll remember with perfect
clarity Daniel's busted lip and bloodied shirt. He'll remember
how that was nothing compared to the complete devastation
on Daniel's face when he learned the news about Natasha. Like
someone handed him a grenade and exploded his life apart.

Sometime in the next month, Jeremy will tell his wife that
he no longer loves her. That it will be best for her and the children if he leaves. He will call Hannah Winter, and he will make
her promises and he will keep all of them.

His son will never settle down or marry or have children or
forgive his father for his betrayal. His daughter will marry her

first girlfriend, Marie. She will spend most of that first marriage anticipating and then causing its end. After Marie, no one will ever love her quite as much again. And though she'll get married twice more, she'll never love anyone as much as she did Marie.

Jeremy and Hannah's children will grow up to love others in the simple and uncomplicated way of people who have always known where love comes from, and aren't afraid of its loss.

All of which isn't to say that Jeremy Fitzgerald did the right thing or the wrong thing. It's only to say this: love always changes everything.

hannah winter

A Fairy-Tale History, Part 2

And They Lived Happily Ever After.

natasha

NOW THAT THE SUN HAS set, the air's gotten much colder. It's not hard to imagine that winter's just around the corner. I'll have to unearth my bulky black coat and my boots. I tug my jacket closer and contemplate going inside to the lobby, where it's warm. I'm on my way in when Daniel walks out the sliding glass doors.

He sees me and I expect a smile, but his face is grim. How badly could his interview have gone?

"What happened?" I ask as soon as I reach him. I'm imagining the worst, like he got into a fight with his interviewer, and now he's banned from applying to any college at all, and his future is ruined.

He puts his hand on my face. "I really love you," he says. He's not joking. This has nothing to do with our silly bet. He says it the way you would say it to someone who is dying or you don't expect to see again.

"Daniel, what's wrong?" I pull his hand away from my face, but I hold on to it.

"I love you," he says again, and recaptures my face with his other hand. "It doesn't matter if you say it back. I just want you to know it."

My phone rings. It's the lawyer's office.

"Don't answer it," he says.

Of course I'm going to answer it.

He touches my hand to stop me. "Please don't," he says again.

Now I'm alarmed. I click Ignore. "What happened to you in there?"

He squeezes his eyes shut. When he opens them again they're filled with tears. "You can't stay here," he says.

At first I don't get it. "Why? Is the building closing for the night?" I look around for guards asking us to leave.

Tears slide down his cheeks. Certain and unwanted knowledge blooms in my mind. I pull my hand out of his.

"What was your interviewer's name?" I whisper.

He's nodding now. "My interviewer was your lawyer."

"Fitzgerald?"

"Yes," he says.

I pull out my phone and look at the number again, still refusing to understand what he's telling me. "I've been waiting for him to call. Did he say something about me?"

I already know the answer. I know it.

It takes him a couple of tries to get the words out. "He said he couldn't get the order overturned."

"But he said he could do it," I insist.

He squeezes my hand and tries to pull me closer, but I resist. I don't want to be comforted. I want to understand.

I back away from him. "Are you sure? Why were you even talking about me?"

He wipes a hand down his face. "There was all this weird shit going on with him and his paralegal, and your file was just on his desk."

"That still doesn't explain—"

He grabs my hand again. I pull it away forcefully this time. "Stop! Just stop!" I yell.

"I'm sorry," he says, and lets me go.

I take another step back. "Just tell me what he said exactly."

"He said the deportation order stands and that it's better if you and your family leave tonight."

I turn away and listen to my voice mail. It's him—Attorney Fitzgerald. He says that I should call him. That he has unfortunate news.

I hang up and stare at Daniel mutely. He starts to say something, but I just want him to stop. I want the whole world to stop. There are too many moving parts that are outside of my control. I feel like I'm in an elaborate Rube Goldberg contraption that someone else designed. I don't know the mechanism to trigger it. I don't know what happens next. I only know that everything cascades, and that once it starts it won't stop.

daniel

Hearts don't break.
It's just another thing the poets say.
Hearts are not made
Of glass
Or bone
Or any material that could
Splinter
Or Fragment
Or Shatter.
They don't
Crack Into Pieces.
They don't
Fall Apart.
Hearts don't break.
They just stop working.
An old watch from another time and no parts to fix it.

natasha

WE'RE SITTING NEXT TO THE fountain and Daniel's holding my hand. His suit jacket is around my shoulders.

He really is a keeper. He's just not mine to keep.

"I have to go home," I say to him. It's the first thing I've said in over half an hour.

He pulls me close again. I'm finally ready to let him. His shoulders are so broad and solid. I rest my head on one. I fit there. I knew it this morning, and I know it now.

"What are we going to do?" he whispers.

There's email and Skype and texts and IMs and maybe even visits to Jamaica. But even as I think it, I know I won't let that happen. We have separate lives to lead. I can't leave my heart here when my life is there. And I can't take his heart with me when his whole future is here.

I lift my head from his shoulder. "How was the rest of the interview?"

He touches my cheek and then tilts my head back down. "He said he'd recommend me."

"That's great," I say, with absolutely no enthusiasm.

"Yeah," he says, enthusiasm level matching mine.

I am cold but I don't want to move. Moving from this spot will start the chain reaction that ends with me on a plane.

Another five minutes go by.

"I really should go home," I say. "Flight's at ten."

He pulls out his phone to check the time. "Three hours to go. Are you all packed up already?"

"Yes."

"I'll go with you," he says.

My heart makes a leap. For a crazy second I think he means he'll go with me to Jamaica.

He sees the thought in my eyes. "I mean to your house."

"I know what you meant," I snap. I am resentful. I am ridiculous. "I don't think that's a good idea. My parents are there and I have too much to do. You'll just get in the way."

He raises himself up and holds out his hand for mine. "Here's what we're not going to do. We are not going to argue. We are not going to pretend that this isn't the worst thing on earth, because it is. We're not going to go our separate ways before we absolutely have to. I'm going with you to your parents' house. I'm going to meet them, and they're going to like me, and I'm not going to punch your dad. Instead, I'm going to see whether you look more like him or your mom. Your little brother will act like a little brother. Maybe I'll finally get to hear that Jamaican accent you've been hiding from me all day. I'm going to look at the place where you sleep and eat and live and wish I'd known just a little sooner that you were right here."

I start to interrupt, but he continues talking. "I'm going with you to your house, and then we're going to take a cab to

305

the airport, just the two of us. Then I'm going to watch you get on a plane and feel my heart get ripped out of my fucking chest, and then I'm going to wonder for the rest of my life what could've happened if this day hadn't gone just exactly the way it's gone."

He stops to take a breath. "Is that okay with you?" he asks.

daniel

SHE SAYS YES. I'm not ready to say goodbye. I'll never be ready to say it. I take her hand and we start walking toward the subway in silence.

She's wearing her backpack on one shoulder and I can see the DEUS EX MACHINA print again. Was it really just this morning that we met? This morning that I wanted to blow wherever the wind took me? What I wouldn't give for God to really be in the machine.

Headline: *Area Teen Defeats Immigration and Customs Enforcement Division of the Department of Homeland Security, Lives Happily Ever After with His One True Love Thanks to This One Weird Legal Loophole No One Considered Until the Last Minute and Now We Will Have a Chase Scene to Stop Her from Getting on the Plane.*

But that's not what's going to happen.

All day I've been thinking that we were meant to be. That all the people and places, all the coincidences were pushing us to be together forever. But maybe that's not true. What if this thing between us was *only* meant to last the day? What if we are each other's in-between people, a way station on the road to someplace else?

What if we are just a digression in someone else's history?

natasha

"DID YOU KNOW THAT JAMAICA has the sixth highest murder rate in the world?" I ask him.

We're on the Q train headed to Brooklyn. It's packed with evening commuters and we're standing, holding on to a pole. Daniel has one hand on my back. He hasn't stopped touching me since we left the office building. Maybe if he keeps holding on to me, I won't fly away.

"What are the other five?" he asks.

"Honduras, Venezuela, Belize, El Salvador, and Guatemala."

"Huh," he says.

"Did you also know that Jamaica is still a ceremonial member of the British Commonwealth?"

I don't wait for an answer. "I am a subject of the Queen." If I had room to do a curtsy, I would.

The train screeches to a stop. More people get on than off. "What else can I tell you? The population is two point nine million. Between one and ten percent of people identify as Rastafarians. Twenty percent of Jamaicans live below the poverty line."

He moves a little closer so I'm almost completely surrounded by him. "Tell me one good thing you remember," he says. "Not the facts."

I don't want to be optimistic. I don't want to adjust to this new future. "I left when I was eight. I don't remember that much."

He presses. "Not your family? Cousins? Friends?"

"I remember having them, but I don't *know* them. My mom forces us to get on the phone with them every year at Christmas. They make fun of my American accent."

"One good thing," he says. His eyes are deep brown now, almost black. "What did you miss the most after you first moved here?"

I don't have to think about the answer for very long. "The beach. The ocean here is weird. It's the wrong kind of blue. It's cold. It's too rough. Jamaica is in the Caribbean Sea. The water is this blue-green color and very calm. You can walk out for a long time and you'd still only be waist-deep."

"That sounds nice," he says. His voice trembles a little. I'm afraid to look up because then we'll both be crying on the train.

"Want to finish the questions from section three?" I ask.

He gets out his phone. "Number twenty-nine. Share with your partner an embarrassing moment in your life."

The train stops again, and this time more people get off than on. We have more room, but Daniel stays close to me as if we don't.

310

"Earlier today in the record store with Rob was pretty embarrassing," I say.

"Really? You didn't seem embarrassed, just pissed."

"I have a good poker face, unlike someone else I know," I say, and nudge him with my shoulder.

"But why embarrassed?"

"He cheated on me with her. Every time I see them together I feel like maybe I wasn't good enough."

"That guy was just a cheater. It's nothing to do with you." He grabs my hand and holds on to it. I kind of love his earnestness.

"I know. I called him earlier today to ask him why he did it." I've surprised him. "You did? What did he say?"

"He wanted us both."

"Jackass. If I ever see that guy again, I'll kick his ass."

"Got a thirst for blood now that you've been in your first fight, do you?"

"I'm a fighter, not a lover," he says, misquoting Michael Jackson. "Did your parents care that he was white?"

"They never met him." I couldn't imagine taking him to meet my dad. Watching them talk to each other would've been torturous. Also, I never wanted him to see how small our apartment was. In the end, I guess I really didn't want him to know me.

With Daniel, it's different somehow. I want him to see all of me.

The lights flicker off and come right back on. He squeezes my fingers. "My parents only want us to date Korean girls."

"You're not doing a good job listening to them," I tease.

"Well, it's not like I've dated a ton of girls. One Korean. Charlie, though? It's like he's allergic to nonwhite girls."

The train jostles us and I hold on to the pole with both hands. "You want to know the secret to your brother?"

He puts his hand on top of mine. "What's the secret?"

"He doesn't like himself very much."

"You think so?" he says, considering. He wants there to be a reason Charlie is the way he is.

"Trust me on this," I say.

We screech around a long corner. He steadies me with a hand against my back and leaves it there. "Why only Korean girls for your parents?" I ask.

"They think they'll understand Korean girls. Even the ones raised here."

"But those girls are both American and Korean."

"I'm not saying it makes sense," he says, smiling. "What about you? Do your parents care who you date?"

I shrug. "I've never asked. I guess probably they would prefer me to eventually marry a black guy."

"Why?"

"Same reason as yours. Somehow they'll understand him better. And he'll understand them better."

"But it's not like all black people are the same," he says.

"Neither are all Korean girls."

"Parents are pretty stupid." He's only half kidding.

"I think they think they're protecting us," I say.

"From what? Honestly, who can even give a shit about this stuff? We should know better by now."

"Maybe our kids will," I say. I regret the words even as they're flying out of my mouth.

The lights flicker off again and we come to a complete stop between stations. I focus on the yellow-orange glow of the safety lights in the tunnel.

"I didn't mean *our* kids," I say into the dark. "I meant the next generation of kids."

"I know what you meant," he says quietly.

Now that I've thought it and said it, I can't unthink it and unsay it. What would our kids look like? I feel the loss of something I don't even know I want.

We pull into the Canal Street station, the last underground stop before we go over the Manhattan Bridge. The doors close and we both turn to face the window. When we emerge from the tunnel the first thing I see is the Brooklyn Bridge. It's just past dusk and the lights are on along the suspension cables. My eyes follow their long arcs across the sky. The bridge is beautiful at night, but it's the city skyline that astonishes me every time I see it. It looks like a towering sculpture of lighted glass and metal, like a machined piece of art. From this distance, the city looks orderly and planned, as if all of it were created at one time for one purpose. When you're inside it, though, it feels like chaos.

I think back to when we were on the roof earlier. I imagined the city as it was being built. Now I project it out into an apocalyptic future. The lights dim and the glass falls away, leaving just the metal skeletons of buildings. Eventually those rust and crumble. The streets are uprooted, green with wild plants, overrun with wild animals. The city is beautiful and ruined.

We descend back into the tunnel. I know for sure that I will always compare every city skyline to New York's. Just as I will always compare every boy to Daniel.

daniel

"WHAT'S *YOUR* MOST EMBARRASSING MOMENT?"
she asks when the bridge disappears from view.

"You're kidding, right? You were there for it. With my dad
telling you to change your hair and my brother making small-
penis jokes?"

She laughs. "That was pretty bad."

"I will live a thousand lifetimes and it will still be the most
embarrassing thing that's ever happened to me."

"I dunno. Your dad and Charlie could figure out a way to
top it."

I groan and rub the back of my neck. "We should all be born
with a family Do-Over Card. At sixteen, you get a chance to
evaluate your situation and then you can choose to stay in your
current family or start over with a new one."

She tugs my hand down from my neck and holds on to it.
"Would you get to choose who the new family is?" she asks.

"Nope. You take your chances."

"So one day you just show up on some strangers' doorstep?"

"I haven't worked out all the details yet," I tell her. "Maybe
once you make your decision you get reborn into a new family?"

"Does your old family just think you died?"

"Yes."

"But that's so cruel," she says.

"Okay, okay. Maybe they just forget you ever existed. Anyway, I don't think many people would switch."

She shakes her head. "I disagree. I think a lot of people would. There are some bad families in this world."

"Would you?" I ask her.

She doesn't say anything for a while, and I listen to the rhythm of the train while she thinks it over. I've never wished for a train to slow down before.

"Could I give my card to someone who really needed it?" she asks. I know she's thinking about her dad.

I kiss her hair. "What about you? Would you stay in your family?" she asks me.

"Could I use it to boot Charlie out instead?"

She laughs. "Maybe these cards aren't such a great idea. Can you imagine if everyone had the power to mess with everyone else's lives? Chaos."

But of course, this *is* the problem. We already have that power over each other.

natasha

IT'S STRANGE BEING IN MY neighborhood with Daniel. I'm trying to see it through his eyes. After the relative wealth of Midtown Manhattan, my section of Brooklyn feels even poorer. Many of the same kinds of stores line the six-block drag that I use to walk home. There are Jamaican jerk restaurants, bulletproofed Chinese restaurants, bulletproofed liquor stores, discount clothing stores, and beauty salons. Every block has at least one combination deli/grocery store, windows almost entirely covered in beer and cigarette posters. Every block has at least one check-cashing shop. The stores are all crammed together, fighting for the same piece of real estate.

I'm grateful for the dark so Daniel can't see how run-down everything is. I'm immediately ashamed of myself for having the thought.

He takes my hand, and we walk along in silence for a few minutes. I can feel curious eyes on us. It occurs to me that this would've become normal for us.

"People are staring at us," I say.

"It's because you're so beautiful," he says back, without missing a beat.

"So you noticed?" I press.

"Of course I noticed."

I stop us in the lighted doorway of a Laundromat. The smell of detergent surrounds us. "You know why they're staring, right?"

"It's either because I'm not black or because you're not Korean." His face is shadowed, but I can hear the smile in his voice.

"I'm serious," I say, frustrated. "Doesn't it bother you?" I'm not sure why I'm pursuing this. Maybe I want proof that if we had the chance to continue, we would survive the weight of the stares.

He takes both my hands, so now we're standing face to face.

"Maybe it does bother me," he says, "but only peripherally. It's like a buzzing fly, you know? Annoying, but not actually life-threatening."

"But why do you think they're doing it?" I want an answer.

He pulls me in for a hug. "I can see that this is important to you, and I really want to give you a good reason. But the truth is, I don't care why. Maybe I'm naïve, but I do not give a single shit about anyone's opinion of us. I do not care if we're a novelty to them. I do not care about the politics of it. I don't care if your parents approve, and I really, truly don't care if mine do. What I care about is you, and I'm sure that love is enough to overcome all the bullshit. And it *is* bullshit. All the hand-wringing. All the talk about cultures clashing or preserving cultures and what will happen to the kids. All of it is one hundred percent pure, unadulterated bullshit, and I just refuse to care."

I smile into his chest. My ponytail poet boy. I never before thought that not caring could be a revolutionary act.

We turn off the main drag onto a more residential street. I'm still trying to see the neighborhood as Daniel does. We pass by rows of adjoined clapboard houses. They're small and aging but colorful and well-loved. The porches seem more overpopulated with knickknacks and hanging plants than I remember.

There was a time when my mom desperately wanted one of these houses. Earlier this year, before this mess began, she even took Peter and me to an open house. It had three bedrooms and a spacious kitchen. It had a basement she thought she could sublet for extra income. Because he adores our mother and knew we could never afford it, Peter pretended not to like it. He nitpicked.

"The backyard is too small and all the plants are dead," he'd said. He stayed close to her side, and when we left she was not any sadder than when we went in.

We walk by another block of similar houses before the neighborhood changes again and we're surrounded by mostly brick apartment buildings. These are not condos but rentals.

I issue a warning to Daniel. "It's a mess from all the packing."

"Okay," he says, nodding.

"And it's small." I don't mention that there's only one bedroom. He'll see soon enough. Besides, it's only my home for a few hours more.

The little girls from apartment 2C are sitting on the front steps when we arrive. Daniel's presence makes them shy. They duck their heads and don't chatter at me like they normally do. I stop by the row of metal mailboxes that hang on the wall. We have no mail, just a Chinese take-out menu wedged into the door. It's from my dad's favorite place, the same one he ordered from when he gave us the tickets for his play.

Someone's always cooking something, and the lobby smells delicious: butter and onion and curry and other spices. My apartment's on the third floor, so I take us to the stairs. As usual, the light for the first- and second-floor stairwell is broken. We end up walking silently in the dark until we get to the third floor.

"This is it," I say, when we're finally standing in front of 3A. In some ways it's much too early to introduce Daniel to my house and family. If we had more time, then he'd already know all my little anecdotes. He'd know about the curtain in the living room that separates Peter's "room" from mine. He'd know that my star map is my most prized possession. He'd know that if my mom offers him something to eat, he should just take it and eat the whole thing no matter how full he is.

I don't know how to relay all that history. Instead, I tell him again: "It's messy in there."

It's a weird kind of dissonance, seeing him stand here in front of my door. He fits and doesn't fit at the same time. I've always known him, and we've only just met.

Our history is too compressed. We're trying to fit a lifetime into a day.

"Should I take my jacket off?" he asks. "I feel like an idiot in this suit."

"You don't have to be nervous," I say.

"I'm going to meet your parents. Now's as good a time to be nervous as any." He unbuttons the jacket but doesn't take it off.

I touch the bruise on his lip. "The good thing is, you can screw up all you want. You'll probably never see them again."

He gives a small, sad smile. I'm just trying to make the best of our situation, and he knows it.

I take the key from my backpack and open the door.

All the lights are on and Peter's playing dance hall reggae much too loud. I can feel the beat in my chest. Three packed suitcases lie just inside the door. Another two lie open off to the side.

I spot my mom right away. "Turn that music off," she says to Peter when she sees me. He does, and the sudden silence is acute.

She turns to me. "Lawd, Tasha. I been calling and calling you for—"

It takes her a second to notice Daniel. When she does, she stops talking and looks back and forth between us for a long time.

"Who this?" she asks.

daniel

NATASHA INTRODUCES me to her mom.

"He's a friend of mine," she says. I'm fairly certain I heard a hesitation before *friend*. Her mom heard it too, and now she's studying me like I'm an alien bug.

"Sorry to meet you under these circumstances, Mrs. Kingsley." I hold out my hand for a shake.

She gives Natasha a look (the *how could you do this to me?* variety), but then wipes her palm down the side of her dress and gives me a brief shake and a briefer smile.

Natasha moves us from the little hallway where we're clustered into the living room. At least, I think it's a living room. A bright blue cloth is crumpled on the floor, and a length of string bisects the room. Then I notice there's two of everything—sofa bed, chest of drawers, desk. This is their bedroom. She shares it with Peter. When Natasha said their apartment was small, I didn't realize she meant they were poor.

There's still so much I don't know about her.

Her brother walks over to me, hand outstretched and smiling. He has dreadlocks and one of the friendliest faces I've ever seen.

"Tasha's never brought a guy here before," he says. His infectious smile gets even bigger.

I grin back at him and shake his hand. Both Natasha and her mom watch us openly.

"Tasha, I need to talk to you," her mom says.

Natasha doesn't take her eyes off Peter and me. I wonder if she's imagining a future where we become friends. I know I am.

She turns to face her mom. "Is it about Daniel?" she asks.

Her mom's now-pursed lips could not get any pursier (yes, pursier).

"Tasha—" Even I can hear the *Mom is about to get pissed off* warning in her tone, but Natasha just ignores it.

"Because if it *is* about Daniel, we can just do it right here. He's my boyfriend." She sneaks a quick questioning glance at me, and I nod.

Her dad walks through the doorway across from us at just that second.

Due to Anomaly in the Space-Time Continuum, Area Dads Have Perfect Timing All Day

"Boyfriend?" he says. "Since when you have boyfriend?"

I turn and study him. Now I've got the answer to my question of who Natasha looks like. She's basically her dad, except in beautiful girl form.

And without the scowl. I've never seen a deeper scowl than the scowl that exists on his face right now.

His Jamaican accent is thick, and I process the words a little after he says them. "That what you been doing all day instead of helping you family pack up?" he demands, moving farther into the room.

Aside from the little Natasha has told me, I don't really know the history of their relationship, but I can see it on her face now. Anger is there, and hurt, and disbelief. Still, the peace-keeper in me doesn't want to see them fight. I touch my hand to the small of her back.

"I'm okay," she says to me quietly. I can tell she's steeling herself for something.

She squares herself to him. "No. What I was doing all day was trying to fix your mistakes. I was trying to prevent our family from being kicked out of the country."

"It don't look nothing like that to me," he retorts. He turns to me, scowl deepening. "You know the situation?"

I'm too surprised that he's talking to me to answer, so I just nod.

"Then you know that now not no time for strangers to be here," he says.

Natasha's spine stiffens under my hand. "He's not a stranger," she says. "He's my guest."

"And this is my house." He straightens himself as he says it.

"Your house?" Her voice is loud and incredulous now. Whatever restraint she had before is slipping away quickly. She walks to the center of the living room, holds her arms open wide and turns a circle.

"This apartment that we've lived in for nine years, because you think your ship is going to come sailing in any day now, is *your* house?"

"Baby. Not no point in rehashing all this now," her mom says from her place in the doorway.

Natasha opens her mouth to say something but closes it again. I can see her deflate. "Okay, Mom," she says, letting go of whatever she was going to say. I wonder how many times she's done that for her mother.

I think that's going to be the end of it, but I'm wrong.

"No, man," her dad says. "No, man. Me want hear what she have to say to me." He widens his stance and folds his arms across his chest.

Natasha does the same thing and they square off, mirror images of each other.

natasha

I WOULD'VE LET IT GO for my mom. I always do. Just last night she said that the four of us had to be a united front.

"It going be hard at first," she'd said. We are going to have to live with her mother until we have enough money to rent our own place. "I never think me life would come to this," she said before she went to bed.

I would've let it go if I hadn't met Daniel. If he hadn't increased by a very significant one the number of things I'd be losing today. I would've let it go if my father weren't using his thick and forced Jamaican accent again. It's just another act. To hear him you would think he'd never left Jamaica, that the past nine years never happened. He really does think our lives are make-believe. I'm sick of him pretending.

"I heard what you said to Mom after the play. You said we were your greatest regret."

He sags and the scowl leaves his face. I can't name the emotion that replaces it, but it seems genuine. Finally. Something real from him.

He starts to say something but I have more to say. "I'm sorry that life didn't give you all the things you wanted." As I'm saying it, I realize that I do mean it. I know what disappointment is now. I can understand how it could last a lifetime.

"Me didn't mean it, Tasha. It was just talk. All of it was just—"

I hold my hand up to stop his apology. That's not what I want from him. "I want you to know that you were really amazing in the play. Just incredible. Transcendent."

He has tears in his eyes now. I'm not sure if it's because I complimented him or if it's regret or something else.

"Maybe you were right," I continue. "You weren't meant to have us. Maybe you really were cheated."

He's shaking his head, denying my words. "Was just talk, Tasha, man. Me really didn't mean nothing by it."

But of course he did. He meant it and he didn't. Both. At the same time.

"It doesn't matter if you meant it or not. This is the life you're living. It's not temporary and it's not pretend and there's no do-over." I sound like Daniel.

The worst part of overhearing that conversation between him and my mom was that it spoiled all the good memories I had of him. Did he regret my existence when we were watching cricket matches together? What about when he was holding me tight at the airport when we were all finally reunited? What about the day I was born?

Tears are streaming down his face now. Watching him cry hurts more than I ever thought it could. Still, there's one more thing I have to say.

"You don't get to regret us."

He makes a sound, and now I know what a lifetime of pain sounds like.

People make mistakes all the time. Small ones, like you get in the wrong checkout line. The one with the lady with a hundred coupons and a checkbook.

Sometimes you make medium-sized ones. You go to medical school instead of pursuing your passion.

Sometimes you make big ones.

You give up.

I sit down on my sofa bed. I'm more tired than I realize, and not as angry as I thought. "When we get to Jamaica, you have to at least try. Go on auditions. And be better to Mom. She's done everything, and she's tired, and you owe it to us. You don't get to live in your head anymore."

My mom's crying now. Peter walks into her arms for a hug. My father goes to them both, and my mom accepts him. As one, they turn to look at me and gesture for me to join them. I turn to Daniel first. He hugs me so tightly, it's like we're saying goodbye already.

daniel + natasha

THE DRIVER LOADS NATASHA'S SUITCASE into the trunk. Peter and her parents have already gone ahead to the airport via a separate cab.

Inside, Natasha lays her head on Daniel's shoulder. Her hair tickles his nose. It's a feeling he wishes he'd have more time to get used to.

"Do you think we would've worked out in the end?" she asks him.

"Yes." He says it without hesitation. "Do you?"

"Yes."

"You finally came around." A smile is in his voice.

"How hard would it have been for your parents?" she asks.

"It would take them a long time. Longer for my dad. I don't think they'd have come to our wedding." A picture of that future day floats up in Natasha's mind. She sees an ocean. Daniel handsome in his tuxedo. Her hand on his face wiping away the sadness at his parents' absence. The joy on his face when she finally says I do.

"How many kids do you want?" she asks, after the pain of that vision recedes.

"Two. What about you?"

She lifts her head from his shoulder, hesitant, but then confesses: "I'm not sure if I want any at all. Would you've been okay with that?"

He didn't expect that answer, and it takes him a moment to accept it. "I think so. I don't know. Maybe you'd change your mind. Maybe I would."

"I have something to tell you," she says, laying her head back down.

"What?"

"You shouldn't be a doctor."

He turns his head, smiles into her hair. "What about doing the practical thing?"

"Practicality is overrated," she says.

"Are you still going to be a data scientist?"

"I don't know. Maybe not. It'd be nice to be passionate about something."

"What a difference a day makes," he says.

Neither of them speaks, because what is there to say? It's been a long day.

Natasha breaks their glum silence. "So, how many more questions do we have left?"

He takes out his phone. "Two more from section three. And we still have to stare into each other's eyes for four minutes."

"We could do that or make out right here."

From the front seat their driver, Miguel, interrupts. "You guys know I can hear you, right?" He looks at them in the rear-view mirror. "I can see you too." Then he laughs a big meaty laugh. "Some people get in the cab and like to pretend I'm deaf and blind, but I ain't. Just so you know."

He laughs his meaty laugh again, and Natasha and Daniel can't help but join him.

But their joined laughter fades as the reality of the moment reasserts itself. Daniel takes Natasha's face in his hands and they kiss soft kisses. The chemistry is still there. They're both too warm, both unsure what to do with hands that seem meant only for touching each other.

Miguel doesn't say a word. He's had his heart broken before. He knows what damage looks like.

Daniel speaks first. "Question thirty-four. What would you save from a fire?"

Natasha considers. It does feel to her like her entire world is being razed. And the one thing that she wants to save, she can't.

To Daniel she says: "I don't have anything yet, but I'll figure it out."

"Good enough," he says. "Mine's easy. My notebook."

He touches his jacket pocket to reassure himself it's still there.

"Last question," he says. "Of all the people in your family, whose death would you find the most disturbing, and why?"

"My dad."

Daniel notes that it's the first time Natasha's called him *dad* instead of *father*.

"Why?" he asks.

"Because he's not done yet. What about you?"

"Yours," he says.

"I'm not your family, though."

"Yes you are," he says, thinking about what Natasha said earlier about multiverses. In some other universe they are married, maybe with two children, or maybe with none. "You don't have to say it back. I just want you to know."

There are things to say to him, and Natasha doesn't know where, doesn't know how to begin. Maybe that's why Daniel wants to be a poet, so he can find the right words.

"I love you, Daniel," she says at last.

He grins at her. "I guess the questionnaire worked."

She smiles. "Yay, science."

A moment passes.

"I know," Daniel says, finally. "I already know."

four minutes

A History of Love

DANIEL SETS HIS PHONE TIMER for four minutes and takes both Natasha's hands in his. Are they supposed to hold hands during this part of the experiment? He's not sure. According to the study, this is the final step for falling in love. What happens if you're already in love?

At first they both feel pretty silly. Natasha wants to say aloud that this is too goofy. Helpless, almost embarrassed smiles overtake their faces. Natasha looks away, but Daniel squeezes her hands. *Stay with me* is what he means.

By the second minute, they're less self-conscious. Their smiles drift away and they catalog each other's face.

Natasha thinks of her AP Biology class and what she knows of eyes and how they work. An optical image of his face is being sent to her retina. Her retina is converting those images to electronic signals. Her optic nerve is transmitting those signals to her visual cortex. She knows now that she'll never forget this image of his face. She'll know exactly when clear brown eyes became her favorite kind.

For his part, Daniel is trying to find the right words to

333

describe her eyes. They're light and dark at the same time. Like someone draped a heavy black cloth over a bright star.

By the third minute, Natasha's reliving the day and all the moments that led them here. She sees the USCIS building, that strange security guard caressing her phone case, Lester Barnes's kindness, Rob and Kelly shoplifting, meeting Daniel, Daniel saving her life, meeting Daniel's dad and brother, *norebang,* kissing, the museum, the rooftop, more kissing, Daniel's face when he told her she couldn't stay, her dad's crying face filled with regret, this moment right now in the cab.

Daniel is thinking not about past events, but future ones. Is there something else that could lead them back to each other?

During the final minute, hurt settles into their bones. It colonizes their bodies, spreads to their tissue and muscles and blood and cells.

The phone timer buzzes. They whisper promises they suspect they won't be able to keep—phone calls, emails, text messages, and even international flights, expenses be damned.

"This day can't be all there is," Daniel says once, and then twice.

Natasha doesn't say what she suspects. That *meant to be* doesn't have to mean *forever.*

They kiss, and kiss again. When they do finally pull apart, it's with a new knowledge. They have a sense that the length of a day is mutable, and you can never see the end from the beginning. They have a sense that love changes all things all the time.

That's what love is for.

natasha

MY MOM HOLDS MY HAND as I stare out the window. *Everything will be all right, Tasha,* she says. We both know that's more a hope than a guarantee, but I'll take it nevertheless.

The plane ascends, and the world I've known fades. The city lights recede to pinpricks, until they look like earthbound stars. One of those stars is Daniel. I remind myself that stars are more than just poetic.

If you need to, you can navigate your way by them.

daniel

MY PHONE RINGS. It's my parents calling for the mil-
lionth time. They'll be pissed when I get home, and that's fine.

This time next year, I'll be someplace else. I don't know
where, but not here. I'm not sure college is for me. At least not
Yale. At least not yet.

Am I making a mistake? Maybe. But it's mine to make.

I look up to the sky and imagine I can see Natasha's plane
there.

New York City has too much light pollution. It blinds us to
the stars, the satellites, the asteroids. Sometimes when we look
up, we don't see anything at all.

But here is a true thing: Almost everything in the night sky
gives off light. Even if we can't see it, the light is still there.

time and distance

A Measured History

NATASHA AND DANIEL try to stay in touch, and for a time they do. There are emails and phone calls and text messages.

But time and distance are love's natural enemies.

And the days get full.

Natasha enrolls in school in Kingston. Her class is called Sixth Form instead of senior year. In order to attend university, she has to study for the Caribbean Advanced Proficiency Exams and her A-level exams. Money is scarce, so she waitresses to help her family. She fakes a Jamaican accent until it becomes real. She finds a family of friends. She learns to like and then to love the country of her birth.

It's not that Natasha wants to let Daniel go; it's that she has to. It isn't possible for her to live in two worlds simultaneously, heart in one place, body in another. She lets go of Daniel to avoid being ripped apart.

For his part, Daniel finishes high school but declines Yale. He moves out of his parents' house, works two jobs, and attends Hunter College part-time. He majors in English and writes small, sad poems. And even the ones that are not about her are still about her.

It's not that Daniel wants to let Natasha go. He holds on for as long as he can. But he hears the strain in her voice across the distance. In her new accent, he hears the cadence of her slipping away from him.

More years pass. Natasha and Daniel enter the adult world of practicalities and responsibilities.

Natasha's mother gets sick five years after their move. She dies before the sixth. A few months after the funeral, Natasha thinks about calling Daniel, but it has been far too long. She doesn't trust her memory of him.

Peter, her brother, thrives in Jamaica. He makes friends and finally finds a place where he fits. Sometime in the future, long after his mom has died, he'll fall in love with a Jamaican woman and marry her. They'll have one daughter and he'll name her Patricia Marley Kingsley.

Samuel Kingsley moves from Kingston to Montego Bay. He acts in a local community theater. After Patricia's death, he finally understands that he chose correctly that day in the store.

Daniel's mom and dad sell the store to an African American couple. They buy an apartment in South Korea and spend half the year there and the other half in New York City. Eventually they stop expecting their sons to be solely Korean. After all, they were born in America.

Charlie pulls his grades up and graduates summa cum laude from Harvard. After graduation, he barely ever speaks to any member of his family again. Daniel fills the void in his parents' hearts in the ways that he's able. He doesn't miss Charlie very much at all.

Still more years pass, and Natasha no longer knows what that day in New York City means. She comes to believe that she imagined the magic of being with Daniel. When she thinks of that day, she's certain she has romanticized it in the way of first loves.

One good thing did come from her time with Daniel. She looks for a passion and finds it in the study of physics. Some nights, in the soft, helpless moments before sleep comes, she recalls their conversation on the roof about love and dark matter. He said that love and dark matter were the same—the only thing that kept the universe from flying apart. Her heart speeds up every time she thinks of it. Then she smiles in the darkness and puts the memory up on a shelf in the place for old, sentimental, impossible things.

And even Daniel no longer knows what that day means, that day that once meant everything. He remembers all the little coincidences it took to get them to meet and fall in love. The religious conductor. Natasha communing with her music. The DEUS EX MACHINA jacket. The shoplifting ex-boyfriend. The errant BMW driver. The security guard smoking on the roof.

Of course, if Natasha could hear his memories, she would point out the fact that they didn't end up together, and that the same things that went right also went wrong.

He remembers another moment: They'd just found each other again after their fight. She'd talked about the number of events that had to go exactly right to form their universe. She'd said falling in love couldn't compete.

He's always thought she was wrong about that.

Because everything looks like chaos up close. Daniel thinks it's a matter of scale. If you pull back far enough and wait for long enough, then order emerges.

Maybe their universe is just taking longer to form.

epilogue

Irene: An Alternate History

IT'S BEEN TEN YEARS, but Irene's never forgotten the moment—or the girl—that saved her life. She was working as a security guard at the USCIS building in New York City. One of the case officers—Lester Barnes—stopped by her station. He told her that a girl left a message on his voice mail for her. The girl had said thank you. Irene never knew what she was being thanked for, but the thank-you came just in time. Because at the end of the day, Irene had planned to commit suicide.

She'd written her suicide note at lunch. She'd mentally charted her route to the roof of her apartment building.

But for that thank-you.

The fact that someone *saw* her was the beginning.

That night she listened to the Nirvana album again. In Kurt Cobain's voice, Irene heard a perfect and beautiful misery, a voice stretched so thin with loneliness and wanting that it should break. But his voice didn't break, and there was a kind of joy in it too.

She thought about that girl making the effort to call and leave a message just for her. It shifted something inside Irene.

Not enough to heal her, but enough to make her call a suicide prevention hotline. The hotline led to therapy. Therapy led to medication that saves her life every day.

Two years after that night, Irene quit her job at USCIS. She remembered that as a child she dreamt of being a flight attendant. Now her life is simple and happy, and she lives it on planes. And because she knows airplanes can be lonely places and because she knows how desperate loneliness can be, she pays extra attention to her passengers. She takes care of them with an earnestness that no other attendant does. She comforts those flying home alone for funerals, sadness seeping from every pore. She holds hands with the acrophobic and the agoraphobic. Irene thinks of herself as a guardian angel with metallic wings.

And so it is now that she's making her final checks before takeoff, looking for passengers who are going to need a little extra help. The young man in 7A is writing in a little black notebook. He's Asian, with short black hair and kind but serious eyes. He chews the top of his pen, thinks, writes, and then chews some more. Irene admires his unselfconsciousness. He acts like he's alone in the world.

Her eyes travel on and flit across the young black woman in 8C. She's wearing earbuds and has a big, curly Afro that's been dyed pink at the ends. Irene freezes. She knows that face. The warmth of the woman's skin. The long eyelashes. The full pink lips. The intensity. Surely this can't be the same girl. The one who saved her life? The one she's wanted to thank for ten years now?

The captain announces takeoff, and Irene's forced to sit. From her jumpseat, she stares at the woman until there's no doubt in her mind.

As soon as the plane reaches cruising altitude, she goes over to the woman and kneels in the aisle next to her.

"Miss," she says, and can't prevent her voice from shaking.

The woman takes out her earbuds and gives her a hesitant smile.

"This is going to sound so strange," Irene begins. She tells the woman about that day in New York—the gray bin, the Nirvana phone case, how she'd seen her every day.

The woman watches her warily, not saying anything. Something like pain flits across her face. There's a history there.

Nevertheless, Irene carries on. "You saved my life."

"But I don't understand," the woman says. She has an accent, Caribbean and something else.

Irene takes the woman's hand. The woman tenses but lets her take it. Curious eyes watch them from all around.

"You left a message for me saying thank you. I don't even know what you were thanking me for."

The young man in 7A peers between the seats. Irene catches his eye and frowns. He pulls away. She turns her attention back to the woman.

"Do you remember me?" Irene asks. Suddenly it's very important to her that this girl, now woman, remember her. The question leaves her mouth and she becomes the old Irene— alone and afraid. Affected but not affecting.

Time hiccups and Irene feels herself torn between two

universes. She imagines that the plane disintegrates, first the floor and then the seats and then the metallic shell. She and the passengers are suspended in midair with nothing to hold them except possibility. Next, the passengers themselves shimmer and dematerialize. One by one they flicker and vanish, phantoms of a different history.

All that remains now is Irene and this woman.

"I remember you," the woman says. "My name is Natasha, and I remember you."

The young man in 7A peers over the top of the seat.

"Natasha," he says. His face is wide open and his world is full of love.

Natasha looks up.

Time stumbles back into place. The plane and the seats reform. The passengers solidify into flesh. And blood. And bone. And heart.

"Daniel," she says. And again, "Daniel."

THE END

acknowledgments

Immigrating to a new country is an act of hope, bravery, and, sometimes, desperation. I'd like to say a big thank-you to all the people who've made long journeys to distant shores for whatever reason. May you find what you're looking for. Always know that the country of your destination is better for having you in it.

Next, I need to thank my own immigrant parents. They are, both of them, dreamers. Everything I've achieved is because of them.

To the teams at Alloy Entertainment and Random House Children's Books: Thank you for believing in this impossible book. Thank you for taking chances with me. Wendy Loggia, Joelle Hobeika, Sara Shandler, Josh Bank, and Jillian Vandall, you are my dream team. I am the luckiest writer in the world to have you in my corner. Enormous thanks also to John Adamo, Elaine Damasco, Felicia Frazier, Romy Golan, Beverly Horowitz, Alison Impey, Kim Lauber, Barbara Marcus, Les Morgenstein, Tamar Schwartz, Tim Terhune, Krista Vitola, and Adrienne Waintraub. Nothing happens without you.

One of the best things about being a writer is getting to meet your readers. To every single person who has read my books, come to a signing, sent me an email, or reached out via social media; to every librarian, teacher, bookstore owner/worker, and blogger: THANK YOU, THANK YOU, THANK YOU. You are the reason I get to have my dream job. Thank you for all your love and support.

Over the last couple of years I've met some wonderful writers who've also become wonderful friends: David Arnold, Anna Carey, Charlotte Huang, Caroline Kepnes, Kerry Kletter, Adam Silvera, and Sabaa Tahir, thank you for your generous support and friendship. I wouldn't have survived this crazy journey without you guys. Thanks also to the LA writer crew and the Fearless Fifteeners debut group. What a crazy year 2015 was! It's been great getting to know you all. Here's to many more years of writing books.

Special and very heartfelt thanks to Yoon Ho Bai, Jung Kim, Ellen Oh, and David Yoon for answering my endless questions about Korean and Korean American culture. Your thoughts and guidance were invaluable.

And then there are my super sweeties, David and Penny. You guys are my small universe. You're my reason for everything. I love you most of all.

about the author

NICOLA YOON is the number one *New York Times* best-selling author of *Everything, Everything*. She grew up in Jamaica and Brooklyn and lives in Los Angeles with her family. She's also a hopeless romantic who firmly believes that you can fall in love in an instant and that it can last forever.

FOLLOW NICOLAYOON ON **t**
@NICOLAYOON ON 🐦
NICOLAYOON.COM

Read the book that everyone, everyone fell in love with.

THE WHITE ROOM

I'VE READ MANY more books than you. It doesn't matter how many you've read. I've read more. Believe me. I've had the time.

In my white room, against my white walls, on my glistening white bookshelves, book spines provide the only color. The books are all brand-new hardcovers—no germy secondhand softcovers for me. They come to me from Outside, decontaminated and vacuum-sealed in plastic wrap. I would like to see the machine that does this. I imagine each book traveling on a white conveyor belt toward rectangular white stations where robotic white arms dust, scrape, spray, and otherwise sterilize it until it's finally deemed clean enough to come to me. When a new book arrives, my first task is to remove the wrapping, a process that involves scissors and more than one broken nail. My second task is to write my name on the inside front cover.

PROPERTY OF: *Madeline Whittier*

I don't know why I do this. There's no one else here except my mother, who never reads, and my nurse, Carla, who has no time to read because she spends all her time watching me breathe. I rarely have visitors, and so there's no one to lend my books to. There's no one who needs reminding that the forgotten book on his or her shelf belongs to me.

REWARD IF FOUND (Check all that apply):

This is the section that takes me the longest time, and I vary it with each book. Sometimes the rewards are fanciful:
- Picnic with me (Madeline) in a pollen-filled field of poppies, lilies, and endless man-in-the-moon marigolds under a clear blue summer sky.
- Drink tea with me (Madeline) in a lighthouse in the middle of the Atlantic Ocean in the middle of a hurricane.
- Snorkel with me (Madeline) off Molokini to spot the Hawaiian state fish— the humuhumunukunukuapuaa.

Sometimes the rewards are not so fanciful:
- A visit with me (Madeline) to a used bookstore.
- A walk outside with me (Madeline), just down the block and back.
- A short conversation with me (Madeline), discussing anything you want, on my white couch, in my white bedroom.

Sometimes the reward is just:
- Me (Madeline).

SCID ROW

MY DISEASE IS as rare as it is famous. It's a form of Severe Combined Immunodeficiency, but you know it as "bubble baby disease."

Basically, I'm allergic to the world. Anything can trigger a bout of sickness. It could be the chemicals in the cleaner used to wipe the table that I just touched. It could be someone's perfume. It could be the exotic spice in the food I just ate. It could be one, or all, or none of these things, or something else entirely. No one knows the triggers, but everyone knows the consequences. According to my mom I almost died as an infant. And so I stay on SCID row. I don't leave my house, have not left my house in seventeen years.

DAILY
HEALTH
LOG

Madeline Whittier

PATIENT NAME

May 2

DATE

Dr. Pauline Whittier

CARETAKER

0002921

ROOM TEMPERATURE

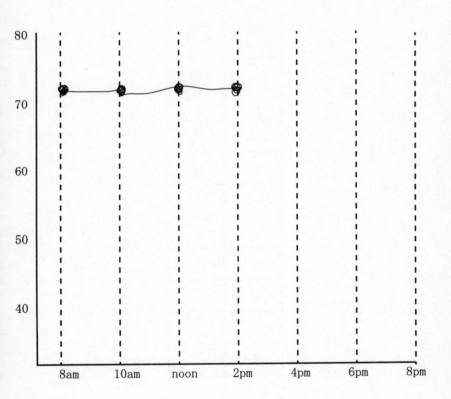

0002921

AIR FILTER STATUS

8am	OK
9am	OK
10am	OK
11am	OK
12pm	OK
1pm	OK
2pm	OK
3pm	
4pm	
5pm	
6pm	
7pm	
8pm	

0002921

BRTHDAE UISH

"MOVIE NIGHT OR Honor Pictionary or Book Club?" my mom asks while inflating a blood pressure cuff around my arm. She doesn't mention her favorite of all our post-dinner activities—Phonetic Scrabble. I look up to see that her eyes are already laughing at me.

"Phonetic," I say.

She stops inflating the cuff. Ordinarily Carla, my full-time nurse, would be taking my blood pressure and filling out my daily health log, but my mom's given her the day off. It's my birthday and we always spend the day together, just the two of us.

She puts on her stethoscope so that she can listen to my heartbeat. Her smile fades and is replaced by her more serious doctor's face. This is the face her patients most often see—slightly distant, professional, and concerned. I wonder if they find it comforting.

Impulsively I give her a quick kiss on the forehead to remind her that it's just me, her favorite patient, her daughter.

She opens her eyes, smiles, and caresses my cheek. I guess if you're going to be born with an illness that requires constant care, then it's good to have your mom as your doctor.

A few seconds later she gives me her best I'm-the-doctor-and-I'm-afraid-I-have-some-bad-news-for-you face. "It's your big day. Why don't we play something you have an actual chance of winning? Honor Pictionary?"

Since regular Pictionary can't really be played with two people, we invented Honor Pictionary. One person draws and the other person is on her *honor* to make her best guess. If you guess correctly, the other person scores.

I narrow my eyes at her. "We're playing Phonetic, and I'm winning this time," I say confidently, though I have no chance of winning. In all our years of playing Phonetic Scrabble, or Fonetik Skrabbl, I've never beaten her at it. The last time we played I came close. But then she devastated me on the final word, playing *JEENZ* on a triple word score.

"OK." She shakes her head with mock pity. "Anything you want." She closes her laughing eyes to listen to the stethoscope.

We spend the rest of the morning baking my traditional birthday cake of vanilla sponge with vanilla cream frosting. After it's cooled, I apply an unreasonably thin layer of frosting, just enough to cover the cake. We are, both of us, cake people, not frosting people. For decoration, I draw eighteen frosted daisies with white petals and a white center across the top. On the sides I fashion draped white curtains.

"Perfect." My mom peers over my shoulders as I finish up. "Just like you."

I turn to face her. She's smiling a wide, proud smile at me, but her eyes are bright with tears.

"You. Are. Tragic," I say, and squirt a dollop of frosting on her nose, which only makes her laugh and cry some more. Really, she's not usually this emotional, but something about my birthday always makes her both weepy and joyful at the same time. And if she's weepy and joyful, then I'm weepy and joyful, too.

"I know," she says, throwing her hands helplessly up in the air. "I'm totally pathetic." She pulls me into a hug and squeezes. Frosting gets into my hair.

My birthday is the one day of the year that we're both most acutely aware of my illness. It's the acknowledging of the passage of time that does it. Another whole year of being sick, no hope for a cure on the horizon. Another year of missing all the normal teenagery things—learner's permit, first kiss, prom, first heartbreak, first fender bender. Another year of my mom doing nothing but working and taking care of me. Every other day these omissions are easy—easier, at least—to ignore.

This year is a little harder than the previous. Maybe it's because I'm eighteen now. Technically, I'm an adult. I should be leaving home, going off to college. My mom should be dreading empty-nest syndrome. But because of SCID, I'm not going anywhere.

Later, after dinner, she gives me a beautiful set of watercolor pencils that had been on my wish list for months. We go into the living room and sit cross-legged in front of the coffee table. This is also part of our birthday ritual: She lights a single candle in the center of the cake. I close my eyes and make a wish. I blow the candle out.

"What did you wish for?" she asks as soon as I open my eyes.

Really there's only one thing to wish for—a magical cure that will allow me to run free outside like a wild animal. But I never make that wish because it's impossible. It's like wishing that mermaids and dragons and unicorns were real. Instead I wish for something more likely than a cure. Something less likely to make us both sad.

"World peace," I say.

Three slices of cake later, we begin a game of Fonetik. I do not win. I don't even come close.

She uses all seven letters and puts down POKALIP next to an *S. POKALIPS*.

"What's that?" I ask.

"Apocalypse," she says, eyes dancing.

"No, Mom. No way. I can't give that to you."

"Yes," is all she says.

"Mom, you need an extra *A*. No way."

"Pokalips," she says for effect, gesturing at the letters. "It totally works."

I shake my head.

"P O K A L I P S," she insists, slowly dragging out the word.

"Oh my God, you're relentless," I say, throwing my hands up. "OK, OK, I'll allow it."

"Yesssss." She pumps her fist and laughs at me and marks

down her now-insurmountable score. "You've never really understood this game," she says. "It's a game of persuasion."

I slice myself another piece of cake. "That was not persuasion," I say. "That was cheating."

"Same same," she says, and we both laugh.

"You can beat me at Honor Pictionary tomorrow," she says.

After I lose, we go to the couch and watch our favorite movie, *Young Frankenstein*. Watching it is also part of our birthday ritual. I put my head in her lap, and she strokes my hair, and we laugh at the same jokes in the same way that we've been laughing at them for years. All in all, not a bad way to spend your eighteenth birthday.

STAYS THE SAME

I'M READING ON my white couch when Carla comes in the next morning.

"Feliz cumpleaños," she sings out.

I lower my book. *"Gracias."*

"How was the birthday?" She begins unpacking her medical bag.

"We had fun."

"Vanilla cake and vanilla frosting?" she asks.

"Of course."

"Young Frankenstein?"

"Yes."

"And you lost at that game?" she asks.

"We're pretty predictable, huh?"

"Don't mind me," she says, laughing. "I'm just jealous of how sweet you and your mama are."

She picks up my health log from yesterday, quickly reviews my mom's measurements and adds a new sheet to the clipboard. "These days Rosa can't even be bothered to give me the time of day."

Rosa is Carla's seventeen-year-old daughter. According to Carla they were really close until hormones and boys took over. I can't imagine that happening to my mom and me.

Carla sits next to me on the couch, and I hold out my hand for the blood pressure cuff. Her eyes drop to my book.

"*Flowers for Algernon* again?" she asks. "Doesn't that book always make you cry?"

"One day it won't," I say. "I want to be sure to be reading it on that day."

She rolls her eyes at me and takes my hand.

It *is* kind of a flip answer, but then I wonder if it's true.

Maybe I'm holding out hope that one day, someday, things will change.

LIFE IS SHORT™
SPOILER REVIEWS BY MADELINE

FLOWERS FOR ALGERNON BY DANIEL KEYES
Spoiler alert: Algernon is a mouse. The mouse dies.

ALIEN INVASION, PART 2

I'M UP TO the part where Charlie realizes that the mouse's fate may be his own when I hear a loud rumbling noise outside. Immediately my mind goes to outer space. I picture a giant mother ship hovering in the skies above us.

The house trembles and my books vibrate on the shelves. A steady beeping joins the rumbling and I know what it is. A truck. Probably just lost, I tell myself, to stave off disappointment. Probably just made a wrong turn on their way to someplace else.

But then the engine cuts off. Doors open and close. A moment passes, and then another, and then a woman's voice sings out, "Welcome to our new home, everybody!"

Carla stares at me hard for a few seconds. I know what she's thinking.

It's happening again.

MADELINE'S DIARY

August 5

The family in the house next door moved away. ~~The~~ The boy cried. He hid in the garden and ate dirt unitill his mom found him but she didn't yell at him for eating it like she usaully does. Outside is so quiet now. Last night I had a dream that they-

didn't really move away.
They got kidnapped
by aliens. The aliens
didn't take me because
I'm sick and they only
wanted healthy people.
They took mommy and
carla away and the
family next door and I
was all alome.

I woke up crying
and mommy came and
stayed in bed with
me. I didnt tell her
What the dream was
about because it would
make her sad, but
I told carla and
She gave me a hug.

THE WELCOME COMMITTEE

"CARLA," I SAY, "it won't be like last time." I'm not eight years old anymore.

"I want you to promise—" she begins, but I'm already at the window, sweeping the curtains aside.

I am not prepared for the bright California sun. I'm not prepared for the sight of it, high and blazing hot and white against the washed-out white sky. I am blind. But then the white haze over my vision begins to clear. Everything is haloed.

I see the truck and the silhouette of an older woman twirling—the mother. I see an older man at the back of the truck—the father. I see a girl maybe a little younger than me—the daughter.

Then I see him. He's tall, lean, and wearing all black: black T-shirt, black jeans, black sneakers, and a black knit cap that covers his hair completely. He's white with a pale honey tan and his face is starkly angular. He jumps down from his perch at the back of the truck and glides across the driveway, moving as if gravity affects him differently than it does the rest of us. He stops, cocks his head to one side, and stares up at his new house as if it were a puzzle.

After a few seconds he begins bouncing lightly on the balls of his feet. Suddenly he takes off at a sprint and runs literally six feet up the front wall. He grabs a windowsill and dangles from it for a second or two and then drops back down into a crouch.

"Nice, Olly," says his mother.

"Didn't I tell you to quit doing that stuff?" his father growls.

He ignores them both and remains in his crouch.

I press my open palm against the glass, breathless as if I'd done that crazy stunt myself. I look from him to the wall to the windowsill and back to him again. He's no longer crouched. He's staring up at me. Our eyes meet. Vaguely I wonder what he sees in my window—strange girl in white with wide staring eyes. He grins at me and his face is no longer stark, no longer severe. I try to smile back, but I'm so flustered that I frown at him instead.

MY WHITE BALLOON

THAT NIGHT, I dream that the house breathes with me. I exhale and the walls contract like a pinpricked balloon, crushing me as it deflates. I inhale and the walls expand. A single breath more and my life will finally, finally explode.

NEIGHBORHOOD WATCH

HIS MOM'S SCHEDULE

6:35 AM - Arrives on porch with a steaming cup of something hot. Coffee?

6:36 AM - Stares off into empty lot across the way while sipping her drink. Tea?

7:00 AM - Reenters the house.

7:15 AM - Back on porch. Kisses husband good-bye. Watches as his car drives away.

9:30 AM - Gardens. Looks for, finds, and discards cigarette butts.

1:00 PM - Leaves house in car. Errands?

5:00 PM - Pleads with Kara and Olly to begin chores "before your father gets home."

KARA'S (SISTER) SCHEDULE

10:00 AM - Stomps outside wearing black boots and a fuzzy brown bathrobe.

10:01 AM - Checks cell phone messages. She gets a lot of messages.

10:06 AM - Smokes three cigarettes in the garden between our two houses.